Longing For Normal

Enjoy the journey!

NORMAL SERIES, BOOK 3

Longing For Normal

A Novel

ELDON REED

TATE PUBLISHING
AND ENTERPRISES, LLC

Longing For Normal
Copyright © 2016 by Eldon Reed. All rights reserved.

No part of this publication may be reproduced, stored in a retrieval system or transmitted in any way by any means, electronic, mechanical, photocopy, recording or otherwise without the prior permission of the author except as provided by USA copyright law.

This novel is a work of fiction. Names, descriptions, entities, and incidents included in the story are products of the author's imagination. Any resemblance to actual persons, events, and entities is entirely coincidental.

The opinions expressed by the author are not necessarily those of Tate Publishing, LLC.

Published by Tate Publishing & Enterprises, LLC
127 E. Trade Center Terrace | Mustang, Oklahoma 73064 USA
1.888.361.9473 | www.tatepublishing.com

Tate Publishing is committed to excellence in the publishing industry. The company reflects the philosophy established by the founders, based on Psalm 68:11,
"The Lord gave the word and great was the company of those who published it."

Book design copyright © 2016 by Tate Publishing, LLC. All rights reserved.
Cover design by Albert Ceasar Compay
Interior design by Richell Balansag

Published in the United States of America

ISBN: 978-1-68301-241-2
1. Fiction / General
2. Fiction / Family Life
16.03.17

1

An early-morning fog had quickly rolled in, camouflaging the east pasture of our Angus ranch to the point where nothing seemed familiar. Cattle grazing in the distance disappeared in the whitewashed atmosphere. *Come on, Lilly. We should pick up the pace—move in closer.*

Out of the stillness ahead, my husband's horse screamed. Was that even possible? I'd never heard more than a gentle nicker from him. He appeared to be stomping at something. Then that powerful Morgan bolted upright, completely vertical on his hind legs, still screaming. Kirk flew off the back of Dandy, in an airborne half somersault, smacking the wet grass in a lifeless clunk.

Lilly instinctively started to back away. Kirk lay there in a contorted heap on the damp ground a few yards in front of us.

Lilly continued in slow reverse. "Whoa, baby." I jumped off and ran to him.

"Kirk!" I got down in his face. "Honey, are you okay? Talk to me!" There was no response. I felt his wrist for a pulse. *Oh, God, help me to know what to do!*

Panic overtook common sense. I put my hand under his head and, without thinking, raised it a bit. No blood. That had to be good. "Kirk! Please talk to me!" I got no response. I felt his wrist again. The pulse was strong, giving me hope that maybe he was just knocked out.

Or was it more? There was the possibility of broken bones. I had to call for help.

I felt for my cell phone—first in my right pocket, then my left. Could I have been sitting on it in the saddle? I slapped both my rear pockets. It wasn't there. "Oh God!" I shouted into the thick air. Kirk's face was upright; his eyes were fixed in a painful stare. "Honey, can you hear me?" He didn't even blink.

Our ranch house was almost a mile away. The nearest neighbor was even farther. What should I do?

Kirk rarely leaves the house without his cell phone. I reached into his right front pocket. *Yes!* I pulled it out, stood, flipped the phone open, and turned my face away from the misty gust. My hand was shaking so violently I wasn't even sure I had tapped the right buttons. Moisture whipped at my face. I clutched the phone to my ear. Had I made the right connection? The 911 operator's spiel had started: "…what is your emergency?"

"My husband has just been thrown off his horse. He's not responding! Get an ambulance out here—now!"

"Ma'am, may I have your name please."

"Katie…Katie Childers. Please hurry!"

When I gave her my address, she must have realized how remote we were. "Ma'am is there a flat area nearby where a helicopter can land?"

"Yes…yes, that'd be great. I probably should give you the combination to our ranch gate."

"Hon…" She paused. "We just talked about a helicopter coming. Helicopters don't need to go through gates."

I felt like a fool. I didn't even know how to respond. I was standing there shivering like a Mexican hairless dog in Siberia. She was talking, but I was still thinking about the absurdity of what I'd just said.

A degree of comprehension finally crept back into my brain. I pressed the phone to my ear. "I'm sending a helicopter now." She emphasized the word *helicopter*. "You might want to stay on—

From my peripheral I thought, I saw some movement by Kirk. I wasn't sure. Maybe I was hoping, so I slammed the phone shut and faced him. Then I kicked myself for doing so. Had I given her all of the information she needed? I felt like Brainless Betty, standing there holding the disconnected cell phone. Kirk was stone still.

I knelt down and put an ear to his chest. The beat of his heart comforted me.

I kept asking if he could hear me, but got no response. The fog had intensified. Would the helicopter even be able to find us? The enchanted silvery-blue vapor that earlier had made our ride dreamlike, even romantic, had become an ugly shroud concealing us from the rest of the world. I felt like a lone calf, separated from her mother, standing there in a misty abyss, chilled and disoriented.

The sun peeped through from the east just as a mourning dove whipped by with its melancholy *woo-OO-oo-oo-oo*. Its chorus of despair further splintered my nerves. I pulled my thin windbreaker tighter around me, trying to fend off the chill.

Then just as I felt all hope was gone for a helicopter to see how to land, the fog was whisked away by a sudden and steady gust. Then the wind calmed, and I waited—scared and sequestered on a vast acreage that somehow looked strange, even though I'd been here many times before. With the thick fog gone, I tried to focus on the surrounding landscape.

Waiting for the air ambulance to come seemed like an eternity. I could see our beautiful Angus beauties grazing on the distant hill. In any other circumstance it would have been a picture-perfect postcard scene. Rural Oklahoma at its best.

As I knelt in the wet grass stroking Kirk's forehead, I began to hear the progressively loud roar of an aircraft in the distance. "Honey, they're coming. Help's on the way. Hold on." Could he even hear me?

The chopper set down forty yards from us, causing a whirlwind of grass blades mixed with moisture from the air to blow our way. I ducked my head next to Kirk's face to protect us from the gust.

Once on the ground, a paramedic jumped out and ran to Kirk. The pilot followed, toting a stretcher and some sort of neck brace. "You know the drill," the paramedic said to the other. "We put the C-collar on, then roll and slide the board under. Whatever you do, don't lift till he's secured."

The eggbeater whip of the chopper blades agitated my consciousness to the point that I was unsure of what was real and what was not. Eerie!

I stood back and watched as they skillfully maneuvered Kirk onto the stretcher. Once they had him secured inside, one of the guys ran back to me. I was still standing there, statue-like with my arms crossed in the vast stretch of open prairie. He grabbed my arm and shouted over the noise of the rotors. "Lady, don't you wanna come too?"

I was shaking and confused about what to do about Dandy. The horse was on the ground twenty feet in front of where Kirk had lain. He hadn't moved. Had he broken a leg—or more? *Dear God, don't let that horse die. Kirk will be devastated!*

"Lady, you comin'?" He tugged on my arm.

I snapped out of my trance and followed him. He helped me climb inside, pointing to a seat next to where Kirk lay. "Buckle up."

I barely heard him. My mind was in a state of disconnect. The helicopter tilted forward, and we were soon ascending out of the awful accident scene. I wasn't even sure to which hospital they would take us. The paramedic was saying something, but the noise was so loud I could only guess at what he was telling me. Something about going into shock. I held Kirk's limp callused hand, feeling utterly helpless.

Minutes later, the landing on the hospital roof was so soft I didn't realize we were actually down. Several people in green scrubs came rushing out to meet us. Once inside, the medical team went to work. I stayed with Kirk until they took him for x-ray. Then I unwillingly let myself be led to a waiting room, still clutching Kirk's cell phone, squeezing it tightly and praying. I sat down in a drab gray chair, at first unaware that I was incessantly tapping my right foot. A hospital volunteer approached, grinned, and asked if he could get me something to drink. "Yes," I said, "water would be good."

"Ma'am, how about coffee? Might calm your nerves a bit."

What? Calm my nerves? I thought caffeine was a stimulant.

But he was right. The coffee somehow seemed to stop my shakes. After downing it, I gathered my thoughts a bit. I called Brandon's cell. He didn't answer—probably was in class. Then I thought about texting him, if only I could remember how to text. Our son Thorne had tried to teach me, but when I looked at the cell phone, nothing looked familiar. I finally asked the guy who refilled my coffee, and he tapped in the words as I dictated. Two minutes later, Brandon's name showed up on the screen as the phone vibrated in my hand.

With tears cascading down my cheeks, I related what had happened. "Can you come? This is serious. Dad could really be in trouble."

"Have you talked to him yet?"

"No, hon, he's still unconscious."

Brandon told me he would cut out of class and be on his way. "What about Dandy?"

"Dandy! Oh, my gosh! When we left in the helicopter, Dandy was still lying on the ground just ahead of where Kirk had landed. Can you—"

"Mom, I'm calling the vet right now. East pasture?"

"Yes, just past the first pond."

"I'll give him the combo to the gate and tell him he's gotta get in there, find Dandy, and take care of him. Oh, hey, what hospital?"

"Deaconess. Brandon, hurry! But please, don't speed. Be careful."

"No worries, Mom. I'll find Thorne, and we'll be there in an hour or so. If Dad wakes up, tell him we're on our way."

I closed the phone and stared at the blank wall in the waiting room. Was it broken bones, a concussion…or…Dear God, I didn't want to think of that possibility. Finally, I walked out to the nurses' station to inquire. All they could tell me was that he was still in surgery. As I walked away, I overheard someone saying something about a spinal cord injury.

A spinal cord injury! Just as I had feared. The ramifications slowly radiated through my consciousness, one horrific thought after another. I lumbered back to the waiting room, unable to concentrate, unable to plan a way out of the mess we were in.

I tried to read some of the magazines on the end table. First, I picked up *Family Circle*—the name alone was disturbing. I tossed it down and picked up *Reader's Digest*, but my mind kept veering off the pages. Our own predicament would trump any story in the magazine.

I walked over to the soda machine, put a dollar and twenty-five cents' worth of quarters in, pushed the Diet Coke button, and stood there, staring into space. Apparently I never retrieved the Coke. I found myself back in the same chair, staring blankly at the ceiling, wondering where God was when I so desperately needed Him.

A lady in a blue volunteer's smock, probably in her eighties, came over and sat next to me. "Girl," she said, placing her hand on my shoulder, "I know you're hurting. If there was something I could do to ease your pain, you know I would."

Her soft words were soothing somewhat, but I was still trying to get my head around the possible situation we were facing. I've always had a fix for every difficulty I've faced—tomatoes that refuse to produce, fifth graders who bully, a child who won't read—but this could be way out in left field for me. I put my hands to my face. With tears welling up in my eyes, I shook my head and somehow managed to say, "Thank you." A minute later, I looked up, and she was gone.

I paced. I sat. I stood. The clock on the wall was frozen. At first I had been eager for the doctor to come in and let me know what he had done and what Kirk's prognosis was. But the more I waited, the more I just didn't even want an update. I was afraid of what it would be. And I was terrified of the imminent consequences—consequences that this time might be totally out of my control.

2

Earlier that morning

It was just mid-October, and already the trees were robed in their coats of many colors. With both boys away in college, the ranch was quiet again. I walked outside, still in my old red pajamas and housecoat, with my usual cup of coffee. The air was thick, the stillness of the surroundings hovered over me like a huge umbrella. I stood near the front gate and watched two cardinals in our cedar tree. A male, clothed in his own crimson pajamas, gently tapped once at his mate's beak. My mouth flew open. Did he just kiss her?

Country living has its advantages. All things natural. The smell of a fresh-mown hayfield. The solitude—our nearest neighbor more than a mile from us. The silence—no sirens, no loud music coming from next door. Then behind me, I heard the creaky front door open.

"I thought I might find you out here."

I turned and saw my cowboy husband standing there, still in his boxers. "Kirk, I just saw a male cardinal kiss his mate in the cedar tree. You should have seen it. It was so sweet."

"Well, you've got quite an imagination." He grinned, walked over and planted a big, prolonged kiss on me. Then he stood back, with both his hands on my shoulders. "That's what a real kiss is. What does a cardinal know about kissing?"

How could I argue?

I set my coffee cup on the fence post by the gate. "Kirk, why don't we do something special today? You've been working your tail off on this ranch lately."

"Well, I've got no help now. Don't have much of a choice."

I put my arm around his waist. "You need a break. It's just the two of us now. Let's do something together today."

I could see he was trying to manufacture an argument, and his mouth opened to start. I put my finger to his lips. "Shh…Listen to this. Have you ever heard such a silence? The wind is gone, the air is thick, and there is a calm enveloping us like a warm breath from God above. Can't you feel it?"

He grinned, kissed me again, and said, "Okay, if you're gonna paint the day like that, I guess I can't say no. What do you wanna do?"

There was no hesitation on my part. "Just be with you. I want to spend this dreamlike day with the one I love."

He smiled—a smile that told me he was glad he married me, even though he sometimes accuses me of living in a mirage. "Since you're in love with this magnificent canopy of quiet solitude we're caught up in, why don't I saddle up the horses and we'll go for a ride today—just the two of us, basking in the stillness that has overtaken our part of the world."

"Kirk Childers! Are you making fun of me?"

He lightly pinched my cheek. "Now why would I do that?" Then his silly half-smile, half-smirk appeared, which makes me never know what to expect next. Then it disappeared, and he said, "How about if you throw together a couple of sandwiches and some of your famous lemonade. We'll put it all in that pommel bag you bought me for Christmas." Another grin broke out on his face. "Then we can ride off into the kaleidoscopic sunrise this morning, leaving behind a trail of awe-inspiring silence for all those amorous cardinals to envy."

"Now I *know* you are making fun of me, cowboy!" I patted him on the behind. "Go saddle up those horses."

He glanced down at his boxers. That one-sided smirk emerged on his unshaven face. I laughed. "But I think you should first go put on some clothes!"

I built a huge sandwich I knew always pleased my man: a thick slab of roast beef—Angus, of course—a red onion slice, a fresh leaf of kale I'd just picked from my fall garden, all wedged between homemade sourdough bread and slathered with lots of mayo. He has never known, but my *famous* lemonade has always come from the store. I grabbed the jug from the bottom shelf of the fridge, where he never looks, and poured some into sixteen-ounce Tupperware glasses with snap-on lids.

I looked out the kitchen window and saw him riding up on Dandy, with Lilly trailing behind. I took the sandwiches and lemonade out and handed them to him. He stashed them all neatly in his pommel bag. "You ready, dream girl?"

I flashed him a sardonic grin. "Are you making fun of me again, or are you saying I'm the perfect girl of your dreams?"

"Aww, Kate, you'll always be the perfect girl in my dreams."

We rode down past the hay barn. The smell of fresh-cut hay was heavenly. So too was the sight of my man riding alongside me. The leisurely gait in the morning air was mesmerizing. My elegant mare, Lilly, is such a gentle creature. She seems to anticipate my every move. The reins are rarely needed to communicate with her. I dropped back a bit to take in the view: a handsome, broad-shouldered man sitting tall in the saddle on one of the most beautifully muscled horses I've ever seen. It was a painting, bringing out each detail of virility in both man and his horse.

The light fog, barely more than a haze earlier, had thickened, and Kirk and Dandy were shrouded in a dense vapor, giving me a sense of déjà vu. Yes, something was familiar. What was it? I'd been in heavy fog before. Maybe that was it. The scene blurred in front of me. Had I been a bit farther back, I think Kirk would have completely disappeared from my sight. Eerie, but oh so picturesque.

I sat there on Lilly, taking in the beauty, allowing the moist air to fill my lungs. I looked down and pulled my light jacket back around me, slapping it shut with the Velcro strips.

Awakened in the hospital waiting room

Then that raucous scream from Dandy caused me to bolt upright in my chair. Reality marched back in like a squadron of soldiers doing double time. I stared at the cold, design-neglected wall of the waiting room. I was alone—again. All was quiet. The clock on the wall surely was lying to me. *When will someone come and tell me what's happening with Kirk? This awful wait is killing me!*

I walked down to the nurses' station. "Any word yet about my husband?" I knew their answer before I even asked, but I had to try.

"Mrs. Childers," the RN behind the counter said, "the doctor will come out and update you as soon as he deems appropriate."

What a chilly answer. I said nothing, just returned to the abandoned waiting room, which was in bad need of a few art pieces. Thorne's art could do wonders for these white-bread walls. I sat down in the same ugly taupe chair, picked up the only magazine I hadn't looked at. *Sports Illustrated* contained nothing to hold my attention. My thoughts backtracked to the argument Kirk and I had about my friend Lana Lou Barrow, Thorne's homeless mother.

Spousal quarrels at a time like this seem so trivial. Now I regret arguing with him. Did I apologize for my pigheadedness? Come to think of it, apologies have never been part of this redhead's way. Will I ever learn to say I'm sorry at appropriate times? What if I never get the chance with Kirk?

Tears moistened my eyes again, and the hands on the wall clock began to blur.

3

Three years earlier

I REMEMBER IT AS if it was yesterday. Kirk took both my hands in his, looked into my eyes, and said, "Katie, what have you gotten yourself into now?" That was nothing new. He's used a similar line several times in the past. He should be used to me by now. We've been married fifteen years. I'm always coming up with what he calls some harebrained idea he thinks isn't feasible. But this time I had a plan. I knew this would work, and my red-haired determination would not allow me to back down.

"Katie, we've got a good life here on this ranch. We've found our niche with fostering kids, and now we've adopted our first one. I don't understand why you can't be satisfied with the progress we've made. Why do you have to get involved in the lives of these kids' birth families? If these people cared a hoot about their offspring, the kids wouldn't be here with us. We should be concentrating on helping them, not their delinquent parents."

My temper was rising, and I think he knew it.

"Come on, let's just enjoy the boys and leave their nutty birth parents out of the picture. We've made a good life right here. You know…you, me, and the boys. It's all we've ever wanted, all we've ever hoped for."

Kirk is a wonderful husband, a good provider for his family. And he knows how to be a super father. But sometimes I think his compassion outside his own family is about nonexistent. There has to be more to life than just making a comfy den for our own family. Other people matter, and if we don't help them, who will?

"You know, getting your friend a job is one thing," he said. "Getting her off the streets and back into normal society is quite another." The next words out of his mouth were first written on his face. I knew what his argument would be. "You expect her to live in that pint-sized A-frame camper? How's she gonna get to work? She has no wheels."

"I've got it all—"

"Kate." Those gentle but work-callused hands reached for my shoulders in the gesture that always whispers for me to hold that thought. "Honey, you have done more than your share to help the woman. It shouldn't be up to you to save the whole world."

I know my eyes probably shot arrows of disgust straight at him. "Your lack of compassion is overwhelming! I'm not saving the whole world. I'm helping one—one only—who happens to be Thorne's mother. We can't ignore her. I have to help."

"Okay, but you have done so already." Kirk looked out from under his sweat-soaked hat that he refuses to ditch for a new one. "Sometimes I think your heart is a lot bigger than your brain."

I was prepared to let him rant for a minute, because I know Kirk Childers, and I know he shares my views about the importance of family—the glue that holds society together. When a family unit breaks down, bad things start to happen. If I can save her family—what's left of it—I will have accomplished something. I know how important my own family is to me. If that should ever start to break down—and I know bad things can happen to anyone—I'd hope someone would come to my rescue.

"Winter's comin' on," he said. "She'll freeze in that tiny cooler chest of a camper. And you know she can't live here with us. DFS won't allow it."

"I've got it all covered. She will live in the A-frame camper in town until she can get on her feet and get her own place. She's already said she would put the old Barrow house in the city up for sale. Her name's still on the deed, even though she hasn't lived there in a few years. Then she can afford to—"

"How's she supposed to sell it? Her good-for-nothin' husband probably would have to sign, and he's doin' life in prison. He won't sign."

"Yes, he will. She's already talked to him and told him she'd send him a couple hundred dollars for cigarettes when it sold, and he agreed."

"So you think she can actually live in our tiny camper till that run-down house finally sells—if it ever does?" Kirk's denim-blue eyes lasered a line of skepticism at me. "That's just nuts!"

"Kirk Childers, you're the one who is nuts! You refuse to listen to my plan. You're being bullheaded!" As soon as I'd let that nasty word slip out, regret started to eat away at my conscience.

I tiptoed up to his face, pushed the filthy sweat-soaked hat back and planted a kiss on him. "That tiny camper will seem like the Biltmore Estate to her after living under her tarp behind the bus station." I pulled the old hat back down over his eyes. "Wouldn't you agree?"

"Uh…what? I don't have a clue what you just said. Something about an estate."

"I said—"

"Okay"—he grinned—"I heard you. I'm just playing with you."

I'll never forget the day life for Lana Lou Barrow was turned around. It was a Friday. I was subbing in third grade at our elementary school in Luther. A thought popped into my head, and I found myself talking to Mr. Johnson, our superintendent, about a job for my friend. I knew it was a long shot, but much to my surprise, he said there was an opening for a janitorial job. Convincing him that a homeless woman should have the job was not easy, but after I told him she was Thorne Barrow's mother, and after he met her, I believe his heart warmed. An interview was arranged, and he hired her on the spot. I later whispered to her, "See, miracles still happen."

I took my homeless friend to the thrift shop and bought her some clothes to wear to work. Kirk and I stocked the camper with as many groceries—mostly nonperishables—as it would hold. Brandon brought several paperbacks for her to read, and Thorne attached two of his paintings on the slanted roof of the A-frame camper.

When we first found Thorne's mother in front of the Greyhound terminal a few years ago, holding out her Folgers coffee can, my heart went out to her. All we knew about her was what Thorne had told us. He said she had walked out of the old Barrow house the day his dad was released from prison, for the third time. John Barrow had come home, found his wife in bed with some biker dude, took a Glock from the top of the refrigerator, and shot and killed the guy.

Lana Lou, I learned later, knew she couldn't support her boys. She didn't have a high school diploma and had never even worked outside the home. The oldest boy was doing time in prison for setting fire to a church, the middle son was strung out on drugs, and eight-year-old Thorne had become a neighborhood bully to the younger children in the area. He was, as she put it, out of control.

"It was wrong to abandon my boys," she once told me. But I think she realized she had already lost in the game of parenting. She told me she secretly hoped a foster home would be the answer for them.

Well, she was right—at least about her youngest. Thorne has thrived here on the ranch with us. He was, admittedly, a little toot at first. But after several trips to the barn for talks with Kirk, he soon lost his swagger. I was able to bring him up to speed on reading and math. He's still just barely an average student, but where he excels is his art.

He's become quite a sensation at the Throckmorton Gallery in Oklahoma City. His Western art is selling at amazing prices, and he's saving all of the money, hoping to have enough to pay for four years of college, plus two more years of graduate school. With the way his art is selling, I have no doubt he can reach his goal. This kid knows what he wants, and he is determined to let nothing stand in his way. We couldn't be more proud.

Kirk pulled our A-frame "chalet" to town and hooked up the propane, electric, and water. I drove to downtown Oklahoma City and the Greyhound terminal. Lana Lou Barrow was holding her Folgers coffee can out for the last time. As I approached, she set the can down and attempted to get up from the sidewalk—the sidewalk that had been her self-proclaimed spot for so long. I took her hand to help her frail body up. "Hon, are you ready to go to your new home?" Her wrist was spaghetti-thin, and I was afraid it would break.

"Katie," she said, "I'm ready, but I'm scared."

"Scared? What could be scarier than living out here on the street? Some of the people down here are pretty creepy—not the friendliest bunch."

The woman emptied the few coins from the Folgers can into her pocket. "I guess I won't be needing this." She started to toss the can into a nearby trash receptacle.

"Wait." I grabbed the can from her hand. "Don't throw that away. You should keep it for the memories."

"Memories?" She snickered. "Why would I want to remember this old cold sidewalk and the winters I've spent out here in freezing rain, sleet, and snow?" A raspy cough erupted from deep down in her lungs. "And the summer's broiling sun—it has baked this paper-thin skin of mine, so now I look like a piece of blackened fish." She ran her bony fingers through her gray-streaked beaver-brown hair. "No, if you want this coffee can, you keep it. I don't want it to remind me of the mistake I made that led to my life of panhandling. I was such a fool!"

I wrapped my arms around her thin shoulders, and a couple of tears escaped from my eyes. "Come on, sweetie, my truck is parked down in the next block." I held on to the Folgers can, knowing it would now belong to her son.

I steered onto Interstate 35, heading north. For the third time, Lana Lou said, "I just can't believe you would do all this for me." She kept saying, "I've been such a fool. I don't deserve it."

It was day one on the job for her. I tagged along and thought I'd work right alongside her for the first day. I was afraid she wouldn't have the strength to do the job. But I was wrong. Frail as she was, Lana Lou seemed to have an unexpected surge of energy. She moved the student desks around and swept the floors. In the restrooms, she slung a heavy wet mop like it was made of dry feathers. She went about cleaning the toilets and urinals with a vigor that amazed me. I tried to help, but she politely informed me it was her job, not mine. I could see the pride the woman had in her newfound employment. After a couple of hours, I knew she would have no trouble handling the work, so I headed back to the ranch, where I was really needed.

The big rock house was quiet. Kirk and Ronnie were doctoring cattle. Brandon was in his last semester as a senior at Luther High, and Thorne was following as a junior. The boys shared an old pickup we had bought for them, and I knew that at about three-fifteen, they would be slinging gravel as they slid around the corner heading up to the ranch house. It was Thorne's turn to drive. Brandon was a pretty cautious driver, but I can't say the same for Thorne. He is carefree, and his driving habits show it.

The ringing of the phone broke the silence. It was Throckmorton Gallery informing me they had sold the last of Thorne's paintings and were asking for more. I was pretty sure he had finished at least one, maybe two more, and I was curious. Thorne likes to paint in the privacy of his room and doesn't want any of us seeing the unfinished product. It had been a couple of weeks since he'd allowed us to see one he'd finished, so curiosity overtook me, and I knew I had to have a look for myself.

Feeling like an intruder, I opened his door, peeked in, and my eyes immediately found the painting resting on the easel in the corner of the room. My right hand went to my chest as my mouth flew open and sucked in air. An 18"x24" canvas was filled with an image of a withered and sunburned hand holding out a red Folgers coffee can. I noticed a thin wedding band on her sun-scorched finger. A fine mist of rain was evident over the entire canvas, with a tiny drop falling from the hand holding the can. *This kid is astonishing!* I found myself wondering how he had managed to paint the amazing mist. A cold-looking mist. I shuddered at the image and knew any painting that evokes that kind of emotion has to be excellent art.

I opened his closet door, where he stored his finished pieces. The one in front made me laugh. It showed the bottom half of a denim clad leg with a brown boot, much like Thorne's own pair that he's worn for over a year, kicking that Folgers can. I found myself wondering if whoever bought either of those paintings would ever know the real story behind them. Probably not.

I tipped the painting forward and found one with a young man about Thorne's age, sitting on a rock in the pasture with tall grass at his feet. A straw was protruding from his mouth, and it was evident from his forlorn eyes that he was deep in thought—troubled. An overcast sky added to the apprehension. Thorne has become famous for the amazing atmospheric conditions which are so prevalent in many of his paintings. Fog, mist, snow—even the last rays of penetrating sunlight—all overtake the paintings to create a feeling of one being totally enveloped in the scene. You can feel the dampness in the air, sense the falling snow, or bask in the warmth of a winter sun. How he does it, I'll never know. He can't even explain it. But the owners of Throckmorton Gallery can't seem to keep his paintings on display. They are sold about as soon as Thorne can deliver them.

I'd just deposited an eighty-five-hundred-dollar check into his savings account for the last painting. It was of an old cowhand—probably a grandfather—riding a chestnut horse with a very young boy behind him, holding on tight and ducking his head into the old man's back. The scene was brimming with brilliant color, and thousands of sun diamonds were glistening off the horse. Apparently, a light shower had just ended with the subsequent burst of sunlight. Rhena Throckmorton told me the painting had sold immediately after being displayed on the wall facing the front entrance. "I didn't even get to enjoy seeing it there," she had said. "It hung there for less than ten minutes." She told me an art collector had walked in, saw the painting, and whipped out his credit card without even asking about the price.

The transformation of this young man from the belligerent know-it-all hayseed he was a few years back to the heart-of-gold young artist he is today is nothing less than a miracle.

4

In the hospital waiting room

I FELT THE PRESENCE of someone next to me. I raised my head off my right shoulder that was my makeshift pillow. It was the sweet lady in the blue volunteer smock. "Oh, hi," I said without emotion. "I didn't hear you come in."

She touched my hand lightly. "Honey, I didn't mean to startle you. You might want to go back to sleep."

"No, it's okay. I hope I wasn't snoring."

She smiled. "It was no more than a baby's breath. Were you dreaming?"

"Well, yes, I think I was. How did you know?"

"I could tell you were having good thoughts. Your face was beaming."

"Yes, I think I was dreaming about our two boys." I glanced up at the clock on the far wall. "They should be here any minute now."

Her beautiful white hair framed her wrinkled face, and her cheery smile returned. "Can you tell me about them?"

I soon found myself babbling on about my family to this stranger—a woman who somehow felt like my best friend.

"Thirteen years! It's been thirteen years now since Brandon, a seven-year-old blue-eyed, blond-haired boy, came into our lives. He was followed by another young boy, Thorne, a year later." I glanced at the unmoving clock again.

"Brandon, the first boy we would foster, and later adopt, was a delight from the first day our caseworker delivered him to us. He was shy at first. But that quickly vanished when my husband made him his personal sidekick on the ranch where we live. Kirk is an amazing father. Every boy should have a dad like Kirk Childers."

I had her full attention. Maybe she had a son like Brandon. Maybe she had been married to a man like Kirk.

"This ranch—it's owned by Kirk's uncle, but Kirk manages it—was the playground for Kirk and Brandon. Kirk's little sidekick was right there, except for the times I pulled him away to work on his reading.

"An eighteen-hundred-acre cattle ranch is a lot of hard work. We also milk a few dairy cows, raise hogs, keep chickens for fresh eggs, and pasture three horses. They have become like family members."

Dandy! My mind veered back to that awful scene. But my friend was waiting for more. I looked down at my own clasped hands and tried to force them to relax. I think she noticed, but I continued.

"I have managed to keep us in a nice supply of seasonal vegetables from my garden in addition to my occasional substitute-teaching at our elementary school in town. So none of us are strangers to hard work, but for Kirk and Brandon, hard work often seemed more like fun, because they just enjoyed each other's company.

"When Brandon first came to us, he insisted on following Kirk everywhere. I played the unpopular role of the one to insist he come in and work on his reading and math, neither of which was grade-level proficient at first. He eventually learned to read well, and books became his best friend—other than Kirk.

"Now Thorne was a different story entirely. At the ripe old age of eight, he was a cocky, sometimes obnoxious skinny boy who wanted no part of ranch work. When Kirk tried to get him to join in and help with the milking or other chores, he tried to cover his incompetence with an arrogant know-it-all attitude.

"Kirk never pushed. In fact, he encouraged Thorne to pursue his own interest, even though it looked nothing like what Kirk thought would be right for a boy his age. It was art—art dominated the boy's time. I'd watch in amazement as he sat at our dining table with pencil, charcoal, and any paper he could find, sketching various objects and ranch scenes, all with a budding God-given talent. Soon afterward, his love for art blossomed, and his sketching evolved into other art media forms, mostly oils."

"So has he become an artist?" Her eyes were sparkling with questions. "What does he paint?"

"Well…" Any mother is more than happy to talk about her child, and I'm no exception. "It was a school art contest that started it all. Thorne Barrow, as he is known in the art world today, is a well-known Western artist, even though he is now just barely twenty."

"What are they like?" She sat up even straighter in her chair. "I really want to hear about his art."

"Many of his now-famous paintings present a comical image. One of his first paintings depicted our border collie, Noah, barking his fool head off at our two-thousand-pound Angus bull. Another one—and this one is from Thorne's own experience—shows a young boy down on his back in a chicken pen, his legs up in the air, his hat flying through the air, and he's being attacked by our angry old rooster."

"Oh," she said, "I can just picture that. The boy must have quite a sense of humor."

"Well, yes, but it mostly shows in his art." I looked again into the eyes of this beautiful lady, so intent on my story. How could I not continue?

"Thorne's paintings are selling quite well. I'm so glad we never tried to pigeonhole him into something he wasn't. I don't even want to think what that would have done to the child."

I glanced at the apathetic hands of the clock again, then back at her. I figured she was surely tiring of my talk about our kids, but her eyes seemed to be waiting for more."

"What a story," she said. "This is interesting."

"I've heard it said that every child is a story yet to be told, and the stories of our two boys are each amazing. Some might have considered their lives to be imperfect—and even useless, coming from such dysfunctional families. 'Outcasts of society'—that's what one ignorant and rude person called foster children. I really believe God has a plan for each child. Discovering that plan and nurturing it is the responsibility of the parents.

"Kirk and I now can clearly see what God's plan has been for both Brandon and Thorne. It is amazing to see how the life blueprint for each boy has evolved, while making room for a volume of love so rare in today's world most people wouldn't understand."

She touched my hand, ever so lightly. "Honey, I want to hear more, but I probably should finish my rounds." She laughed. "Other people's stories may not be as interesting as yours." She patted my hand. "I'll be back for more if you're still here."

5

Waiting for the doctor

I WALKED OVER TO the window. The view hadn't changed—just a parking lot full of motionless cars and pickups, dutifully lined up in their preplanned and equal spaces.

There were other calls I knew I should make. My folks—I had to call Mom and Dad. I desperately needed them now. They were only twenty minutes or so away. I pulled Kirk's cell phone out of my purse to make the call. The battery was dead.

I assumed someone at the nurses' station would allow me to use the phone. But I somehow felt glued to the window. Did I really even want to tell them? The thought of having to talk about this awful day made me nauseous.

And what about Kirk's dad? Would he even be sober enough to take my call? Kirk hadn't seen him in several years. Kirk's mother divorced him when Kirk was just a teen; then she was killed in a car wreck not long after. Mr. Childers—I don't even know his first name—has never called or come to see Kirk. Kirk has tried to call him a few times, but the conversation goes nowhere. The man is always drunk. Kirk says his dad was abusive to his mom. I'm not sure Kirk would even want me to try to talk to him.

And then there's Uncle Carl. *Oh dear God!* What could I tell him? What would we do about the cattle? Oh, and what about all the other farm animals? Our milk cows! I"wasn't sure Kirk even milked them early this morning…No, he didn't! I remembered it was six in the morning. He greeted me out by the front gate in his boxers, and then he got dressed and went down to saddle up the horses for us to go for a ride—that ride.

If we'd never decided to go horseback riding, this would never have happened. And I'm the one who insisted we go. In the fog! Oh, and poor Dandy! I wonder if Brandon got hold of the vet to check on him—

Brandon! I shouldn't have told him how bad Kirk was. He'd drive like a maniac trying to get here. I looked at the wall clock again. The boys should have been here by now. It's been over three hours since I talked to him. He said he would pick up Thorne and they'd leave right away. *Dear God, please don't let them get into an accident. I can't take any more bad news.*

The scene outside the window was depressing. My head was down, so all I saw was the bottom of some green scrubs and some funny-looking booty-covered feet approaching.

"Mrs. Childers?" I looked up and saw a doctor standing in front of me. At least I assumed he was a doctor. He was a somewhat robust man, probably in his sixties, mostly gray hair—or what I could see of it under his surgical cap. "Mrs. Childers?" he repeated.

My stomach did a flip-flop. I had eagerly waited for this time. Now I dreaded it. "Yes," I said.

He motioned me to a chair and sat down beside me. "I'm Dr. Brockman." Then he paused. And it was then I knew…I knew right away he didn't have good news.

"I just wanted to give you a quick update on your husband. He's still in surgery. I'm assisting Dr. Graystone, one of the finest neurosurgeons in the Midwest."

Both of my hands went back up to my tear-stained face. I found it difficult to look the man in the eye. I didn't want to hear what I knew was coming.

"Mrs. Childers—I believe it's Katie, right?"

"Yes," I managed to say.

"Katie, I want you to know Kirk is awake—has been since right before we started the surgery."

I looked up at him and gasped. "You're doing surgery on my husband and he's wide awake?"

He smiled and lightly touched my hand. "Yes, but that's a good thing—

"How can it be good?" I blurted out, loud enough for the nurses down the hall to hear. My red-hair temperament was about to show it's ugly self.

"Trust me on this," he said. "We need him awake for this type of surgery. You see, the fall your husband took crushed his vertebrae. We needed him to be able to talk to us while we were working. He hasn't been in pain." He looked deep into my eyes. "Katie, I have to be honest with you…"

Honesty, today, was something I wasn't sure I wanted.

He continued, "This is not looking good. We need a miracle here." He squeezed my hand. "Miracles do happen—I've seen them myself. But short of a miracle…" The dreaded words spewed forth and permeated the air between us: "Kirk will never walk again."

At that moment, everything came to an immediate halt. I swear the TV on the wall went silent. The voices down the hall died. My own blood seemed to freeze, and chill bumps appeared on the dance floor of my arms.

The doctor's gray eyes pierced my inner being. "This type of injury can never be reversed." He blinked. "Maybe someday we'll learn how, but for now, we simply don't have the ability."

My right hand went to my chest, and I sucked in the air from his words. "No!" I tried to say. My tongue was stuck to the roof of my mouth.

"The break, Katie, is at the fifth vertebrae. We call it a C5 break. We're hoping he will eventually be able to have limited movement in his shoulders and, thus, his arms. I can't promise that, but many C5 patients, in time, are able to feed themselves, and even operate an electric wheelchair. Had the break been just higher up, he would be totally paralyzed from the neck down. He would be in serious trouble—his speech, and even his breathing."

"You mean like the actor…" I couldn't remember his name. "Like…Superman?" "Christopher Reeve…" He smiled. "Yes, but in Kirk's case, we're hoping for some movement in his shoulders. Believe me, the prognosis for Kirk is better than was the case for Christopher Reeve, but it's still not good—at all."

I was reeling. How could this be? Just this morning, everything was going our way. With both of the boys in college, Kirk and I were even starting to enjoy our empty nest a bit. We talked more now. We spent more time together. It was like when we were first married, and my serious nature had made somewhat of a turnaround. I even became a bit giddy on occasion. We laughed a lot. We went fishing—just Kirk and me. We took in a movie every month or so. We went for an early-morning ride in the fog…

Oh God! If we just hadn't done that!

"Katie?" Dr. Brockman was trying to get my attention. "Katie, I have to get back in there with Dr. Graystone. I just wanted to let you know where we stand now with your husband."

"Thank you, Doctor. I'm glad you and the other doctor were available to operate quickly."

"Normally," he said, "with a break of this nature, there would be so much swelling in the area we'd have to wait a few days to go in. But Kirk's swelling was minor, and his x-rays showed dangerous bone fragments that Dr. Graystone felt had to be removed immediately to prevent further damage. So that's what we're doing now. You should know it may take another hour or so. I'll meet with you again after we've finished and give you more information then. Understand, though, it will probably take weeks, even months, for us to know how Kirk will respond. I wouldn't expect much in the short term. Right now we'll be closely monitoring his breathing, which, at this point, looks good."

"When will I be able to see him?"

"As soon as we've completed the surgery, he'll be taken to an intensive care room, where he'll remain for—"

"Does he know? I mean, will he be aware he may never"—I could hardly bring myself to say the words—"he may never… walk again?"

"Yes, he knows. We talked while Dr. Graystone was working on him." Dr. Brockman grinned. "He was mostly concerned about his horse. Kept asking if someone could go check on him. I take it he loves that horse?"

I could only nod my head as I tried to blink back a tear.

"You should be able to see him after we get him up to ICU and stabilized. I'll come and get you then."

I was stunned! I didn't even thank him. With my hands framing my damp eyes, I felt him touch my shoulder, and then he walked away.

My world had just imploded. It rocked my spirit with a jolt I could have never, in a million years, anticipated. I've always been one to see a problem, sometimes before it even happens; plan my strategy for fixing it; and immediately put it in place. Nothing gets past me. My parents always knew I was an independent little redhead. I was the one who always had my term papers completed days, sometimes weeks, before the due date. I had my four-year class schedule planned out at the beginning of my freshman year in college. I was in control of my destiny. I allowed God to be my guide, but I demanded He let me know the path I was to take well in advance. No last-minute change of plans for this girl.

Mr. Johnson, my school superintendent, once said, "Katie, you see problems in the classroom well before anyone else, and you immediately go to work on them."

Whenever I see either of the boys run into a difficult situation, I am always right there with an answer. I know what to do, and I make sure it gets done. There have been times when Kirk has said he wishes I'd let him figure a few things out on his own. Bossy? No, I don't see it that way. Someone has to fix things, and it's always been me.

But I had no answers to this problem. I could not fix this one.

6

Alone again

I FOUND MYSELF CURLING up on those armless chairs. The tears began to roll out and drip onto the ugly upholstery. *God, why did this have to happen? Life as I have known it is all but gone. How will we be able to carry on? The ranch—what will happen there? Where will we live?*

I continued to question God. *How can I possibly pay these hospital bills? Will I even be able to give the proper care to my husband?*

Then I became angry. *But, God, I've got two sons in college. This is just not fair! I've always been able to see trouble coming, plan for it, and put my plan into action. I am totally unprepared this time.* The tears wouldn't stop.

Why did you allow this to happen?
Why?

There were no answers. God did not come to my rescue and offer a solution. Soon my questions seemed to all run together. I sat there feeling so alone, but it somehow had become a peaceful solitude. The quietness in the room hovered over me. Something was happening here. I had no explanation for it, but a change was happening. My anger was being pushed aside, and my mind was slowly entering a period of recess, a healthy retreat from the past hours. All I wanted now was to think about the good times—the times when the boys were still home, Kirk was still feeding the cattle, and I was serving my hot-out-of-the-oven cinnamon rolls to my men.

With nothing more for me to do but wait, my thoughts raced back to a time when the sun was still shining on our world, a time of laughter, and even a time of family quarrels. Yes, even quarreling somehow didn't sound so bad now.

Two years earlier, back at the ranch

The sound of the boys' pickup braking and sliding on the gravel out front brought me running back into the big room. Then the old truck's horn honking signaled Thorne's signature arrival. I went to the fridge and poured their usual glasses of milk. Without that welcome of mine, I think they'd think something was wrong—and they'd be right.

Thorne was the first to burst through the door and run to the table to retrieve his milk. I looked straight at him until he caught sight of my glare. "Thorne Barrow, you scare the bejeebers out of me with your driving! You've got to slow down."

"Yeah, he drives like a maniac." Brandon pulled his hands out of his pockets and punched Thorne's shoulder with the force of a two-ton bull. "He almost hit a black Lab just outside the ranch gate. I think it belongs to Old Lady Wiggins up at—

"Brandon! That's rude! You mean Miss Cassie—Cassie Wiggins."

"Yeah, Miss Cassie—you know, up at Miss Cassie's Café. Anyway, Thorne saw the dog heading across the highway, and what'd he do? He gunned it!"

"I wasn't gonna hit the dumb dog, Brandon. Geez! Give me a break. I knew what I was doing. I just wanted to spook the goofy mutt. He should have been on a leash and tethered to his owner's hand."

"Whatever. You guys just need to slow down. Dad catches you driving like that, and your driving privileges will be curtailed."

I pulled out a pan of brownies from the oven, still warm. "Brandon, you need to sit down with me tonight so we can finish the FAFSA. You're running out of time."

"Mom," Brandon said, "we've got a whole week before it's due. You can chill."

Brandon's never been late on anything in his life. I knew he wouldn't let this slip either. "You know, buddy, that's not a bad idea."

"What?"

"You said I could chill, so I think I will. You guys can make yourselves sandwiches for supper. I'll kick back in my recliner and finish the novel I started reading last night. Thorne's mother about ran my legs off this morning. I didn't know the woman could move so fast. Here I've been, feeling sorry for her with that awful cough and her skin-and-bone frame. I don't know where she got that burst of energy."

Thorne was hanging on every word I'd just said, but Brandon was wolfing down the brownie and milk. Then he reached for another one, laid it down, and said, "Mom, I'm thinking about changing my major."

"Changing your major! You haven't even started college yet."

"Yeah. So? Better to change it now, than two years from now. Right?"

"Well, sure, but I thought you wanted to be a math teacher."

"Okay, I love math. But I want to go into ranch management. Maybe Uncle Carl will buy another ranch, and I could manage it for him, just like Dad does this one."

"Brandon, that's a long shot. It takes millions to buy a ranch like this. It seems like an impossible dream, but I know you have always loved ranching, so why don't you talk to Dad about it. See what input he might have." I moved the last brownie away from the boys so there would be one left for Kirk.

"I've been reading the OSU catalogue they sent me. It's a really cool college. They offer several agricultural majors, more than any school I know of."

"Well, after all, that *is* what OSU is known for." The teacher in me wouldn't give up. "Maybe you could teach ranch management in college."

"Yeah, right!" Thorne blurted out. "Professor Brandon Childers—somehow I just can't see that."

"Shut up, Thorne. I can't see you doing a lot of things." Brandon rocketed the last of his brownie toward Thorne.

Thorne ducked. "Yeah, and I can't see you ever hitting the side of a big red barn. Baseball, basketball—forget it. You'd never make the team."

"All right guys! That is enough! The food fight and the slandering have to stop!"

Brandon turned his back toward Thorne, stuck his size 11 Nike up on the chair next to him, and looked at me. "Farm and ranch management sounds interesting, and another one I'd like is livestock merchandising. Forage and livestock production would be good too. If I majored in crop and soil science, I might learn how to maximize the pastureland so we wouldn't have to feed so much hay. Hay's expensive to buy."

I gave up. "Well, talk to Dad about it."

I couldn't help but be somewhat disappointed, because I knew Brandon would make a wonderful math teacher—something the schools are really short on. But I'd also be the first to say you have to be happy and love your chosen field. I knew Brandon loves working with the cattle. He always has. He needs to be able to make a decent living. Public school teachers don't make a lot of money, but it is a good, dependable income. It's also rewarding to be able to steer young children in the right direction with a good understanding of math, science, reading, and the arts.

As soon as Kirk walked in the door, Brandon unloaded his educational plans. Kirk's eyes beamed, and a big Kirk Childers grin dominated his sunburned face. The two of them chattered nonstop for the next hour about ranch management, livestock sales, and crop and soil science. I knew my hopes of Brandon pursuing a teaching career were gone.

With this change in direction, Brandon finished preparing his FAFSA in record time. The supper table became a one-subject conversation between Brandon and his dad, leaving Thorne and me in silence. Several times I'd catch Thorne looking at me and rolling his eyes, as if to say, *Don't they have anything better to talk about?*

Final exams were in two days. Because of Brandon's perfect attendance and near-perfect grades, he was exempt from finals. Not so with Thorne. He should have been hitting the books fervently in preparation for finals, but instead, he spent every spare minute after school and on weekends painting. Kirk had already asked him twice about his upcoming finals, and I knew the response I'd get when I knocked on his door. I walked in, thinking I'd share my motherly advice.

I was prepared with my speech about how these finals were critical to him getting accepted into OSU for his undergraduate work. I would tell him that it would be his stepping-stone to his eventual goal of a graduate degree in art. He'd already picked out the world-renowned School of the Art Institute in Chicago. That's what I was prepared for. What I wasn't prepared for was the incredible painting I saw propped on the easel in the corner of his room.

A view from behind showed a lone cowboy sitting on his horse at the fork of two trails. The young cowboy held his hat in one hand and was scratching his head with the other. One trail led off toward a one-room clapboard schoolhouse in the distance, with ominous dark clouds hovering above. An obvious thunderstorm was about to hit. The other led in a very different direction, toward a herd of Angus cattle behind a barbed-wire fence. The entire scene was shrouded in a cold mist, giving me a chill. Somehow my attention was drawn to a single drop of rain dripping from the brim of the young man's hat. I looked closer at that drop.

No way!

He had painted an inner sparkle in the obvious shape of—of all things—a question mark!

Thorne was seated at his desk on the other side of the room and turned toward me. "I'm calling it *Brandon's Decision.*"

"Thorne, that is absolutely amazing! How do you do it? The mist—it is almost as if I can feel the dampness."

"Did you take a good look at the drop of rain dripping off the hat?" His walnut-brown eyes fizzed with excitement.

"Yes!" I said. "The sparkle in it is in the shape of a question mark. What an inimitable touch!"

"A what?" He glared at me. "Is that bad?"

"No." I ran over to him and squeezed his shoulder. "It simply means it can't be imitated. You couldn't have said it in any other way. That question mark says it all. And only a few will catch that detail."

"Yeah, first glance probably won't do it." He winked. I'd never seen him do that before. "So you like it?"

"Oh, sweetie, it is beautiful! Has Brandon seen this yet?"

"No, I was gonna give it to him for his graduation present."

I totally forgot about talking to him about final exams. I was so overcome with emotion. What kind of kid gave this much thought to the decisions his brother was making? Most kids only think of themselves. Outside the world they inhabit, nothing else matters. And then if the subject matter was not enough to make one think, the sheer beauty of the painting itself—the incredible reds, oranges, and blues of the boy's Western shirt and the denim blue jeans, all penetrating the moist air—would garner a prolonged stare from anyone. The image bounced off the canvas in a gorgeous spectacle of pigment like I've never seen. My eyes went back to the raindrop with the question mark sparkle inside. Where did he come up with that? Imagination and an eye for beauty—that's what makes up Thorne Barrow.

The door burst open. "Hey, Mom, what's for supper?" Brandon's appetite, rivaled only by Kirk's, was enough to keep me busy as a full-time house chef.

"Brandon," Thorne yelled, "get outta here!"

"I'm not in your precious hidey-hole. I just opened the door."

"Well, close it! I don't want you in here."

"What's your problem, Thorne? You think you're gonna flunk them finals?"

"Shut up, Brandon!"

I went over and told Brandon he should respect Thorne's privacy, and then I gently pushed him away and gave the door a shove.

"Geez!" Brandon said as the door closed. "Someone's got a burr in their britches."

I was scheduled to substitute for Mrs. Henry in fourth grade. The last week of the school year is not a good time for a substitute teacher. The kids are bouncing off the walls, ready for summer break and the pool at Wildhorse Park.

As I walked into the room, I saw Thorne's mother arranging the desks back in rows and picking up a few scattered paper scraps and dropped pencils from the floor. "Hi, Katie," she said. "I was just thinking 'bout you. Would you mind stopping by the trailer after school today? I need to talk to you."

"Well, of course not. What did you have in mind?"

"Katie, I want to ask your opinion on something"—a nasty cough erupted from her lungs—"but this is not the place."

Mrs. Henry always kept the best lesson plans, but that didn't seem to make a lot of difference. The kids had no intention of learning anything. The girls fussed with each other, and the boys were even more disruptive. For the most part, I just counted the hours until lunch, then again till the three o'clock bell.

As I pulled up to our camp trailer we'd loaned Lana Lou, I saw her sitting out on the metal door steps, obviously deep in thought. "Hey sweetie, what're you doing out here in this heat?"

"Oh," she said, "it's even hotter inside."

I grabbed a rusty old folding chair from the yard and sat down next to my friend. "So what do you have on your mind, girl?"

"Katie, I got a call from the Realtor yesterday—my sweet neighbor here lets me use her phone—and he has a contract on my old house in the city."

"Wonderful! So when does it close?"

"The Realtor said it was a cash contract, so I should have my money in a week or so." She coughed and grabbed at her chest. "Do you think there is a possibility I could get my boy back with me if I can find a place of my own here in town?"

"Well, sure," I said. "I don't see why DFS would have a problem with that. I mean, you've got a good job, and you'll have a place of your own. What's more, the kid dearly loves you."

"I know he does, but…"

"But what?"

"Katie, I know I can't give him everything you and Kirk do."

"What are you talking about? Thorne doesn't need much. He just wants to be with his mother."

"Maybe." Another cruel cough erupted from deep in her chest. "But the thing is, I can't give him a father. And Kirk is so good for him."

"Look, sweetie, it's not like either one of us would be abandoning him. You'd be welcome to come out to the ranch anytime you want, and I know Kirk would always keep in touch. He loves Thorne. Just last night, he whispered to me, 'I'm so glad I didn't try to make a rancher out of him. Art will be his ticket to a secure financial future.'"

"So it would be okay with you if I try to get custody of my boy?"

I went over and hugged her. "Well, of course I'd be okay with that. He needs his mother, and you need him."

7

It was Saturday. Landon Throckmorton had called and wanted to know if Thorne had any more pieces to bring in. I found him in his room, putting the final touches on *Brandon's Decision*. I stood in the doorway, watching. Amazed.

Thorne must have felt surveillance from behind. "Get outta my room!" he shouted. Then he turned around and saw me. "Oh, it's you. I thought it was Brandon. What's up, Katydid?"

"Katydid! Where did you come up with that?"

He looked at me and grinned. "Well, you usually are singing a tune, just like them noisy bugs out in the yard."

I put my hand on my hip and feigned irritation. "I think that is the first time I've ever been compared to a bug."

"Okay, so it's not a very good comparison." He laughed. "Them bugs all sing in tune."

"Come on, funny guy, put your stuff away and come with me."

"Where we goin'?"

"Landon called and wants more of your art. The last one of yours just sold for forty-five hundred."

"Which one?"

"He said it was the one with the old cowboy wearing the oilskin duster riding his horse. You know, the one with heavy snow coming down sideways."

"Forty-five hundred! For that?" Thorne shook his head. "I didn't think it was very good. I guess people will pay big bucks for about anything."

"Well, put your stuff away and grab your paintings. Landon said if we can bring him more, he'll just write you a check for the one that sold right then and not have to mail it."

"Yeah, sure. Just let me finish this." After a couple of knife strokes on the country schoolhouse, he wiped the artist knife on a rag and laid it down. "Yeah, I'll go in with you, but he's not getting this piece. It's for Brandon."

Rhena Throckmorton met us at the door. Thorne was carrying one painting, and I held the other one.

"Young man, what do we have here?" She reached down to pull the painting toward her. Her mouth flew open, but no words came out. Then she took the large painting in both hands, held it up, and said, "Oh, Thorne! Oh my!" She set it on the floor, leaned it up against the wall, and stood back for a better look. "Oh, this is incredible! And look at that outstretched arm and hand—the sun-fried skin, the wrinkles on the hand, that worn-thin wedding band, and that Folgers coffee can! That can is an exact image of the real thing."

Thorne stuck both hands in his pockets. "So you like it?"

"Like it? This is absolutely amazing, Thorne. Have you given this one a title?"

Thorne ducked his head and mumbled, "I'm just calling it *Mom?*"

Rhena brought her hand up to her closed mouth. A stare lasered straight toward Thorne. Then she walked over and wrapped her arms around him. "Oh, Thorne!" She had already seen Lana Lou and knew the history. "This tells a story, and it's told beautifully in these vivid oils." She placed her hands on his shoulders. "I'm guessing this was very hard for you to do."

Thorne didn't answer.

Landon appeared from the next room, saw his wife standing in front of Thorne, and came over and put his hand on her shoulder. His eyes shot over to the large canvas. "What have we got here?"

Rhena stood and looked toward the painting. "Landon, just feast your eyes on this. Isn't this incredible? He's calling it simply *Mom?* And that's with a question mark."

Landon stood back, still staring at the piece. "*Mom?* Yes, what a great title. This will go out of this gallery as soon as we hang it."

"No, Landon! No. We're not putting it up in here. This goes in our home. I even know exactly how I'm going to frame it and where it will hang."

"Rhena, that wouldn't be fair. We don't even have a price for it."

"What would this sell for *if* we were to frame it and price it?"

Landon hesitated. "I'm afraid to say—now that I know you want to keep it."

A big baritone voice resonated from behind us. "I'll give you eighty-five hundred when you frame it."

We all turned, surprised to learn we'd not been alone. The man pulled out his wallet and reached for a credit card.

"No! I can't sell this." Rhena glared at him. "This one's mine."

"Ten grand."

Rhena walked over to him; he was obviously a regular customer in the gallery. She pointed her pistol finger at his face. "You can't have it. It's going in my home!"

"Fifteen thousand, Rhena."

"I said no!"

"Twenty thousand!"

Rhena Throckmorton stepped up to the man; a cold stare shot straight for his eyes. "Landon, get my checkbook!" Without breaking her stare at the man, she said, "Write out a check to Thorne for twenty-five thousand."

Landon stood still. The hum of the air-conditioning was the only sound. I looked back at Rhena just as she turned toward her husband. "Now!" she said with the authority of a queen.

Once again, the baritone voice boomed, "I'll give you—"

Rhena turned back to him. "Mr. Claybough, you won't give anything for this painting. It is *sold*!" Then she grinned at him. "You got that?"

Claybough retreated. "Okay, I see the boy's mother holding another piece. Can I see it?"

I was still in a state of shock. The volley between the two of them had left me breathless. "I…uh…yes." I turned the painting, showing a boot kicking the Folgers can. My brain was still overloaded with the twenty-five-thousand-dollar figure.

"Okay, how much for this one, Rhena?" Claybough was still staring at the painting in my hands.

"Ten thousand, Mr. Claybough," she said.

The man flinched. "Ouch! Might be a little steep on that one."

Rhena stood tall, both hands sparkling with diamonds. She pointed at him. "Eighty-five hundred—unframed."

Claybough pulled out a credit card. "Five thousand, Rhena!"

"Sold!" She reached for his credit card and started toward the desk.

I handed the painting to Rhena. She placed it next to the desk and swiped Claybough's card. I looked at Thorne. A big grin dominated his face, and his eyes were wide open with excitement. "Mr. Barrow," I said, "looks like you're going to have to go back home and get to painting again. You have nothing more to sell."

Claybough signed for the purchase and walked out with the painting of the boot kicking the Folgers can. I was still in a state of shock. "Five thousand?"

"Katie"—Rhena grinned—"the piece sold for the right price. It didn't really tell a story." She looked over at the one she'd just bought. "This one may even be worth more than we just paid for it, but it was all I felt like I could afford."

I was still trying to catch my breath.

"Yes," she said, "this piece employs about every tool an artist can use to create those rich colors, the exact shading, and the brushstroke techniques that make the subject pop right off the canvas. If that isn't enough, the composition—the subject—is enough to bring a tear to any eye. This piece is chock-full of emotion. No one could possibly just glance at this and go on to the next. It grabs you and holds you in a dead silence." Rhena looked back at me. "I've never seen anything comparable!"

Thorne and I walked out of the gallery with a check that would finish paying for the remainder of his tuition, plus room and board, for four years at OSU. Now if he can just get a high-enough score on his SAT to be accepted. I knew I was going to have to really push him on that. On the way home, I stopped at Best of Books, a bookstore I was familiar with, and bought *The Official SAT Study Guide*, second edition. I looked at the young man there in the pickup with me, staring out the window, blithe to the task ahead of him. My voice was just a whisper. "We've got a lot of work to do, buddy."

I was disappointed when we walked in the ranch house and found no one there. I already had the big check in my hand, ready to be waved in front of Kirk. Or Brandon...Or...I knew I had to tell Lana Lou, but she didn't even have a phone. I picked up the phone and rang Kirk's cell. No answer.

News like this couldn't wait. I went back to the pickup and drove up to where I knew the boys would be rounding up the steers to take to market. Kirk was on one side, heading the steers into the pen, and Brandon was riding Puzzle, going after one headed back out to pasture. I waited until they got the last one penned. Kirk closed the gate and headed my way. I got out of the truck with the check in my hand and started toward them, waving it like a white surrender flag.

"What you got there, Katydid?"

"Katydid? Now it's you! You been conniving with Thorne?"

"Yeah, I heard him call you that last week. Thought it was pretty cute."

"Kirk, look what I've got here in my hand!" I grasped the two sides and held it up for him to see the front of the check.

He pulled his sweat-soaked hat down to shade his eyes and squinted. Then a whistle of surprise shot out between his lips. "What is that?"

"That, Mr. Childers, is for two—just two—of Thorne's paintings!"

"No way! Are you kidding me?"

I was in the middle of relaying the entire gallery story to him when Brandon rode up and growled, "Where was Thorne when we needed him? The slacker sits in his room while we're out here bustin' our—"

"Watch it, buddy!" Kirk grabbed the check out of my hand and held it behind his back. "How much do you figure you're gonna get paid for helping out here today?"

"Probably not enough. Why?"

Kirk brought his hand out from behind his back, held the check between his index and middle fingers, and about a foot in front of Brandon's face. "You think you might come close to makin' this kind of money?"

As Brandon's eyes focused on the check, his mouth flew open. "What the…"

Kirk took his own hat off and swatted the air in front of Brandon's face. "Now, you gonna belittle Thorne for not comin' out here and helpin' us?"

Brandon's eyes bugged. "How many paintings did he have to sell to get that kind of money?"

Kirk grinned and tipped his head back slightly. "Two, Brandon. Just two."

8

It was Thursday, the last day of school. I had been substituting for Mrs. Garrison in second grade for the last three days. She thought they had timed the delivery of their second child so she'd be off for the summer break, but baby Garrison decided to come a bit early. I was glad to get the job. We needed the money.

Lana Lou caught me as I walked down the hall toward the front door. "Katie, I've got some really good news!"

"Let's hear it, sister."

"You remember my neighbor Blanche?"

"You mean the lady who owns the property where the trailer is parked?"

"Yes, she's the one. Blanche moved to Ohio to be close to her son and daughter-in-law. The movers came and picked up her furniture and things yesterday."

"Oh no! Now where are we going to find a place to move your trailer?"

A big grin spread over her wrinkled face. "Katie, Blanche is letting me rent the house. She even left a few things there for me. I have the key, and I can move in anytime now. She's not even charging me as much as some of the places we've looked at that weren't as nice. With my salary here at the school, I can afford this house."

I was almost as excited about it as she was. I hugged her and started the wheels turning in my head. "Hon, we'll need to go shop at some garage sales around town tomorrow. We'll find you some furniture and whatever else you need to set up house."

The weekend garage sales started early the next morning, and so did we. Kirk cleaned out the loose hay from the pickup bed. Lana Lou and I didn't stop until we had her a bed and a dresser, a kitchen table with two chairs, a like-new La-Z-Boy recliner, and a green sagging old green sofa that didn't match anything else. She didn't care. She was all but jumping up into my pickup each time we'd come away from a sale. I was so happy to see her enthusiasm.

On the way back to the camper, she told me Blanche had left all the appliances in the house, even a washer and a dryer. Things were certainly looking up for my friend. I carefully backed the big pickup to the front porch. I started to get out but caught sight of her sitting there in the passenger seat with a big grin on her face and staring at me. "Can you believe this?" I said. "You've got your own home, complete with furniture, appliances, and kitchen things." I grinned. "You've come a long way, baby!" A nasty cough erupted from deep in her chest.

Mr. Johnson saw us trying to carry the dresser in and came over to give us a hand. "You know, Katie, this little lady somehow manages to do more work than anyone I know. She runs circles around the teenager I hired to help. And look at her now. The woman isn't afraid to take on anything."

"She's proven to be a hard worker," I said.

He offered to help move the rest from the truck, but I told him Kirk and the boys should be here any minute. He opened the door to get in his car. "Call me if you decide you need more help."

As he drove away, I said, "That's some boss you've got there, Mrs. Barrow."

"Can't be beat. I've got you and him to thank for my job."

We didn't wait for Kirk to help. We moved most of the stuff into the house ourselves. But some pieces of furniture were just too much for us. Kirk hadn't shown up yet, so I headed back to the ranch to get the guys to come on and help us with the rest.

Thorne grabbed one of his paintings from his closet to take back with us. After the guys got the big sagging sofa inside, Thorne hung the painting above it—three horses galloping along in a thunderstorm. The colors in it clashed terribly with the old green sofa, but Lana Lou thought the whole room was nothing short of a decorator's dream. I sat down to try out the sofa and sank so far down in it I thought my butt would reach the floor. I didn't complain. Instead, I looked at my frail friend and said, "And to think you paid for all this with cash."

She grinned. "Thanks to you and Blanche, I haven't had to pay rent. I've been able to save my money. Oh, and my Realtor said we will close on my house next week, so I'll have my money then. Maybe I could buy a newer sofa. I can see you're gonna have a tough time pullin' yourself out of that old thing."

We heard a mower start up. "Sounds like someone's mowing your grass."

Lana Lou walked over to the window and peeked through the blinds. "It's your son. Brandon's mowing my yard!"

"Where did he get a mower?"

"Oh, Blanche left it for me. She said she wouldn't need it in Ohio. She's bought a condo. They take care of all the yardwork for her."

I managed to pull myself up from the old sofa, walked over to her, and put my arm around her. "You know, sweetie, God is really turning things around for you."

"I know, Katie. I'm so happy."

Then another awful coughing spell erupted. She beat her chest, hacked, and gasped for air. Then she plopped down in the big recliner, exhausted.

I gathered up some household items to take to Lana Lou. As soon as I saw her, I knew something was wrong. Her smile was gone. She led me to the kitchen, where she poured us both a cup of coffee. We sat down at the kitchen table.

"John won't sign for me to sell the house."

I thought I saw a tear welling up in her eyes. "Oh no. What made him change his mind?"

"I think he got to talking to some of his fellow inmates, and they convinced him he should have half the proceeds."

"So what are you going to do?"

"I don't know. The contract price is already so low I wouldn't get much out of it. I'd hoped to be able to buy this house from Blanche. She said she'd sell to me when I got my money."

I looked at her with a bit of evil in my eye and said, "Girl, just let him sit there behind bars with no cigarettes for a while. He'll sign."

9

The clock on my nightstand glowed with the numbers I'd been staring at intermittently for the past hour. Now it was fifteen minutes past midnight, and Thorne wasn't home yet. I nudged my snoring husband. "Honey, I'm worried. Thorne hasn't come in yet."

Kirk glanced over at the clock. With a heavy voice, he drawled, "Awh, where is the little goober?"

"Didn't you tell him to be home by eleven?"

"Yeah, I made it perfectly clear to him. Curfew was at eleven—sharp!"

Brandon had dated occasionally and was always home right at or before curfew time, even on prom night. But this was the second time Thorne was late. I asked Kirk what he thought we should do. He simply rolled over and mumbled under the covers, "Give him heck about it tomorrow morning."

"But what if he's had an accident or something?"

"Babe, he's got his cell phone."

"How can you be so nonchalant about this?" My irritation was building. "You dads can just roll over and go back to sleep. We mothers are cut from a different fabric. We can't ignore something like this. He may be in danger and needs our help, and you just turn over and go back to sleep?"

Kirk threw the covers to one side. "So what are we supposed to do, Kate? Get up, get dressed, and go hunt him down?"

"Well, yes," I snapped. "If you think you can pull yourself out of bed."

"Embarrass him in front of his girlfriend? That'd really score some points with him."

I'd already turned the light on and was reaching for my jeans and sweatshirt. I looked back at the bed. Kirk hadn't moved. "So you're just going to lie there and let me go look for him?" Now I was beyond annoyed; I was fuming. I grabbed my jeans and started pulling them on, hoping I could still zip them up after the big supper we had.

I felt a tap on my shoulder, turned, and Kirk was handing my cell phone to me. "Why don't you just give him a call?" He cocked his head to one side, grinned, and stood there with that patronizing posture of his that I've come to hate. "See if he's had trouble," he said. "It'd be a whole lot easier, and not quite so embarrassing for him."

Just as I reached for the phone, we both heard it. Gears downshifting, squealing brakes, and a vehicle obviously out of control. I stood there with my jeans still unzipped, "Okay, Mr. C., this battle's got your name all over it. I'm going back to bed."

Final exams for Thorne were about to begin, and I knew he hadn't studied. I'd reminded him twice, and both times, all I got was, "Me and Misty are gonna study together today after school. Besides, they ain't gonna be that hard."

"Well, from listening to your grammar now," I said, "you just might flunk your English test."

It seemed this Misty had taken over Thorne's ability to think straight. His grades had been dropping ever since this blonde Barbie had come into his life. Rhena Throckmorton had called, wanting more pieces for the gallery, but Thorne hadn't touched a brush since I deposited the big gallery check into his account. The supper table was a dash-in–dash-out event for him. I knew his teenage hormones had effectively eclipsed his dreams. It was time again for another Kirk-Thorne talk.

But that never happened.

There was a call the next day from Betty Sawyer, Thorne's caseworker. "Katie," she said, "I've got good news."

"Great, Betty, I could use some good news. What's this about?"

"I've just signed the papers. Mrs. Barrow has regained her parental rights. Thorne can now be returned to her. You and Kirk have been such a good match for him. I know he'll do well now back with his mom."

I was quiet.

"Katie, I have to hand it to you. Had you not befriended Lana Lou like you did and gotten her back in the mainstream of society, this would never be happening. You are to be commended for the compassion you showed and all the hard work involved in her rehabilitation."

I was still without words. Betty had to ask if I was still on the line.

Still speechless, I sat down in the nearest chair. I knew this is what we had been working toward for so long. My friend needed her son, and he needed her. I knew this, but my heart was doing battle with my brain. Thorne—well, Thorne was Thorne: cocky, carefree, and often fickle. And yes, I wanted him to be with his mother—just not quite yet. We still had some work to do on him. He'd managed to pass all his final exams, but I wanted to work with him to get his SAT score up to a respectable number. His last score wouldn't get him in any college, much less OSU, as I'd hoped. Would Lana Lou be able to help with that?

And this brainless Barbie he'd been spending every spare minute with was not good for him. Would Lana Lou know how to handle that? And what about his painting? Would he just drop it completely now that this Misty had filled his sights and manipulated his hormones?

No, this was just not a good time for him to leave us. This kid had way too much potential to drop everything we'd worked for. Lana Lou—sweet as she is—knew nothing about steering a child like this to a finish line. He needed to be with us! At least for a while longer.

Kirk knew something was wrong as soon as he walked in the door. I ran to him and tipped my head into his chest. My emotions were so conflicting I couldn't even start to tell him what had happened.

"Sit down," he said. "Whatever it is, it can't be all that bad."

I finally blurted out, "We're losing Thorne!" Then I told him about Lana Lou regaining her parental rights.

Kirk had a bewildered look on his face. "But isn't that what you've wanted all along?"

"Yes, but this is not a good time. We were already starting to lose him. His grades have dropped, he's quit painting, and it's all to be blamed on that little prurient Barbie doll. Lana Lou won't know how to handle that."

Much to my surprise, Kirk agreed with me. "Babe, why don't we all sit down with Thorne and talk about these things you're worried about? Let's bring his mother in, and we'll all sit down and discuss it. I'd be the first—okay, maybe the second one to say I've seen a change in the kid. And not for the good either."

The next day, we moved Thorne's things to Lana Lou's house. I thought about bringing a cake to celebrate with her, but somehow I just couldn't bring myself to do that. A celebration right now just didn't seem right.

Lana Lou, Thorne, Kirk and I sat down together in the living room of her rented house. I sat on the floor, because I knew the ugly old sofa would have me barely off the floor anyway. Kirk and I did most of the talking. Thorne could see we were concerned.

I looked into Lana Lou's eyes. "This kid has so much potential! He's got college ahead of him and a career in art most struggling artists would die for. I just hate to see him throw it away—

It was Lana Lou who interrupted. "Thorne," she said, pointing her twig of a finger at him, "you listen to what they are saying. Talent like you have can't be wasted on a girl at this point in your life. You just need to put that girl on the back burner and put your art and school up front." She wasn't through with her speech. "I've never had a say in discipline with you or your brothers. Your dad always shut me up. But I'm tellin' you, son, you better listen to Miss Katie and me. This Misty girl is causing you a heap o' trouble, and you'd do well to drop her like a hot potato."

Thorne searched his mother's eyes, grinned, and said, "That won't be necessary." He hesitated. "She dropped me last night."

We were all silent, but he could see we had questions. "Yeah, she hooked up with this big dude who came in to the store where she worked, and he put his magic spell on her. Anyways, I was beginning to see she was only dating me 'cause I told her how much money I was makin' off of my paintings. Then she found out all my money was goin' into a savings account and I wasn't gonna spend a dime of it on her. So she dumped me."

"Well, Thorne," Lana Lou started to say, "it's best—

A coughing spell interrupted her. She beat her chest and then gasped for air. Her once-sun-browned face lost what little color it just had. I thought she might pass out, but I didn't know what to do to help her.

10

It was graduation day, and the auditorium had been decorated like I've never seen it before. Various university posters plastered the side walls. The Luther Lions logo formed the backdrop of the stage, with poster pictures of each of the graduating seniors displayed on separate easels down in front of the raised stage.

Luther is a small town where most people know everyone in town and the surrounding area. When asked, I was proud to tell them Brandon would be going to OSU, where Kirk and I had both graduated.

I kept looking around for Thorne and Lana Lou, and just before the ceremony began, Thorne, in a flash, slid into the chair next to Kirk's. "Where's your mom?" I asked.

"Mom didn't feel like coming," he whispered. "She is really sick. Can't breathe. I've been taking care of her. She's been in bed for three days now. I've been cookin' for her and bringing her water and her meds."

"Oh gosh!" I said. "I feel terrible not checking in on her. I can bring some meals by for you two. Do I need to take her to the hospital?"

"No, she won't go. I already asked her. She said there is nothing they can do. The COPT is really bad."

"You mean COPD."

"Yeah, she won't use her oxygen. Says it burns her nose."

"So now I understand why you told Brandon you couldn't come to the taco party."

"Yeah, Katie, she's really sick. I'm real worried."

I put my arm around him and squeezed his shoulder.

The superintendent of schools rose from his seat on the stage and officially opened the program. "Ladies and gentlemen, I am proud to present this year's graduating class—

I didn't hear anything else he said. Visions of my friend lying in her bed, barely able to breathe, made me want to run out the door and down the block to her house. I had wanted to check in on her yesterday, but with all of the end-of-school activities and graduation, I didn't take the time. We had invited several of Brandon's friends to the ranch for a taco party last evening, and my day was spent in the kitchen preparing for ten energetic about-to-graduate seniors, all with appetites to match their level of energy.

As I was sitting there thinking about what I could do to help Lana Lou, the speeches began. Brandon made us proud with his salutatorian address. He was beat out for valedictorian by only two-tenths of a point—and the two-tenths advantage was by his girlfriend.

As soon as graduation was over and we'd visited a bit with friends, Kirk and I hurried over to Lana Lou's. Thorne had already raced over well ahead of us.

He greeted us at the door and led us to the bedroom. She was pale, gasping for breath, but smiled as I took her hand. Kirk and I prayed with her. I could see it would take a miracle for her to pull through. Again, she refused to let us take her to the hospital.

"Katie"—she squeezed my hand—"I know I'm dying…" A rattle deep inside her chest hinted at her critical condition. She was struggling but continued, "and I just want to be here—in my house, with my son."

Her breaths were erratic. I felt her wrist and could barely feel a pulse. Her beautiful walnut-brown eyes searched deep into my own. A profound sense of emotions flowed silently between us. Finally, she whispered, "Thank you."

I placed my hand on her forehead and pulled back her hair a bit. I looked at her neck and saw the mottling. I knew it was the end. Thorne was standing on the other side of her bed. He looked at me and realized the finality of the moment. He reached down and slowly kissed his mom on the cheek as she drew her last breath.

I knew there were several phone calls I should make. The first, of course, was for an ambulance to come pick up Lana Lou's body. Then I called Mr. Johnson, the school superintendent who had hired Lana Lou. Fifteen minutes later, he was knocking on the door. With compassion in his eyes, he grabbed Thorne and hugged him in silence. Thorne ducked his head, and I watched this brave young man as he fought back a pending flood of tears.

The thought crossed my mind that I should notify family. But what family? We were her only family. I knew enough about John Barrow, her scoundrel of a husband, to know I would never let him know of his wife's death. But what about her other two sons? The oldest, Johnny, I knew was serving life in prison for the kidnapping and physical abuse of Thorne a few years back. The hinges to the gates of Hades would frost over before I'd let him know.

I asked Thorne about his other brother.

"You mean Josh?" he said without much feeling. "He's not family anymore. I don't have any brothers, except Brandon."

Brandon! We hadn't even called to tell Brandon. I didn't know if he was still with the other graduates or had driven on home. I called his cell phone. He was still at the school with a few of his friends. Five minutes later, he walked in the door, went immediately to Thorne, and bear-hugged him. I don't see many kids now with that kind of compassion for others. Most are concerned only about what others are thinking of them.

Brandon got in his pickup and opened the door for Thorne from the inside. The outside handle was broken. After a few seconds of grinding, he finally got the old truck started, and they drove back to the ranch. Kirk and I followed after meeting the ambulance. Then we locked up the house—the one my friend had been so proud of.

I got busy and prepared Thorne's favorite supper. Angus burgers, french fries, and chocolate pie. It was at the supper table when Thorne brought up something I'd never given a thought to. "You know"—he was choosing his words carefully—"Mom didn't have any money." A tear popped up in his left eye. "I want her to have a nice funeral."

I was trying to prevent my own tears from gushing out. "Sweetie, I think I know what you want to ask, but I'd like for you to go ahead and say it anyway."

He wiped at his eyes with his shirt sleeve. "Can I take money out of my savings to give her a real nice funeral?"

I knew my answer before he even asked. "Of course you can, Thorne. We'll take you into town so you can pick out exactly what you want. Then we'll withdraw whatever it takes from your account." Then a thought struck me. "All it would take to replenish your account would be a couple more paintings. The Throckmortons are waiting for more pieces from you—when you're ready."

"I'm ready," he said. "I started one last night."

Kirk's cell phone rang. It was Brandon, stranded again in the old beater pickup, eight miles from home. Kirk and Brandon had spent many evenings working on the thing. First it was the brakes. They had to be replaced. Then the U-joints—whatever that is. Then the windshield wipers' motor had to be replaced. Brandon couldn't drive it anywhere there was mud—and we have a lot of that around here. The accelerator sticks just when you need to ease through the mud and muck. Then you're stuck! Just last night, Kirk had spent two hours doing something to the carburetor.

"What now?" I said.

"Sounds like maybe the fuel line is plugged." Kirk slammed the flip-phone shut. "We need to go. I don't want him to be out there trying to thumb a ride."

11

Thorne Barrow may have been his mom's only blood family at the funeral, but that didn't mean much. All of the school staff was there—teachers, principal and superintendent, cafeteria workers, bus drivers, and many of the students. This little town of Luther amazes me. People came who hardly knew Lana Barrow. Some had heard about her story. Some knew her son's story. Some only knew me as a substitute teacher. Every neighboring rancher whom Kirk had ever talked to came to the funeral. What an outpouring of love from a community who values family and friends. I determined right then that I'd never live anywhere else.

Thorne had done a marvelous job of orchestrating his mother's funeral. I had just stepped back and let him do it all. That's what he wanted. The music, the flowers, the minister—all his doing. The artist was evident in everything he arranged. But what took me by total surprise was a phone call he'd made on his own—a call to Lena Throckmorton. He asked permission to display the painting that she had purchased, the one she had paid twenty-five thousand dollars for. The one with the malnourished and brown, sun-damaged arm with a bony hand stretching out and holding a Folgers coffee can. A brass plaque with the title was affixed to the large frame of sun-bleached driftwood. This emotional piece was displayed on a beautiful walnut easel that Landon Throckmorton furnished.

Thorne apparently had asked Lena Throckmorton to say a few words at the service. She got up, stood so elegantly by the easel with the painting, placed her hand on the top of the piece, and started.

"This, people, is the work of Thorne Barrow. For those of you who know much about art, you can easily see the quality of this piece. I had the privilege of purchasing this from Thorne a couple of months ago. I predict it will escalate greatly in value, even from the sum I paid for it.

"The real value I see is more than what meets the eye here. This young man had a story to tell. Yes, it's the story of his mother. How he found her, homeless, living on the streets and begging for money from strangers.

"That's only the beginning of the story. The rest tells about a woman most of you know. Katie Childers. Katie and Kirk Childers not only took this homeless mother's son in to their home and steered him into becoming the famous artist he is today, but Katie also made Lana Barrow her friend, finding a job for her, providing a home for her, and giving her back the dignity she had lost for so many years.

"I'd like for each of you to take a closer look at this painting and understand that her son chose to capture the story of Lana Lou Barrow with a title that brings tears to my eyes every time I walk by this beautiful work of art in my home—*Mom?* Yes, that's with a question mark. When Thorne first found his mother out there panhandling, he wasn't even sure he was looking at his mother. The last time he had seen her, she was healthier, made breakfast for him, sent him off to school, and proudly displayed his early pencil drawings on her refrigerator.

"Friends, this is not your usual piece of art. Yes, it has all of the elements of great art, as far as technique is concerned. Balance, composition, the light that is incorporated, and how the viewer's eye moves throughout the piece—it's all there. But there is more, much more—something else that makes a piece of art a masterpiece. Plain and simple, if you simply cannot take your eyes off it, if it strikes your soul to the very depths, then you are looking at a masterpiece.

"Folks, you are looking at a masterpiece."

Lena sat down. There were no dry eyes in the crowd. Silence wafted throughout the room like lazy clouds in a sky of blue. Then a music student from Luther took up her violin and started playing "Amazing Grace." Yes, I thought, it was truly amazing grace that carried my friend through the gates of heaven.

Then it was Thorne's turn to speak. I knew he had prepared a beautiful speech; he'd worked till late at night on it. He stood, walked over to the easel, and touched the shriveled hand in his painting. He turned, briefly looked at the audience with an ever-so-slight perfunctory smile, and, with tears filling his eyes, he turned back to the painting and simply said, "Mom, I love you." There was a hush felt throughout the auditorium. He could say no more.

He turned, ducked his head, and slowly walked back to his seat, holding the three handwritten pages he had planned to read. I knew when he was writing the speech, he was having a difficult time. Tears filled his eyes and occasionally dripped onto the paper. I wondered then how he could possibly get through reading it at the funeral.

Oh, but what a handsome man he had been, standing there by the painting. Kirk had taken him to town for a haircut and outfitted him with a new tailored black two-button Brunswick suit, a charcoal pinpoint shirt, and a madder-blue silk tie. His shoes were black and hand-polished for the occasion. He stood tall, his sooty-black hair draped over his forehead and just above those beautiful deep-set walnut-brown eyes. He was quite a striking figure in this come-as-you-are town. His appearance definitely set him apart from anyone else in the school auditorium. It was at that moment I knew this young man would make his mark in the world. I was looking at a future celebrity in the art world. Yes, I was proud, but my heart hurt for him. He loved his mom so much.

12

Back at the hospital

I WAS STARTLED BY some loud voices out in the hall. There was a heated argument. Some guy was lacing his words with profanities, and a girl was lashing back with her own colorful refutations. I listened for a few minutes. Then the squabble escalated, and I was afraid their anger was about to lead to physical violence.

I walked over to the door of the waiting room. "You two need to take your disagreements somewhere else!"

"Butt out, lady!" The guy scowled at me, his face beet red, a vein popping in his neck. "This is between me and my girl, so you mind your own business!"

"No, slick!" My own anger was surfacing. "You've made it my business by shouting your ugly obscenities here in this hospital, where there are people in pain, suffering, and maybe trying to sleep."

Nothing gets my dander up quicker than the use of God's name in a vulgar attempt at expressing oneself. The guy wrapped his arm around the girl's neck, forcing her farther down the hall. She squirmed and tried to free herself from his headlock.

I stepped forward and watched as he punched her in the ribs with his other hand. Common sense would have told me to turn and head toward the nurses' station to call for help. But common sense must have been hidden under this head of red hair. I quickly moved up behind the couple and blurted out, "Take your filthy hands off the girl!"

He ignored me.

"I said, turn her loose right now, or I'm callin' security."

The guy turned toward me, still keeping a tight grip around the girl's neck. I stepped up to him, pulled the dead cell phone out of my pocket, flipped it open as if to dial, and only then did I recognize the girl. It was the girl Thorne had dated back in high school, her thick mascara smeared, a bruise on her left cheek, and her hand tugging at the bully's arm at her neck.

I was so shook up I couldn't even think of her name, but I could see she recognized me. The stampede of footsteps behind me broke the silence. A couple of men in hospital scrubs grabbed the guy.

The RN I'd talked to earlier asked if I was all right. I could feel the blood leaving my face, and I broke out in a cold sweat. The floor and walls of the hallway began to spin, and I could feel my body going down.

When I woke up, my volunteer friend was sitting by my side. Disoriented, I said, "Where…where am I?"

"It's okay," she said, "you're in good hands. It seems you may have had a sudden drop in blood sugar. You went down, and a nurse brought you here to this room. It looks like they've got your sugar level back up, gave you some orange juice. You don't remember?"

I stared blankly at her. "No, I don't recall that. Last thing I can remember is some stinking coward was bullying a girl out in the hall."

She laughed. "They told me you were right in his face, giving him the what-for!" She shook her head in a way older women sometimes do. "I gotta hand it to you. You've got guts, girl!"

I started to get up, but my friend told me to lie back down. "You have no place to go, so you should just rest here a bit more before you go back out and try to confront another 250-pound linebacker." A smile broke across her face, and she put her hand up in an attempt to hide it.

I thought about Kirk and said, "I need to see if the doctor has come back with news about my husband."

"Honey"—she pushed her oversize plastic glasses up a bit—"the nurses know where you are. They'll direct the doctor to you when he comes for an update."

I felt even more helpless, lying there in a strange place, Kirk lying somewhere on an operating table with surgeons working on his crushed body, and my boys—"Where are my boys? They should have been here by now."

"Honey, like I said, the nurses know where you are. They'll direct your sons in here as soon as they arrive. Now, I want to hear what happened to this boy of yours. Thorne—is that his name?"

13

"Oh yes—Thorne. At times he lives up to his name. As Shakespeare put it, 'the thousand natural shocks that flesh is heir to.'" The kid has caused us some anguish and some sleepless nights, but most of the time, he has brought us joy. He certainly is making a name for himself in the art world, and he's just beginning college. It was his dream to do graduate work at School of the Art Institute in Chicago. I hope it can still happen."

"You call him your son. Did you adopt him?"

"Yes, we did. And yes, he was almost eighteen. That didn't matter. He was already family. How could we refuse to adopt him after his sweet mother passed on?

"Unlike the last time, when we adopted Brandon, the courtroom was empty. We stood before the judge—the same judge that had presided over Brandon's adoption. It became obvious that he remembered us. After his usual rhetoric relating to an adoption, he looked at us and smiled. "Mr. and Mrs. Childers, you are to be commended for your dedication and love for children." He slammed his gavel down and said, "You are now the proud parents of this young man."

"Our caseworker, Betty Sawyer, couldn't understand why we would want to adopt a child who was about to turn eighteen. 'What's the point?' she had said cold-heartedly. 'He's almost an adult.'

"I glared at my longtime friend, feigned insult, and then said, 'The point is, Betty, Thorne has been a part of our family from the day you brought him to us.'

"She knew me well enough to know I was in no way insulted. 'Katie,' she said, 'you and Kirk know better than anyone I know how to build a family. I could not be happier for Brandon and Thorne. I just wish all of my cases could have happy endings like this.'

"Betty was instrumental in obtaining the legal documents required to adopt Thorne. John Barrow had to be convinced to give up his rights to his son. But we weren't worried about him refusing. Thorne was about to turn eighteen, and parental rights would not even come into question at that point.

"Brandon had been sitting at the back of the courtroom. He got up as we walked by, punched Thorne on the shoulder, and said, 'Welcome to the family, little brother.'

"I have heard people make comments about adopted children, as if they are not much more than invited guests in the home. I've heard this question asked more than once, 'Where's his real mother?' That pretty much brings my blood to a boil. A *real* mother is the one who cooks his meals, helps him with his homework, plans a birthday party for him, keeps an eye on him throughout the night when he's plagued by a croupy cough, turns her worrier up a notch the day he gets his driver's permit, lies awake at night when he's late coming home from a date. Don't tell me I'm not his real mother!"

"Katie," she said, "that says it all. Yes, that is exactly the definition of a real mother."

I sat up, looked at the imaginary watch on my left arm, and pulled out Kirk's cell phone for the time, forgetting the battery was dead. Then I looked back at her, questioning.

She smiled. "Girl, don't worry about me. I'm not on a clock anymore. My relief volunteer is already making rounds. I have nothing better to do."

"Are you sure? I don't want to bore you with all this."

"No, no, I'd love to hear more."

I couldn't understand why she'd want to hear more, but I knew talking was just the medicine I needed. It was cathartic, at a time when I needed it the most.

"Well"—I thought back to the time in question—"it had been over two years since Brandon's *other* mother had had any contact with him. There had been no birthday cards, no Christmas gifts, no phone calls, or even e-mails. So I was surprised when I heard her voice on the phone. 'Katie,' she said, 'I've got a graduation present for Brandon. I'd like to come out to the ranch and give it to him.'

"When we adopted Brandon, we had given Denise limited visitation rights, as long as Brandon agreed. The first year after his adoption, we had heard nothing from her. She was in China with her jet-setting oil-baron husband. For years afterward, an occasional phone call or a short e-mail was all he would hear from her. In all those years, he had received one Christmas present and two birthday cards, which were at least a month late."

I said, "Denise, you caught me by surprise. We haven't heard from you in a long time. We thought you had dropped off the face of the earth. I'm surprised you even remembered Brandon was graduating."

I thought I heard a slight moan on the line. Then she said, "Martin and I have been spending most of the time at our home in the Bahamas, except for the six months we were in Brazil. Martin's rigs are still there, and he flies down about once a month to check on the drilling. I went with him a couple of times, but—

I said, "Denise, I don't care to hear any more about your world travels, and neither does Brandon. Now, you were saying you want to come and bring a graduation gift for him?"

Her voice got louder. "Uh…I can do that, or I can take this big monster back to the dealership—maybe that's what I should do anyway."

"Her irritation on the other end of the line came through loud and clear, but probably unmatched by my own. Dealership! What did she think she was doing? She hadn't said a word to Brandon for over two years, not even a birthday card. Now she's gone and bought him a vehicle—probably a new one at that! And probably paid cash for it, or whipped out her American Express card.

"Honey," my volunteer said, "was his birth mother really that wealthy?"

I laughed. "She fell into wealth—literally! It was at an AA meeting she was required to attend. She met this wealthy oilman—

"Well, for heaven's sake, why couldn't she keep her son?"

"Well, you see, her new husband considered Brandon to be extra baggage in their jet-setting lifestyle. So it was either Brandon or her meal ticket. She chose the meal ticket."

My friend pursed her lips and shook her head, obviously disgusted. I raised my hand, like a student asking to speak. "Honey, are you sure you want to hear any more of this?"

"Yes, don't stop now." She grinned. "Sounds like you're just getting to the good part."

"Well, you just tell me when to shut up, okay?"

She stuck her index finger up and to one side like I've seen older ladies do. "No, this is good for you. It keeps your mind off your present situation, and it keeps me wanting more of the story." She laughed. "And I don't even have to pay for the entertainment."

"Okay, well, where was I?"

"The unexpected graduation gift…"

"Yes, well…"

I calmed down as soon as I remembered that old clunker we'd bought Brandon—the one that had left him stranded more than once. So I said, "Okay, Denise, just come on out. Brandon and Kirk are out mending fences, but I can probably get him on his cell phone when you get here."

The loud crack in my ear told me she'd slammed the phone down. Past experiences with Denise Whatever-her-name-was-at-the-time had told me she was the reason for Webster's word *capricious*. Back when Betty was Brandon's caseworker, she told me Denise couldn't be trusted, and she never knew what to expect from the woman.

I was thinking, *Who knows if she'll come on out and bring this graduation present or take it back to the dealership.* At that point, I really didn't care—but a new set of wheels would sure make things easier around here. Kirk and I had talked about it, and we dreaded the thought of Brandon heading off to college with that old clunker. But then Kirk had reminded me that my old car I had in college was no better. He'd spent many afternoons camped out in the parking lot of my dorm, working on the old thing.

"So did she follow through and bring him a graduation present?"

"Honey, you sure you want to hear this? I feel like I'm spilling my guts out to a new friend who probably has better things to do than listen to me."

"Are you kidding?" My friend grinned. "This is better than the paperback novel I'm reading at home. Please, continue."

The RN on duty peeked in the door just then. "Mrs. Childers, are you doing okay now?"

"Yes, I'm fine now. Thanks."

"I can get you more juice or something from the employee fridge. We keep it pretty well stocked."

"No, thanks. I'm fine."

She left, and my friend rolled her index finger for me to continue.

Denise did, in fact, follow through. Exactly one hour later, my cell phone sounded with the familiar ringtone Kirk had placed on it for me, right after we bought it—"You're Still the One" by Shania Twain never fails to get my attention, and I'm always hoping it is Kirk calling.

Instead, it was Denise. I held the phone out from my ear a bit to reduce the sound of her infamous loud voice. "Katie, I'm sittin' up here at this flippin' gate. You wanna give me the combination so I can come on in?"

I wasn't about to give her the combination. The electronic gate is there to keep people like her from coming in. So I said, "I'll be up in a second, Denise."

Kirk and Brandon were in our truck over in the east pasture, and Brandon's old beater was in the shop again, so I jumped on our trusty old four-wheeler and headed up toward the gate. I stood up on the running boards as I drove—

"Oh girl!" My friend grabbed at her stomach and laughed. "I can just see that!"

"Well, that's the mode of transportation for us farm girls. Anyway…as I got closer to the gate, I couldn't believe my eyes. On the other side of the gate was a brand-new Dodge three-quarter ton Turbo Diesel, crew cab, and—oh my gosh—four-wheel drive!"

I stopped and punched in the code. The gate opened, and I motioned for Denise to come on through. Behind her was Martin in an identical pickup.

They both drove through, and I was eating their dust, so I stopped to let the dust settle and called Brandon on his cell. "You need to come on up to the house. Denise is here and has a graduation present for you."

"Denise!" he blurted out. "Tell her I don't have time to come up and see her—just like she never had time for me!"

"Uh, Brandon…I think you'll want to come up and see what she has for you."

"Yeah, like I really care!"

"I think you might." I said, 'Get your butt on up here now before she decides to take it back."

I heard him utter what sounded like a curse word under his breath—something I'd never heard him utter. "Okay, tell her I'll be there as soon as we finish this."

I said, "No! You're not going to leave me stuck up there with her by myself. You get on up to the house now!"

When I pulled up to the front gate, Denise was already at the front door. Martin remained in the other pickup truck. As I walked past the vacated truck, I could see tan leather and what looked like a navigation system in the dash, and as I looked up, I saw that the top of the cab was lined across the front with slanted yellow lights. Was this Brandon's graduation present?

I walked over to the front door and invited Denise in. "Martin," she said, "wants to stay in his truck. He's got several phone calls to return."

After some dreaded small talk, Denise finally said, "Do you think Brandon will like it?"

I didn't know exactly how to respond. She had never actually told me the graduation present was in fact the beautiful diesel pickup sitting out there in our driveway. "Well, I'm sure he'll appreciate whatever it is."

Denise had been looking out the window toward the truck. She turned quickly, flippantly tossing her salon-crimped shoulder-length blood-red hair and said, "It's a Dodge, of course!"

I was glad to hear Kirk pulling up in our truck, getting me out of my jam. "Hang on," I said. "I think I hear them now."

When Brandon walked in the door, he barely acknowledged Denise and started walking back to his room. I hollered for him to come back in. "Denise has a graduation present for you."

He slowly walked back in to the big room. Denise went to him, got right up in his face, and held a set of keys up to within inches of his nose. "What's that?" he muttered, as he backed away a bit.

"It's your graduation present, you idiot!" She was jiggling the set of keys in front of him now.

He backed off a bit more and stuck both hands in his pockets. "What am I supposed to do with those keys?"

My friend laughed again. I knew she was enjoying this story, so I went on.

"Denise was becoming a bit impatient with him. She reached out, gently grabbed him by the shirt, and pulled him back toward her. She reached down, pulled his right hand out of his pocket, and slammed the set of keys in the palm of his hand. He looked toward me as if he needed some backup.

I shrugged my shoulders and grinned.

At that point, Denise took Brandon's arm and led him to the front door. "Those keys in your hand, Brandon, fit that new Dodge truck out there. That's your graduation present from me and Martin."

Brandon stood stone still, didn't crack a smile. It was a bit embarrassing. I jumped in and said, "Brandon, I think you probably should say something. Maybe a big 'Thank you.'"

He looked at me with question marks in both eyes. "Is this for real?"

"Well, I don't know," I said. "Let's go see if they really do fit."

At that point, Brandon rocketed out the door. As I was following behind, I saw him run to the truck, open the door, and jump in behind the wheel. We immediately heard the big diesel engine rumble. It was a sound different from the old beater truck we'd managed to buy him. That is, when it would even come to life and make a sound.

Only then did we see the ear-to-ear grin appear.

My friend pushed up those big glasses that had slipped on her nose. "So she really did give him a new Dodge truck? Even after not having hardly anything to do with him before?"

"Yes, she did."

Denise reached into her huge Prada Daino tote bag and pulled out a vehicle title and registration papers. "We've already tagged it and paid the sales tax." There was no emotion, just a matter-of-fact businesslike moment.

"I accepted the papers, looked at the title, and saw it was, in fact, made out to Brandon Childers."

"Diesel fuel is pretty expensive," she said, "so give him this prepaid gas card. There's five hundred dollars on it."

I stood there like a turkey in a downpour, looking up toward the heavens. God, can this be real? As much as I had despised the woman for years for the way she had neglected her son, I found myself reaching for her with a big Oklahoma-style hug.

Martin Van Buren never showed his face. Without any goodbye to Brandon, Denise walked back to the other Dodge truck, got in, and we haven't seen or heard from her since.

"Well, if that don't beat all!" My friend said.

I saw her glance down at her watch. "Honey," she said with the softest voice, "I probably should be going, but I'd love to hear more. If you're here tomorrow, maybe you can finish this story for me. I feel like I already know your family."

"Oh, I'll probably be here. But hopefully, it will be up in my husband's room."

14

The same RN popped her head in the door. "You still okay?"

"Yes, I'm fine. May I go back out to the waiting room? I'm afraid I'll miss the doctor when he comes to talk."

"Sure," she said. "I just thought you might be more comfortable staying here. You know, the chaise lounge you're sitting on looks pretty inviting. I'm tempted to sneak back here at times."

"Well, if it's okay, I think I'll go back out to the waiting room. Oh, by the way, whatever happened to the couple who was arguing out in the hall?"

"I heard someone called the cops and they escorted the two of them out. I guess the guy gave them quite a time. They said the girl was beat up pretty bad, but she refused to be admitted."

I thought, Thorne's Brainless Barbie got herself into a heap of trouble when she met up with that hooligan.

I found the same chair I'd been planted in earlier. There were others in the room now. My stomach told me I needed to get something to eat, but there was no way I was going to run down to the cafeteria and miss the doctor—or the boys. Where were those boys? Something had happened. I just knew it.

My emotions were teeter-tottering between sadness for poor Kirk and what he must be going through now and worry for my tardy boys.

Every time anyone walked by, I looked up, hoping it would be Dr. Brockman. For the hundredth time, I glanced at the clock. Where were the boys? They should have been here long ago. I picked up that copy of *Reader's Digest* again. The page I opened to was a story about a famous racehorse having to be put down due to a broken leg. I quickly dropped it back to the table.

"Mrs. Childers...

It was Dr. Brockman. My heart skipped a few beats. I jumped up from my chair. "Yes, how's Kirk doing? Is he out of surgery?"

"Surgery, although lengthy, went as expected. Kirk is now in ICU. His vital signs are all stabilized at this time."

"So I can go up and see him now?"

"Yes, but first, I need to fill you in on Kirk's prognosis." He looked around and saw other people in the waiting room. "Katie, follow me to the conference room. It's just down at the end of the hall.

"As I told you earlier, Kirk suffered a break in his spine. Actually that part of his spine was crushed. Part of the reason the surgery took so long is we had to remove all of the bone fragments. Then we had to support and stabilize the vertebrae and bones in the spine. The location of the break is critical to any mobility. The good news is some C 5 patients eventually are able to feed themselves and even operate a power chair. That's what we can hope for. It will take months of therapy to get there. As time passes, with regular rehabilitation and additional surgeries, there probably can be some improvement in Kirk's mobility. The bad news is from this point down"—he reached around and touched an area just below his neck—"he will have no feeling, no use of his legs, and no control over his bodily functions. He will need twenty-four-hour, round-the-clock care."

"Oh dear God," I burst out. "This is even worse than I imagined."

"Katie, you're right, it is bad. But remember, it could be worse. If the break had been higher up, we would be in serious trouble.

Breathing would have to be with the help of a ventilator. At this point, we're hoping that won't be a problem for Kirk. Whoever will be his caregiver—

"Oh, I'll be the one to care for him. Will someone train me?"

"Yes, you'll be trained to meet his needs, at least after a while. Kirk will need to be transferred to a facility specializing in spinal cord injuries. There's such a facility right here in the city. At the end of his stay there, he should be admitted to a full-time care facility for the next month or so. But right now, I know you are anxious to see him. I'll go over more details with you later.

"Just give me one minute to call upstairs and make sure everything is ready. Unless I get back to you, you'll be able to go on up in about five minutes or so. ICU is on the fourth floor. Just make a right as you exit the elevator. He'll probably be in the first room on your left—at least that's what I've requested. There's a glass wall there, so you'll see him as you walk up to his room. His head is restrained, so he may not see you at first. Just give it five minutes before you head upstairs. Okay?"

All I could do was nod.

As I dropped back down in my chair, I felt moisture forming in my eyes again, so I grabbed another tissue from the box. With my elbows on my knees and both hands holding the tissue, I sank my face into the lotion-infused tissue. I tried to pray, but I was interrupted by thoughts of Dandy. Our dairy cows needed to be milked; how I could possibly manage the ranch and take care of Kirk too? The boys—had they gotten into an accident? It had been over five hours since I talked to Brandon. "Oh Jesus!" My voice was muffled by the tissue.

I felt a hand on my shoulder and heard a familiar voice: "Jesus is here, Mom, and so are we."

I jumped out of my chair like a jackrabbit being shot at, dropped the tissue, and looked into Brandon's face. "Brandon! What took you so long?"

Thorne reached around his brother and hugged me. "We stopped by the ranch, saw the cows needed to be milked, and after that, we went into town to the vet's office to see what he'd done about Dandy."

I froze. "And?"

Brandon's eyes met mine. His sad face said it all, and I knew. "Mom," he whispered, "he's just waiting on the word from Dad. It looks like he's gonna have to be put down. Both front legs are shattered."

My hand went to my heart. "No!" I choked on my next words. "That will kill your dad. We can't do it."

"Mom! It's not up to you. It's up to Dad. Let him decide. But really, there is no decision. It will have to be done."

My emotions were all over the map. I knew he was right. Dandy probably was lying somewhere back at the ranch still in a lot of pain. Then my mind flipped to Kirk, lying somewhere—I guess upstairs—in a room. ICU. Was he alone now? Awake? Was he in pain? *What is he thinking right now?*

It was Thorne who folded and stashed that emotional map for me. "Mom, we milked the cows, separated the cream, and cleaned the equipment. After we saw the vet, and he told us where Dandy was layin'—

The teacher in me wanted to correct him. I wish I could just let those insignificant grammatical errors go, especially at a time like this. I said nothing. Unfortunately, I think my eyes spoke on my behalf.

Thorne knew me pretty well. "Okay, *lying*." He grinned and winked. "Brandon called Uncle Carl. He drove over and met us down in the pasture. I'd filled up a bucket with water to take to Dandy, and Brandon brought some carrots from the fridge. I hope you don't mind."

I was staring right through him. My mind was still trying to figure out how I was going to fix the mess we were now in. Thorne got right up in my face. "Mom?"

I finally came back to earth. "Mind? Oh, the carrots? Of course not."

"Anyway…we got him to drink a bit, but he wanted nothing to do with the carrots. Uncle Carl drove back up to the barn, got a bucket of oats, drove back down—

"Yeah, but he refused that too." Brandon placed his old scuffed Durango work boot on top of the left one. "Hey, can we continue this conversation some other time? I wanna go see Dad."

"Yes, of course. Dr. Brockman just came and told me Dad's out of surgery and in ICU. He hasn't come back, so I'm assuming it is okay for us to go on up. But probably we should make it just one person at a time."

Brandon took my right hand. Then Thorne moved to my left side and squeezed my other hand. We walked toward the elevator, my boys on each side of me. What would I do without them?

Alone inside the elevator, I told the boys more about Kirk's condition. "Guys, Dad is in serious trouble. The doctor says that short of a miracle, he will never walk again. He has what they refer to as a C5 break, meaning his fifth vertebra was crushed with the fall. It has interrupted all spinal cord activity from that point downward. He will have no motion from there on down."

Brandon's eyes were saucer-like. "Where is the fifth vertebrae exactly?"

I turned and put my finger on his spine where the doctor had showed me. "Dr. Brockman thinks Kirk may eventually have some limited movement in his upper arms due to his shoulders being above the break area in the spine. He did say some C5 patients are able to operate an electric wheelchair."

Thorne stood ramrod still, and Brandon's face turned ashen. It was then I realized I had not pushed the fourth-floor button. We were going nowhere.

Brandon also noticed and reached down to punch the button. He broke the tomblike silence in the seven-foot square. "What will we do? I mean, about the ranch. Doesn't sound like Dad will be able to work it at all."

I ran my fingers through my hair and felt some pieces of grass, probably blown in there earlier when the helicopter landed. "Guys, I don't have a clue. Kirk's not only lost the ability to walk, he may have also lost the ranch he loves so much. I just don't know." I stood there gazing aimlessly at the lights above the door.

"Mom!" Brandon whispered. "This is our floor." I had waited for hours to get to see Kirk, and now my body seemed frozen, my mind in a trance. I felt the elevator begin to spin.

Thorne touched my arm. "Mom, come on, let's move."

The boys must have seen me starting to reel a bit, and both grabbed my arms. "You okay, Mom?" Brandon pulled Kirk's cell phone out of my clinched hand. "Here, give me that."

Thorne turned and faced me. "Brandon, we might need to call a nurse. She looks like she might faint."

"No, I'm okay, guys. Let's just get in and see your dad."

Brandon guided me out of the elevator and to the right. We walked a few steps, and I saw Kirk lying there through the glassed-in wall. Some pulleys with heavy weights occupied the foot of the bed. There were numerous machines with banks of blinking lights.

Thorne opened the door. Kirk's head was squeezed in an apparatus to prevent movement, but he rolled his eyes toward us. I broke loose from the boys' grasp and ran toward him. His drug-induced glassy eyes brightened a bit as I approached. I stooped down and carefully kissed him. Then a cloud of guilt enveloped me. "Oh, Kirk, honey, I'm so sorry!"

The dam broke, and a flood of salty tears fell down my cheek and into my mouth. "Honey, it's all my fault. Can you ever forgive me?"

He looked at me. Then his eyes wandered around to the boys and back toward me. "What are you talkin' 'bout?" His speech was slurred. "Kate, you…you…you're not makin' sense. Why, you think it was your fault?"

"I was the one who insisted you take the day off and we do something together."

He grinned. "Well…we did. So what's your point, Katydid?"

There it was again. Couldn't he find a better pet name for me? But this time, it made me laugh. *Yes, I've got my Kirk back!*

A big black nurse with bleach-blonde hair popped in and interrupted. "Umm…I think the doctor has requested only one visitor at a time."

The pain meds clearly were having an effect on Kirk's personality. He glared at her, snarled, and said, "You can take them doctor orders and stick 'em in the shredder! They're all stayin'!"

Thorne looked over at Brandon, and they both cracked up. The nurse joined in the laughter and then said, "Okay, but make it short. I don't wanna lose my job."

She left the room, and I bent down and kissed Kirk again. I asked him about the contraption that was holding his head stable. "Yeah," he said, "I watched the doc screw it into my skull."

I gasped. "You didn't!"

"Yep, I was awake the whole time. 'Course they gave me pain meds, but Doc said he had to keep me awake so I could talk to them as they worked on my neck."

I looked over at the boys. Thorne's eyes mirrored my own reactions. "Oh, honey! That is awful!"

"Naw, it wasn't that bad. Them pain meds they gave me did a good job."

Brandon moved over closer to Kirk. "Dad…"

"Yeah, son?"

"I'm gonna work the ranch for you. You don't need to worry."

"Brandon, you're in college. How you gonna do that and stay in college?"

"Dad, I've already got it all figured out. I'm gonna move back home and work the ranch. I can take most of my classes on the Internet."

"No, Brandon, that's not fair to—"

"Dad! It's a done deal. You know I can do it. I've been working right beside you all these years. You taught me well."

I saw a tear creeping from Kirk's eye. Brandon stooped down and kissed his dad on the cheek and said, "I love you, Dad."

"I love you too, son."

Thorne squeezed in beside Brandon. "Dad, I'll help too. I know you tried to teach me—and yeah, I still hate that kind of work—but I'll do it. I promise."

Kirk blinked a couple of times, maybe to clear his vision from the tears. "Hey buddy, I want you to stay in school and stick with your art. Promise?"

"Maybe. But I can come home on weekends and help Brandon. That's a promise."

I had been standing back, listening, taking it all in. I raised my closed fist up to my mouth and exhaled heavily. *Oh!* It would take this whole family to make this work—no, it may take even more. It may take our friends and neighbors too. *God, you know I can't do this by myself.*

I could see we were losing Kirk. His eyelids kept drooping. He was fighting to stay awake, so I asked the boys if they would mind heading back to the ranch and see what needed to be done there. "I should stay here with Dad."

"Sure, Mom," Brandon said. "We can do that. We'll do the milking and stuff tomorrow morning and then come back over here."

The same nurse stepped inside. "Okay, you guys are fixin' to make me get fired. I've got orders to keep it to one—only one—visitor at a time. So someone's gotta go!"

It was Kirk's resurrected baritone voice, loud and clear: "Okay, so maybe that oughta be you, sister!"

"Say what!" She pointed a finger at Kirk. "You ain't in no position to be tellin' me any such thing." She laughed. "Now you just tell them boys they gotta vamoose now!"

Kirk grinned. "No worries, ma'am. They were on their way out when you came in bellowing out your orders. Hey guys, see you tomorrow."

The nurse turned to me, grinned, and put her hand on my shoulder. "I can see this patient is gonna be a pain in the behind. I may have to get my ugly hat on—maybe my boxin' gloves."

As she was leaving, I walked outside the room with her. "He seems to be doing pretty good. I can't believe he is making jokes and acting like everything will be just dandy—oh, I didn't even tell him about his horse! The vet says he's gonna have to be put down."

She looked deep into my eyes. "Honey, if he don't ask, don't tell him—least not now. Let's keep the jokes comin' long as we can. They'll be plenty of time for serious talk."

I looked back in at Kirk. His eyes were closed, and his heavy breathing told me sleep was masking any anxiety about his future. It was me who was worried. If he had been anxious, I couldn't tell. How could he have been making jokes at a time like this?

A thought occurred to me. He and Thorne were more alike than I ever thought. Both are carefree, taking each day as they come. Kirk once told me, "Kate, why worry about tomorrow when we're not even finished with this day?"

Well, I still see that as being irresponsible and foolish. But now, how can I plan any of our tomorrows?

15

For the next three hours, I paced while Kirk slept. Could Brandon manage the ranch and still get his education? What about his scholarship? Would that go away if he wasn't a resident student?

I would have to stop substitute-teaching, for sure. Kirk would need me to be there 24/7. Could I even manage to care for him properly? What would that involve?

What about transportation? Our old pickup would never do for Kirk. Could I trade it for a van—one with a wheelchair ramp? How would I even get him from the bed into the wheelchair?

I ran my fingers through my hair again. How can I plan for something when I don't even have all the facts?

I dropped into the leather recliner the RN rolled in to Kirk's room. "Not exactly like your bed at home," she said, "but maybe you can get some sleep anyway." She walked out, and I still didn't ask her her name. Her badge had flipped around.

Kirk's heavy breathing had become a light snore. The constant blinking and beeping of the machines by his bed lulled me away from the present, and I found myself back a few years. Back when our family was still operating as planned—well, pretty much as planned. If only we could command our dreams to become present reality.

Two years earlier
The end of summer was on us, and the pastures were turning brown once again. We got Brandon set up in his dorm at OSU. Kirk had driven our pickup, but I'd insisted on riding in the new truck with Brandon. The smell of those lush leather seats got me to thinking: *Will this kid appreciate all his good fortune? Will he come back the same humble and loving person?* Right then, I'd said a prayer that he would.

Thorne entered his high school senior year the same carefree, impulsive Thorne everyone had come to love. The guy had more phases than the moon. We never knew what to expect from him. His grades remained pretty consistent, mostly Cs, with an occasional B in the easier subjects. But it was his art that was so unpredictable. One piece might bring fifteen thousand dollars at the gallery, and the next one would go for five hundred or less. "What's with that?" I asked Landon when I took in more pieces. "Why does he blow hot and cold? I don't understand."

"Katie," he said, "Thorne just needs to focus on his art. He's young. He'll become consistent, but right now, he's got too much growing up still to do." He ducked his head a bit and said, "He *is* still planning on college and then art school, isn't he?"

"Yes, Thorne has every intention to go to college—hopefully OSU, where Brandon is going. And then, he hopes to go to the School of the Art Institute in Chicago. I've just got to make sure he keeps his grades up. The little stinker thinks he doesn't have to study."

"Well, give him time to mature a bit. He'll become more consistent with his art. I can see in some of the pieces he just doesn't have his heart in them, and then there are others he cares deeply about—and those are the ones bringing in the big bucks. He'll do fine. Actually, most artists are very much like him. They do much better when they really care about a subject. Take the one Rhena bought, *Mom?* We could see Thorne's emotion in that piece. It was something he *had* to get on a canvas, and it showed. Encourage him to paint the things that grab at his heart and won't let go. He's got the technique—an amazing technique, unlike any other artist I know. All he needs to do is concentrate on painting what really moves him."

"So you're saying for him to paint his emotions."

"Absolutely! If he's angry about something, paint it. If something tickles his funny bone, paint it. But I can tell you from experience, painting from sadness or a heart full of grief is what opens up the gold mine."

"I can see that."

"Katie, you've told me you are writing a book. Right? So you probably understand a reader wants to put themselves in a novel. They want to *live* the situation in their mind. It's the same with a piece of art, especially Western art, but also in other forms. Buyers willing to shell out big bucks for a painting want to *live* in that painting themselves. It has to come alive to them at first glance.

"You would probably use a good bit of dialogue in a novel—same with a painting. It has to talk to them. A novel without dialogue would be pretty dull, even in the most intriguing of settings. What is it you writers say? It should show, not just tell?"

I could see Landon was right. When Thorne has painted simply a pretty picture, it just sits there. Silent. But when he paints from deep within his soul, I am mesmerized by it. It talks to me and shows me something new.

The dream, continued

When the girls weren't batting their heavily mascaraed eyes at him, Thorne focused on his art. He surprised me with a beautiful painting for my birthday. It was a ranch scene with Kirk's horse, Dandy, rearing up on his hind legs. The entire canvas was shrouded in a heavy fog—a silvery-blue vapor, which Thorne has mastered to duplicate on canvas of God's own work.

It gave an eerie feeling and showed off the beauty of that Morgan horse we've come to love. He was standing there in the fog on his hind legs—so majestic, so powerful, and so handsome. It was the largest piece Thorne had ever attempted. It was on a 40"x40" canvas that Landon had given him.

Kirk made a stunning frame out of old barn wood and mounted the untitled painting. He brought in a ladder and hung it above the fireplace with the gorgeous Arkansas rock as a background. It goes unnoticed by no one entering that room.

Kirk's Uncle Carl stood motionless, looking up at it for the first time. "Katie," he said, "that painting is so fitting to this ranch house—the size, the colors, and, of course, the subject."

We've had friends over, and the conversation always centers on the painting. It is a stunning focal point of the big room. Some see it and start telling a story of their own horse.

Our self-made artist was taking some pretty easy classes his senior year, so I wasn't constantly harping on him to study. I wasn't sure his SAT score would be high enough, along with his barely average grades, to get him into OSU. Kirk didn't see it as much of a problem as I did.

"Hey," he reminded me, "the kid can make more in two days than I've ever made in two months."

That grabbed my attention. "Making money is not all there is to life," I said. "He needs a good education just to function in this world now. Education is more than book learning. It is preparation for entering a complex world. If he's a well-known artist, he'll find himself speaking in public, maybe the media. He can't come off like a grammarless bumpkin." I was wound up. "He's got to handle his finances properly. There are college classes for that. And then there's this thing called common sense. Education can help there—

"Yeah," he cut in, "and common sense tells me we should push a bit, but just not too hard. Grades are important, but they're not everything. I think what he needs right now is a bit of approval from us. We need to show him we're proud of his accomplishments. The guy's just lost the mother he loved dearly. Let's just concentrate on making him love us just as much. That'll go a long way in making him want to get his education."

How could I argue with wisdom like that?

I stirred a bit when I heard a couple arguing out in the hall. How dare they break me away from such sweet memories? They moved on, and I quickly returned to my dream.

It was the next morning, and I had suggested we spend Saturday at the National Cowboy & Western Heritage Museum in Oklahoma City. The museum is where Thorne got the break that led to his career in art. He had won the school art contest, allowing him to display his winning piece there.

We hadn't been back since, and I knew their art exhibits were rotated periodically. The Prix de West Invitational Art Exhibit and Sale was something Thorne had talked about, and he would be thrilled to spend an entire day there wandering through the gallery with pieces by some of the most famous Western artists. Kirk agreed.

Saturday morning, the three of us arrived early, because I knew Thorne wouldn't want to be rushed.

Kirk told Thorne he could spend as much time as he wanted in the gallery. "If we get tired," he said, "we can take a break and have lunch in the restaurant they have right here in the building."

The restaurant, Blueberry Hill, serves a scrumptious lunch, buffet-style. We got tired and hungry, but Thorne couldn't pull himself away from the fabulous pieces of art on display. Some were for sale, and were way off the chart as far as our budget was concerned. One piece, titled *Star of the Storm* by Curt Walters, had a price tag of eighty-five thousand dollars. It was oil on canvas and depicted an approaching storm over the Grand Canyon. The storm had cast amazing special light effects bouncing off the canyon walls in brilliant hues of reds and blues. Thorne stood absorbed in the detail. And it was absolutely beautiful, but I've seen our own Thorne create some of those same effects in a few of his pieces.

Bill Anton was one of Thorne's favorite artists. He carefully studied a piece by him. Then Tim Cox's *Straight from the Well* caught his eye. He stared at it for a full ten minutes and then went back to it again later. But it was an artist by the name of Scott Burdick who captured Thorne's real admiration. Thorne stood in front of Burdick's piece titled *Rose Cly* for probably an hour or more. It was a 60"x40" oil and priced at twenty-two thousand dollars. It was an old woman—probably Navajo—standing with her arms crossed, with a cat at her feet. In the background was what appeared to be an outhouse, and beyond was a typical rocky landscape one might find in New Mexico or Arizona, nothing really special about the background.

I was amazed at Thorne's fixation on the piece. I asked him what it was that had fascinated him so with that particular painting. Without moving his eyes from the piece, he said slowly, "It's the character in her wrinkled face and the way she's standing there staring off in to the distance with her arms crossed. Makes you wonder what she's seeing. And the cat is so totally oblivious to whatever it is she's seeing."

"Oblivious, huh?" Right then, I turned my worrier off about him ever being seen as an unschooled bumpkin in a world of intellectuals.

He finally turned toward me. "I just keep staring at her face. There is wisdom in that sun-browned old face." I could tell he was deep in thought. "And that hair! White as snow! The wind is blowing some of the strands into her face and isn't bothering her one bit. She is focused on something out there far to the right, and it is killing me to not know what it is."

Where did he learn that? Acute perception in art can't be learned. It has to be a natural gift. I touched his shoulder and whispered, "You got it, buddy. That is exactly what makes for great art. Put a bit of mystery in each of your paintings, and you'll be consistently demanding higher prices."

After nearly four hours in the art exhibit, Kirk steered Thorne around to one of Kirk's favorite displays, the American Rodeo Gallery. I knew Kirk would take his time in there, so I stepped into the Museum Store to browse the souvenirs, books, and jewelry. Ten minutes later, the guys found me there thumbing through a book about the women of the West. I was surprised to see them back so soon, but I knew Kirk wouldn't be interested in anything in the store, and I was right.

He headed for the door and motioned for Thorne to follow. "Hey buddy, I don't think you got enough time in the art exhibit. You wanna go back in?"

What a man I married! I was pretty sure he wasn't interested in seeing any more art pieces, but he knew this was the way to our boy's heart. This country needs more dads like Kirk Childers.

I joined the guys again, and after another hour or so back in the Prix de West exhibition, we headed toward the front entrance. My feet were killing me. As we walked through the grand hall of sculptures, one had caught Thorne's eye—*Grizzly Pride*, a piece by Gerald Balciar. I asked him what it was that captured his interest so. "It's the feeling of maternal security I see in those cubs for their mother."

Wow! That struck a chord with me. I was so proud. He was looking into the heart and soul of the artwork, not just the physical beauty and artist's technique.

Thorne moved on to a piece by Harold T. Holden, an Oklahoman. Another bronze, titled *Backdoor Diner*, showed a young calf trailing and nursing its mother from behind. He laughed. "Not much emotional charge in this one," he said, "but I like the title. It's pretty funny."

On the way back to the ranch, Thorne had been quiet for most of the way. I was sitting in the back seat, and he was in the passenger seat up front. He reached over and punched Kirk on the shoulder and said, "Thanks, Dad. I know you did that just for me. You would rather have stayed longer in the rodeo gallery, with stories about all those famous rodeo stars."

I could see the launching of a grin on Kirk's face, and I knew he was thinking the same thing I was. It was the first time we'd heard Thorne call Kirk Dad. *Yes*, I thought. *mission accomplished*. It takes so little to bond with a child—in this case, a young adult. We just have to be attentive to *their* desires, not our own. Kirk looked over at Thorne, winked, and said, "We'll go back again. You just let me know when they're gonna rotate the art exhibit."

I opened my eyes wide. The rhythm of the machines beside Kirk's bed had suddenly stopped. My own heart thumped at the thought of what could have happened. In the dim light, I thought I could see Kirk's chest move. All was quiet, and I was about to jump up and call for a nurse. But the nurse was already there.

She must have noticed the fright in my face. "Honey," she said, "you just go back to sleep. I'm only making some adjustments. Everything is okay. He's doing fine."

I've had many dreams before, but I don't think I've had them disrupted and then taken up again at the same time and place. Could it be I just didn't want them to end? I pulled the light blanket back up around my shoulders and found the dream continuing in less than a minute.

And there I was again—back home, before our world imploded. In the days, weeks, and months following, I began to see a change coming to our home—one that tickled my heart. Thorne started helping Kirk with the milking chores. He'd never done that in all the years he'd been with us. That had been Brandon's job, and Thorne would have no part in any of the daily ranch chores. On the other hand, I would often find Kirk in Thorne's room, deep in conversation about the painting Thorne happened to be working on at the time. I stood just outside the door and listened.

Thorne pointed toward the painting with his artist's knife. "Dad," he said, "can you see the disgust on the cowboy's face?"

Kirk moved closer, staring at the painting. "Yeah, sure. He's ticked off because the dog keeps nipping at the horse's hoof. His face says it all."

Thorne held the knife up and tapped into the air, as if to make a point. "See, if you just take a casual glance at this piece, all you'd see is a cowboy on a horse with a dog biting at the horse's back leg. But when you look closer, you see the guy's ever-so-slight expression. It's barely visible. He loves his dog, but he wishes he'd quit the nipping. I want my art to tell a story. This one's not much of a story, but you know what I mean. That's what Landon tells me. He says, 'You've gotta have a story in each painting—and it's even better if you can have a story within a story.'"

Another welcome change I saw was Kirk and Thorne taking in Friday-night football games at school. Kirk has never liked football or other team sports, and neither has Thorne. Brandon and I had tried to catch most of the home games, mostly because I was expected to, being a teacher. But Kirk and Thorne were never interested. Something was changing.

They'd almost always stop by Mama Cassie's for one of her greasy burgers, fries, and a milkshake prior to the game. I liked that. It meant I didn't have to cook. Now what can make two guys start doing something neither of them cared much for in the past? It was the bond that was building between them. They just liked being together. But I could see each one was working at building the bond. Some things don't come naturally.

When Brandon called from college, I told him about Kirk and Thorne taking in the home football games, and even a few of the out-of-town games. "No way!" he said. "I find that hard to believe."

"Well, believe it."

"But Dad hates football, and Thorne wouldn't know a touchdown from a basketball tip-off."

"Well, I'll bet he does now."

It was Saturday. Kirk had always found some kind of work to do here on the ranch, rarely taking any time off except Sundays. Work on a ranch this size is never done. There are always fences to mend, cattle to doctor, newborn calves that need help, not to mention hay-baling time and pasture maintenance. A few months ago, Kirk lost his helper when Ronnie enlisted in the marines. We were proud of him for serving his country, but it left Kirk with double the work. And now that Brandon was away at college, Kirk's work kept piling up.

So when I heard the back door slam, I assumed it was just another workday. But then Thorne was right behind him, and Kirk hollered, "Don't count on us for lunch. Thorne and I will be out for most of the day." I had no idea where they might be going.

I figured I'd take advantage of a nice, quiet day alone and picked up the novel I'd started last week. About five that afternoon, I heard a car pull up in front of the house. I looked out the window and saw a blue pocket-sized roadster. The sun was bleaching out the scene so I couldn't see who was in the car through the tinted windows. Curiosity got the best of me. Why was no one getting out of the dinky car? I laid my novel down and headed out the door. Just as I opened the front gate, I saw Kirk attempting to crawl out from the passenger side. With one long leg out, he put his hand down on the area of the door well, pushed, and finally pulled his six-foot-two body out of the low-slung car. A sardine can on wheels.

I laughed at his lack of dexterity. "What on earth were you doing in that dwarf of a car?" Then I saw Thorne pop out from the driver's side. "You have got to be kidding! Where did you guys come up with that thing?"

Thorne was about to burst with excitement. "It's mine!" He was hopping up and down on his tiptoes.

"No way!" I said. "How did that come about?"

"I sold a painting and bought this with the money I got from it."

Kirk finally had managed to stand erect and was stretching, clearly tired from having been curled up in the tiny car. I was still laughing. "You might need to go see a chiropractor after riding in that."

My comment was ignored. Thorne walked over to Kirk, and they high-fived each other, both obviously very happy. Kirk looked back at me. "We took the painting he'd just finished by the gallery. While we were there, a buyer came in and bought it on the spot. Landon wrote out a check for Thorne right there." I saw delight in those denim-blue eyes—eyes that always distract me, to the point where I lose my train of thought.

I finally got back on track with the situation at hand. "So you went out and bought this silly Tom Thumb car—just like that?"

"Yep, it's what Thorne has been wanting." Kirk slid his hand over the canvas top. "I had asked him if he wanted to buy himself a better pickup. The one he'd inherited from Brandon is past repair. He didn't want a truck, so I told him we'd shop for whatever he wanted."

"Yeah, Mom, it's a Mazda Miata. Come look."

And there it was: *Mom!* I'd heard him call Kirk *Dad* a couple of times, and now he had included me in that family of pronouns. I'm not sure, but my own delight over that surpassed Thorne's excitement over his little car. I walked over, peeked inside, frowned, and said, "Only two seats? Where am I supposed to sit?"

He looked over toward Kirk. "Oops!" He was grinning. "Guess we didn't think about that."

Kirk tried to bail him out. "He really got a good deal on this. It's six years old, just got barely over fifty thousand miles on it. Consumer Reports has rated these cars consistently tops since Mazda brought them out in early ninety. Kate, look at this ragtop. It looks brand new. Car's a one-owner, and he's kept it garaged and serviced regularly."

I didn't care much for the miniature car, but my heart warmed at the transformation I was seeing in my two men. I knew that car would be the last thing Kirk would pick out. But it wasn't about Kirk, and Kirk recognized that. I could feel a tiny tear trying to escape from my eye. Again, I thought, *Every kid needs a dad like Kirk Childers.* I couldn't be more proud.

16

I ROUSED FOR A second but went right back to sleep, and those sweet memories continued.

The end of May was quickly approaching. Thorne would be graduating in two days, and he had just received a letter from the admissions office of Oklahoma State University. I pulled it out of our mailbox up by the ranch gate and thought about ripping it open right there. I knew his SAT score was still not what it should be, and his grades were only average. He'd played no sports in high school, had no extracurricular activities that would impress an admissions officer, and his only letter of recommendation came from his art teacher.

My curiosity was killing me, but I knew it was Thorne's moment, not mine. I drove back to the house and laid the letter on his desk. At the supper table, I had to ask about it.

"Yeah, I saw it." he said. "I got accepted."

"Just like that? Where's the emotion, the excitement?"

"Mom," he said, "I wasn't worried. Were you?"

I sat there, dumbfounded. We had talked about the possibility several times that he might not get accepted. "Yes, I guess I was worried. What I don't understand is, why aren't you excited about it?"

He grinned. "Okay, I gotta confess. I called the admissions office two days ago to check on my status, and they told me I'd been accepted."

"And you didn't tell us!"

He pulled the letter out of his hip pocket. "Well, I knew you'd eventually see the letter. They said they'd already mailed it. I'm surprised you didn't rip it open."

"Well, I thought about it. You don't know how close I came to doing just that."

"Yeah, I think I do. I know you pretty well."

Where does this guy get such a stolid attitude? Nothing fazes him. I had a feeling, had he been rejected, his response would have been the same. Sometimes I wish I could be more like that. I fret, fume, and try to figure out everything myself—most of which is out of my control, anyway. Thorne just waits and rolls with the punches.

If I don't see those punches coming, I'm better off.

Last year, Brandon graduated high school. Now it was Thorne's turn. I had asked him if he wanted me to invite several friends to the house for a graduation party like we did with Brandon. He told me he didn't want a party, so there I sat, three hours before the ceremony started, wondering what we could do to make this special for him. I'd asked him several times what he wanted to do. All I got was, "It's all good, Mom. You don't need to worry about it."

I'd been hearing that same phrase a lot lately—not only from him, but also from Kirk. And just last week, Brandon had said the same thing when he called. "Mom," he said, "you don't need to worry about my grades, my spending money, what I've been eating, who I'm hangin' out with."

Had I really become that much of a worrywart?

I'd asked him if he thought he might be able to come to Thorne's graduation. He'd already told me he was starting a new summer job to help pay for his room and board. All he said was, "We'll see." So I asked him if he still had the gas card Denise had given him, or if he needed money for gas to come home. "Don't worry 'bout it, Mom," he mumbled. There it was again—the nasty *w*-word. Maybe I just needed a vacation. Sit on the beach somewhere reading *Gone with the Wind* again. Who was I kidding? I don't even like the beach, and I probably couldn't sit still for a 900-page novel. Maybe our big catfish pond with a fishing pole in my hand instead. Yes, I'd like that better.

Thorne's high school graduation

Thorne had gone to the school in advance of the graduation ceremony. I had to admit, that tiny pocket car looked like it was made just for him. What a handsome guy. And he never has to struggle getting in or out of it like Kirk did. Oh, to be young again!

Just as we were driving up to the ranch gate, I saw Brandon's Dodge whip in on the other side of the gate, conveniently blocking us. I turned to Kirk. "That turkey never would tell me if he was coming or not."

"You didn't know?"

"And you did?"

Kirk reached over and touched my hand. "Yeah, I knew. But Brandon didn't want me to tell you. He knew you'd just fret and fume about what kind of meals to fix. Kate you worry too much."

"Okay," I blurted out. "Maybe you're right. I'll try to zone out and let everyone else figure things out." Kirk looked over at me, dipped his head, and those blue eyes hiding under his bushy eyebrows said volumes.

Brandon popped down out of the big pickup. I could see there was a girl in the passenger seat. "Who do you have with you?"

"Oh, her…That's Amy. But don't worry, Mom, she can have my room tonight. I'll sleep on the couch in the big room."

There it was again. I'm beginning to hate that word. "Why would I worry, Brandon?" I said with a bit of sarcasm.

"You know how you are, Mom." Had he been standing just a few inches closer to my open window, I'd have reached over and messed up that prickly porcupine hair of his.

The graduation was just as spectacular as last year's. Parents were seated on the front row, and as each graduate picked up their diploma, each one walked by and gave their mom a red rosebud. Thorne stopped by me and took the time to pin mine on my lapel. All of the other students had simply handed the rosebud to their mom. Our Thorne is definitely one of a kind. He had won no special honors like a few of the others had, but I was no less proud. What beautiful people both of my boys had turned out to be!

After the ceremony, Kirk stopped and visited with a dozen or more people. As soon as I got a chance, I told him we needed to get on home because I hadn't planned anything for dinner for the boys—and this Amy girl.

"Brandon didn't tell you?" Kirk said.

"Tell me what?

Brandon and Amy invited Thorne and a couple of his friends to a Skillet concert in the city tonight. He said they would leave right after the graduation ceremony."

"Skillet?" That one threw me. "What on earth do they do with a skillet?"

"No," Kirk laughed. "Skillet is a Christian rock band. Don't you ever listen to any of Thorne's music?"

"I guess not." I was still confused. "Why would they want to name themselves Skillet? That's pretty silly."

"You'd have to ask them, Kate. I just know even I like their music. John Cooper, the lead vocal, is great. I like their song 'Hero.' They just received a Grammy nomination for two of their albums."

What's the song about? Are there any actual lyrics, or is it just an overdose of loud noise these teens are calling music?"

"It's about mankind's need for a hero, with the hero being Jesus Christ. It's the first single on the album *Awake*. And the music is good. You should listen to it."

"How do you know so much about this group?"

"I keep up, Kate. You know, you should take time to listen to both of our boys. Our time with them is slipping away. They're not children anymore. We've gotta keep that link."

"Well, you make me feel totally out of the loop, like a granny from Goobersville. Did I just age forty years without knowing it?"

"I'm not about to answer." He winked at me. "But if you want, I can help you with your walker when we get out of the truck."

I had nothing in my hand to throw at him, and I couldn't even think of a comeback. Maybe I was getting old.

The boys and Amy were past midnight getting back home. And no, I didn't wait up for them. Neither did I prepare anything for them to eat when they got back. I just did as I'd been told—I chilled.

17

Back to reality: Deaconess Hospital

THROUGHOUT THE NIGHT, nurses appeared and disappeared. I'd just get to sleep and another one would come in, making adjustments, checking the monitors, and waking Kirk each time. He seemed to go right back to sleep. I did too for a while, but now I was fully awake, and new questions popped into my head—Was Dandy still lying out there in the pasture, the vet waiting for instructions from Kirk? Would the boys find enough to eat? There was the leftover lasagna they could heat up. Maybe I should go home and fix some meals ahead for the boys, but how would I get home? I realized I'd not called my folks. Should I call and wake them now? Shouldn't I call our pastor—but now at three o'clock in the morning?

A blast of reality struck me like a cannon. The questions popping in my head now centered on the eventuality of our predicament. *Can I really care for Kirk as I should when he finally gets to come home? Where would he want his bed? In our bedroom, or maybe in the big room, where I'd be able to watch over him? Will we even have a home?*

Apparently, I had just dozed off again when I felt someone touch my hand. "Katie." It was my mom. "Honey, we're here."

"Mom! How did you know? I don't think I ever called you."

"No, you didn't. Brandon did."

"Oh, I'm so sorry—

"Don't be."

My dad moved around and kissed me on the forehead. "You've had enough to think about. Brandon knew that, so he called last night, filled us in on what he knew." I looked over at Kirk; he was sleeping again.

"Dad, this is really bad. We are in so much trouble—

I heard a faint moan by Kirk, accompanied by heavy breathing.

"Kate, let's step out in the hall." Dad rolled his eyes over toward Kirk.

I followed him, with Mom behind us. I took hold of Dad's hand. "Dr. Brockman says he has a break at the C5 level of his spine. It wasn't only broken—it was crushed. He was in surgery for over seven hours. Dad, Kirk is paralyzed. They say he will never walk again!"

My tears started streaming again down the familiar path of both my cheeks. Dad wrapped his arms around me, while Mom burst out with her own tearful cry. "What will you do, Katie?" Between the snivels, in broken words, she asked, "How…can you…manage to care for him? And keep the ranch going—

"Carol!" Dad ended our hug promptly and gave Mom his familiar *That's inappropriate* look. Mom compliantly quieted. Then Dad took both my hands and squeezed gently, "Katie, honey, you know we'll help out any way we can. We'll make this work. I promise."

"Dad's right, Katie," Mom interjected. "Whatever you need, we'll be there to help. I can help you with laundry, cooking, and whatever else I can do."

"Thanks, Mom. But right now, let's go back in and see if Kirk's awake."

It was about ten o'clock when the boys arrived back at the hospital. Brandon walked in first and looked over at Kirk. "He sleepin'?"

I pulled my stiff body out of the recliner and stood up. "I think so." Once again, Thorne stood behind Brandon. "Did you guys find anything to eat at home? There was some leftover lasagna in the fridge."

"Yeah, Mom, don't worry 'bout us. There's always food in the house. How's Dad doing?"

I could see Thorne was still behind Brandon, not saying anything. Something wasn't right. I could sense it. "Oh," I finally said, "the nurse was just in a few minutes ago and said his vitals all look normal. He's even breathing on his own now. That's a good sign."

"Why those weights at the foot of his bed?"

"They're there for traction. It's supposed to stretch his spine and relieve any pressure on the break. It's supposed to help with the swelling."

Thorne still hadn't said a word. I reached around Brandon and said, "Come here, Thorne. Something's wrong, I can see it in your eyes."

Brandon chimed in, "He's all bent out of shape. I had to drag him out of bed to go help with the chores. Then he wouldn't come out. He was holed up in there again with his precious paints. When I finally got him to put the paintbrush down, he was grouchy the whole time. I tried to show him how to bottle-feed the new calf, but—

"Shut up, Brandon!"

"Anyway, he wouldn't listen. You know, he was just being his usual self—

"Brandon," I scolded, "this is not the time or place to argue about such trivial things."

"Yeah, well, he's being a real jerk!"

I looked over at Kirk to see if the boys' quarreling had brought him out of his slumber. When I turned back around, Thorne was nowhere in sight. "Where did your brother go?"

Brandon rolled his eyes, "Who cares? He always skips out when the heat's on."

It was a few minutes past noon. My head was down and cradled between my hands. The doctor had given me some literature about quadriplegia, which I learned is called tetraplegia in Europe. As I continued reading, the needle on my worry gauge suddenly red-lined. How would we ever get through this? The truth is, we wouldn't—we couldn't. There was simply no way I could make this all work. Just yesterday everything was going our way. Two lives under control and loving each other more than ever.

I felt a hand on my shoulder. I looked up and froze.

"Uncle Carl!"

Panic overtook me like ice-cold water from a showerhead that hadn't had time to run up warm. With a chicken-egg-sized knot in my throat, I could only stare up at the man I had known for so many years. *What could I possibly say to him?* The owner of the ranch. The ranch—our only source of income. My thoughts were racing ahead at amazing speed and were about to result in a head-on collision.

I attempted to say something. I didn't know what. The lump in my throat blocked any words.

He reached down, took my hand, and then—a gesture that warmed my heart—knelt down beside me. "Katie, you'll get through this."

"No, Uncle Carl, I don't see how."

"Yes, hon, I'm here. *We'll* get through it. Don't worry."

A river of tears emptied over both of my bottom eyelids. He plucked a tissue from the bedside table. "Katie, Brandon came by earlier today and told me what happened. We talked it over. For over an hour, we discussed the outcome of the ranch. Between me and him, we will take over the entire operation, and you don't need to worry. Let's just see that my nephew gets the best treatment available, and we'll pray for a miracle."

I dug my face into his shoulder. My tears and sobs continued unabashed. He wrapped his arms around me and held tight. "Katie, Kirk's sleeping. Let's step outside the room so we don't disturb him."

A kinder and gentler man I've never known, except maybe Kirk. It must be in the genes. We walked out, and I closed the door behind us. "Uncle, this is really bad."

He hugged me again. "Katie, you're right—it is bad—but if I know my nephew, he will not want sympathy. He'll want us to support him but allow him to learn to live with his new inabilities. That's the Kirk I know."

"You're probably right. It's just that I am so scared. Never in my wildest dreams did I think we'd ever be facing this."

He looked deep into my eyes. "Well, we are—and yes, I said *we*." He placed his hands on my shoulders and got close up in my face. "That's what families are for. We'll make this all work. You'll see."

I filled him in on what the doctors had told me, and we walked back in the room. "So you said Brandon came to your house?"

"Yep, you and Kirk have raised a good one. The kid is ready to take on the ranch responsibilities, I have no doubt about that. And he will. I'll help all I can, but I'm convinced Brandon can step right into Kirk's shoes. I've never seen a young man so willing—and capable. He's strong and smart—and honest. You should be proud."

"Oh, I am. I just hope he'll be able to keep up with his studies. Most classes can be done by Internet, but some will have to be on campus."

"We talked about that too. I'll be there for him when he needs to be away. And we can hire some help when needed."

Uncle Carl put his hat back on his head, pinched my cheek, and said, "Tell Kirk I'll be back soon. Wilma was out shopping when Brandon came by. She'll want to come back with me next time."

He left, and I looked over at Kirk, still snoring lightly. My anxiety had softened a bit now. Maybe this could work.

But that semipositive outlook lasted only a few seconds. The ramifications of quadriplegia stormed back into my mind like an F5 tornado. I dropped back into my chair, shaken and disoriented. My short-lived courage splintered.

18

IN THE DAYS and weeks following, I found my emotions mimicking the pendulum of a large grandfather clock. One visitor would come in and provide incredible comfort and hope for our future, offering unlimited and continued help with managing our daily life. I'd be on an optimistic high. The next visitor would come in, offer a tearful and prolonged bundle of pity, and I'd find myself swinging in the opposite direction to a pessimistic low. At one point, after a walking sympathy card had left the room, leaving me depressed again, my courageous husband, lying there, unable to move his head in any direction, whispered, "Kate, you gotta pull yourself outta that funk you're in."

"Really? How can you say that? Have you not examined your own situation?" Then I was sorry I said such a thing. I went over and kissed him. "Honey, that was mean of me to say. I'm sorry."

"I don't care what you said." He winked at me. "I just like the way you kiss. You're the best there is."

"And just who are you comparing me to?" Those denim blue eyes of his rolled around, teasing, searching for some unknown person. I grinned and then stood back, took a long look at him, thinking what an amazing man I had married. He definitely knew how to pull me out of the mulligrubs, even amidst his own terrible predicament.

Later in the day, Pastor Lindall came in. He was cheerful, and he and Kirk traded several of their favorite jokes. No tears. It was refreshing, and Pastor knew it was what Kirk needed. Actually, he knew Kirk pretty well. Could it be his lighthearted attitude was meant more for me than for Kirk?

Pastor moved over to me and wrapped his arm around me. He must have seen the worry lines in my face, and then he placed his index finger under my chin and gently pushed my head up a bit. "Remember, Katie, when the world pushes you to your knees, you're in the perfect position to pray."

"Pastor," I said softly, hoping Kirk wouldn't hear, "the world as I knew it doesn't even exist anymore." The dam burst, and my cheeks were flooded once again.

"Katie," he said, "don't discount what God can do. You may think your life is spinning out of control, but God has a plan. We just don't understand it yet." He reached over, pulled out a tissue from the box on the table and dabbed at my wet cheeks.

I covered my mouth with my left hand, and I muttered a muffled moan. "But I'm at the end of my rope. I see no way out."

He took my hand and whispered, "Katie, when you get to your wit's end, you'll find God lives there."

"Will I? Right now, I'm not hearing from Him."

He squeezed my hand a bit. "God promises a safe landing, not a calm passage. Let Him work this situation out. You'll see He has a plan. You just need to sit back and allow Him to take the wheel."

In the moments that followed, Pastor Lindall pulled a fresh yarn from his bottomless repertoire of jokes and somehow managed to break me loose from my despair. A few minutes later, we were both laughing at something that had happened when he first came to be our pastor, nearly ten years ago.

He prayed a brief and uplifting prayer before he left. I've never understood why some people would want to pile on more pain and tears on a person who is struggling, especially with severe health issues, or even death. When Pastor left, the dreadful hospital room seemed brighter. The grays gave way to color, and my hopelessness gave way to optimism.

Afterward, I made myself busy straightening up the room, topping off the water for the flowers Pastor had brought, and unnecessarily checking the IV bags hovering over the bed. When Kirk was awake, his eyes followed my every move. At first, I found it annoying, but then I saw something in those roving eyes that was comforting to me. There was a pleasant look on his face as he continued to observe my movements around the room. When I decided I'd paced the floor enough and there was nothing more for me to do, I slipped back down in the recliner and looked over at him. Those gorgeous eyes, accompanied by a warm smile, penetrated deep into my soul. Amid utter catastrophe for him, that he could smile—a heartfelt smile, no less—was amazing. What a man!

After a single knock on the door, Dr. Brockman walked in, saw Kirk sleeping, and turned to me. "Good morning, Mrs. Childers."

"Please, Doctor, just make it Katie. I've been bombarded by my students with the *Mrs. Childers* bit way too much." Then I voiced a sudden thought. "But I guess those days are over now. Kirk's going to need me full-time."

He grinned, "Yes, Katie, he probably will." He walked over to Kirk's bed, took a minute to look at and decipher the blinking lights and digital readouts on the three machines. Then he pulled up the charts attached to the foot of Kirk's bed and read the nurses' reports. "Looks like our guy is responding just as we'd hoped. He's breathing on his own just fine. His blood pressure looks good. The post-surgery CT scan shows everything to be in exactly the same position we left it." Dr. Brockman closed the chart and returned it to its place.

"You know, Katie, we're lucky no one tried to move Kirk. Most of the EMTs know how to move a patient with possible neck and spinal injuries. Had they tried to raise his head a bit out there on the ground, it could have pushed one of those broken pieces of bone higher up and caused even more damage. The slightest movement of the head is extremely dangerous. We could have been looking at a C3 injury instead of C5."

I froze! Any words were locked deep inside me.

"What's wrong, Katie? Your eyes are like small Frisbees, and you're turning awfully pale."

I opened my mouth, but nothing came out. Chill bumps popped up—first on my arms, and then raced over the rest of my body. I felt my hair stiffen and stand at attention. "Oh God," I managed to say.

Dr. Brockman took my hand. "What is it, Katie? What?"

"I…out there on the ground…"

The doctor was waiting. "Out there on the ground, before the EMTs arrived, I remember, I put my hand under Kirk's head and raised it up—you know, trying to get him to respond." The familiar flood of tears started again. "Do you suppose I'm the cause…"

Dr. Brockman reached for my other hand. "No, Katie, you can't blame yourself."

Panic had already kicked in. I ran over to Kirk, and even though he was sound asleep, I put my head down to his face. "Oh, honey, I'm so sorry. I didn't know. Can you ever for—

"Katie! It's not your fault."

"But you said…"

Dr. Brockman gently urged me away from Kirk's face. He was still sleeping. "Katie, the C5 break was already there—

"But—

"No, listen to me—the break was already there. As soon as Kirk hit the ground, the break was there. Now I admit, it could have exacerbated the situation, but it didn't."

I was shaking uncontrollably. The chill bumps that had danced over me were now a million icicles pricking my arms, neck, and face. His voice seemed to be coming from a distance.

"It didn't," he said as he squeezed my hands. "It didn't."

19

THE MOVE OUT of ICU to a standard room on the third floor was a small step forward. Over the next several days, Kirk had numerous friends pop in. The doctor said it was okay, and Kirk seemed to enjoy the visits. He was always positive and loved the joking and teasing most of them brought. On the other hand, I endured. Yes, I was glad these people had taken the time out of their day to drive the thirty-something miles into the city to see him, but the decisions I was being faced with pulled my thoughts away from the chitchat bouncing off the walls in the hospital room. In fact, to me, it was a bit annoying—okay, a lot.

When one of Kirk's visitors had exited the room, Kirk could see I was deep in thought—well, actually that would be an understatement. "Kate," he said, "you've been awfully quiet. Embarrassingly quiet. No one is going to understand. Not even me."

"Honey, I'm just trying to figure out what we'll do—

"Aww! I thought so."

I plopped down in the chair beside his bed and realized I may have had a look of despair on my face. "I mean, do you think Brandon can manage the ranch? And even if he does, it's not right for us to take the pay for him doing the work. Should we just tell Uncle Carl we'll move out of the ranch house? Maybe rent a small house here in the city, close to doctors. But how would we have money for that? Maybe you could get Social Security disability. But would it be enough?"

"Kate, stop it!" His head was locked in tight with that device attached to his skull, but those cowboy-blue eyes were making up for any lack of head movement. "Stop trying to figure all this out." Then he slowly spoke each word separately and distinctly: "We will be all right—no matter what."

"I think you just told me to chill." I grinned. "Seems like I've heard that before."

"Yep, Katydid, you catch on fast."

I stood up, huffed, and said, "Okay, that does it. This girl's getting out of here. I'm going over to Mom's to see if she wants to go take in a movie. Maybe we can both chill."

He grinned. "Maybe that'd be a good idea—for you both."

I grabbed my purse. "Uh, Kate, you don't have any wheels. Remember, the truck's still at home."

I sat back down with my purse dangling off the side of the chair, and blew the hair out of my eyes. "Maybe Mom could come over and get—

"Call her."

I had barely gotten in Mom's Honda when she started questioning, "Katie, what are you going to do? Kirk can't work the ranch, so does that mean you will have to move? And what about—

"Mom, I'm not in any mood to discuss the what-ifs. Let's just enjoy the afternoon together." Then I had to laugh. I knew where I got my fusspot attitude. "Today this Nervous Nellie's gonna chill—and you should too."

"Okay," she said. Sso which movie you think will *chill* us?"

"I saw a trailer of one on TV in Kirk's room yesterday. *What to Expect When You're Expecting*. It's gotta be good, with Cameron Diaz starring in it. It's a romantic comedy."

"Sounds good, Kate. Now where's it showing?"

"Head over to Quail Springs Mall. I think it's showing there."

There were surprisingly few people at the mall, and the theater was no exception. We both enjoyed the movie. "Mom, you know they probably made that movie just for you and me."

"Why's that?"

"The theme. I think those couples in the movie came to the same conclusion."

"What?"

"They all finally understood that no matter what you plan for, life doesn't always deliver what's expected."

After a stop at Starbucks for a chocolate cookie crumble frappuccino, Mom dropped me off back at the hospital. "Kate, I need to run on over and visit my friend at Baptist Hospital," she said. "She had surgery yesterday. Give Kirk a hug for me."

"Mom…"

"What?"

I smiled. "Keep the conversation positive."

I knew my mood had changed. The timeout was good for me. Kirk was fully awake when I walked back in the room. "So how was the movie?"

I grinned. "Wasn't what I expected."

Kirk's room down on the third floor sparkled with the morning sunshine. The east windows are my favorite. Dozens of flower arrangements filled the windowsill and the table beside the unoccupied bed. I'd read the cards attached to each. The note from my parents attached to a dozen red roses simply read, "For our favorite son-in-law." I'd laughed after reading it, because Kirk is their only son-in-law. There was a large vase of orange gladiolus from our country church and numerous potted plants from neighboring ranchers.

The ones from our neighboring ranchers got Kirk's attention. "I didn't know they cared."

Another florist delivery lady brought a beautiful arrangement of daisies—my favorite. "Kirk, I don't know where we're going to put all of these. We're out of room." It was from my school principal and his wife.

Then still another florist delivery came. This one was different from all the rest. It was a small turquoise bowl with a fishhook barrel cactus. A cluster of bright-yellow pineapple-shaped blossoms topped the prickly plant. I opened the card and was so overcome with emotion I could barely read it to Kirk. It said,

> *Dad, when you first met me, I was in fact a little prick—just like this cactus.*
>
> *But you convinced me someday beauty would come from this thorn. I have you to thank.*
>
> *Love you,*
> *Thorne*

Kirk's eyes worked overtime, roving from me to the cactus, then back to me. Finally, he said, "Let's put that one right here in front of me on this table."

Hand gestures used to play a part of Kirk's speech. I've often told him he couldn't possibly talk without using his hands. But now I'm beginning to easily see through the windows of his eyes. Even if he wasn't able to talk, I think I'd still be able to interrupt his thoughts. So now, they were telling me more than his words were. His love for the guy had blossomed, just like the odd-looking cactus. Who would have ever thought a die-hard cowboy like Kirk Childers would ever learn to enjoy the company of a somewhat obnoxious kid who wanted nothing to do with cattle, or even the horses—one who'd rather sit in his room and paint? I'm still amazed that a bond could ever exist between the two.

20

The next week mimicked the last—constant interruptions day and night. I don't know how anyone gets any rest in a hospital. Kirk convinced me I should ride back home with Brandon. "Stay home a few days. You're not getting any rest here."

"Honey, I can't stay home. I need to be here with you."

"Naw, you should stay home a couple of days—maybe three or four. Then when you come back, you can bring the pickup. That way, you'll have some wheels while here."

"Well, I can't stay away from you that long."

"You got a cell phone, don't you? Just call."

I stared at him. "How would that work? You can't even pick up a phone."

"Oh yeah, I forgot."

I shook my head. "We're both going to have a lot of adjustments to make."

"Aww." Then he drawled an old John Wayne line: "I'm up to it—are you?"

I went home, stayed one day, and I did call. I called the hospital and talked to my volunteer friend I'd met earlier. "Honey," she said, "I'll go to his room. You call there, and I'll hold the phone for him to talk." What a sweet lady.

The following day was sunlit, not a cloud in the sky. I was in a Pollyannaish state of mind. The drive back to the hospital gave me time to reflect on all the good things I'd been blessed with. When we were first married, we'd asked God to bless our home with children. That had happened—just not as we'd planned. Two handsome boys, now men, fulfilled the answer to our prayer. Yes, the timing was odd. We'd been cheated of time with them as infants, but that just meant I got to skip the diaper stage.

As soon as I walked back in Kirk's room, his eyes met mine and quickly moved away. He drawled, "What are you doing back here?"

Somehow that just hit me wrong. "What do you think?" I blurted out. "I'm here to be with you—take care of you."

"Look, Katie, the hospital hires a full staff of nurses, doctors, cleaning people, cooks, and there are even volunteers to fill in any gaps in service. I think I'm getting all the care I need. I don't need you to further baby me." Those otherwise-placid eyes bore into mine. "What I need is for you to go back home and take care of business there. I'm sure we've got a mailbox full of bills to be paid, and the grass probably needs mowing."

I dropped down in my chair and let my big heavy purse drop on the floor beside me. "And this is the greeting I get?" I felt the blood rise to my freckled face. "First of all, Brandon mowed the grass yesterday. And secondly, I paid bills before I left and put them back in the mail."

Kirk's eyes turned toward the window in a deliberate attempt to ignore me. I sat there, fuming. How could he be so insolent? The sound of the monitors beside his bed penetrated the otherwise silence—silence, but without calm. Unspoken lyrics passed between us—frenzied from my side of the room and deflective from Kirk's side. The monitors continued their rhythmic song of apathy. A sparrow on the ledge outside the window glared at me with condemning eyes.

There was a faint chirp inside my purse, indicating an incoming text. I reached down and pulled the phone out and flipped it open. It was Brandon, saying he and Thorne were now back home for a three-day break. I closed the phone, slammed it back down in my purse, got up, and said, "The boys are home. I'm going back." I headed out the door, but my conscience soon smacked at me, so I went back and gave Kirk a quick and obligatory kiss on the cheek.

On the drive back to the ranch I stared vacantly at the all-too-familiar road and was injected with an overdose of guilt. How could a day turn around so quickly? From sunlit-yellow to iron-gray.

I know Kirk Childers, and I know what he said was not meant to hurt me—but it did.

21

"Hey Mom," Brandon said, "I didn't expect to see you home so soon. How's Dad doing?"

"Dad's doing okay. Where's Thorne?"

"As usual, he's holed up in his room—won't come out. I cracked his door open a hair and asked him to help me with feeding the animals and milking. All I got was, 'Get outta my room, Brandon!'"

"Seems like I've heard that phrase before," I said. "He's probably working on a painting."

"Yeah, well, I was tryin' to *work* on the chores around here so we could go see Dad." Aggravation was etched in his face. "I get no help outta him." The aggravation began to tint with a bit of gall. "Oh, but you don't need to remind me, Mr. Thorne Barrow is an *artist*—makes a lot more money than I'll ever make."

"Brandon, suck it up! You've set your sights here on ranching. Thorne's hitched his wagon to a distant star. Do what you do best and let him do what he does best."

"All I'm asking is that he give me just an hour of his precious time. This is a big ranch—requires a lot of work."

"Okay, buster, what's left to do? I'll get my old jeans on and help you finish up."

Lilly and Puzzle were waiting patiently for their allotment of oats. What a stunning sight, each in their own stall. The stalls had been recently mucked. Fresh water automatically fed in— one of Kirk's ingenious solutions. He'd used the fill valve controls of a toilet tank, retro-fitted to furnish a continuous supply of water to a small water trough in each stall.

The sun peeped in through the opening in the stable wall and shone down on their gorgeous coats. But the two looked a bit misplaced without Kirk's beautiful Morgan in the stall next to them. I was staring into the empty stall, and I thought Brandon could read my thoughts. "Mom, we had to have the vet go ahead and put him down. It couldn't wait for Dad to give us the word."

"I figured that. Dad hasn't even mentioned it. I think he knows."

"Mom, one thing was a bit odd. Thorne was with me when the vet injected the fatal dose in Dandy. Of course, it was a sad time for me, but Thorne stood there and bawled his eyes out. Then he was quiet the rest of the day. In fact, he hasn't been the same since. He refuses to go anywhere on this ranch except to his room."

I held my hand out for Lilly. She immediately ducked her head under my hand for me to rub her nose. "Well, that is odd. I didn't know he cared about Dandy."

Brandon touched my arm, and our eyes met. "Mom, I don't think it was the horse."

I tried to swallow the lump in my throat. "You may be right."

After the chores were done Brandon drove me back to the house and then headed toward town to sell the week's accumulation of crème. I headed toward Thorne's room, knocked on the door, and said, "It's me, Thorne. Can we talk?"

"Yeah, Mom, come on in."

He was standing at his easel with a brush in his hand. Background color dominated most of the canvas, but he had already meticulously sketched in what I could easily see would become the head and neck of that handsome Morgan horse. I would recognize those distinctive forehead markings anywhere. A primitive half-star, squashed a bit on one side, with the other half of the squashed star falling down and to one side. Dandy's head was turned toward—oh my gosh, an outstretched but limp hand. I recognized the wedding band.

My fingers shot up to cover my mouth, because I could easily see where this theme was going.

"What you think so far, Mom?"

I was awestruck. "You have an amazing ability to make a painting talk—using a language of your own."

"So what's it saying to you so far?"

My emotions had already started to speed out of control. "I can't…Thorne, I can't even talk about that right now." I stepped back. "It's definitely talking. But I can't."

I moved in closer to this amazing guy, patted him on the shoulder, and made my way out of his room, hoping the dam wouldn't burst before I could get to the tissue box.

I think I know Thorne. Does anyone else? His exterior is quite deceiving—obnoxious, narcissistic. But the real Thorne Barrow comes out in his paintings. A gentler demeanor with unabated compassion is hidden in the oils. The story in one of his paintings will linger in my head throughout the day, just as this latest—even unfinished—image did. As Lena Throckmorton has said, "That, friends, is what good art is all about."

22

The following Monday evening, Brandon told me he would be driving back to Stillwater to finish up the details for converting his current class schedule to Internet classes. I knew Thorne would be riding back with him, because he had left his Miata at school.

The next morning, I made some scrambled eggs, fried some thick-sliced bacon, and set the breakfast table for three. Brandon sat down, bowed his head for his usual silent prayer before digging in. His plate of bacon and eggs disappeared almost before I got a chance to sit down.

"Where's your brother?" I asked as he was refilling his plate with the last of the eggs.

"Don't know. Haven't seen the little goof-off."

"Brandon! We talked about that. Cut him some slack."

"Why should I? He's a lazy bum!" Brandon quickly killed off what was left of the bacon and stuffed the last bite of eggs in his mouth. Then he jumped up and said, "I'll go tell him I'm leavin' in five minutes. He better be ready."

I was pouring myself a second cup of coffee when I heard Brandon yell from the back door, "See you, Mom. I'll be back later tonight." The door slammed, and a minute later, I heard his big diesel pickup roar to life.

The house was quiet. With the boys gone, I had planned on working on paperwork with our insurance company. The hospital and doctor bills were piling in. I had no idea where we would come up with the money for co-pays, deductibles, or whatever they call them, or the other related expenses. As I was sorting through the mountain of mail, I thought I heard a bedroom door close. My heart skipped a couple of beats. I listened, but then all was quiet again.

I quietly set my cup down on the table and then tiptoed into the hall. Noah started barking at something outside. Maybe the guys forgot something and had to return.

I went back to the kitchen and looked out the window. Brandon's truck was nowhere in sight. My heart was pounding. If only Kirk could be here. "Brandon, is that you?" My voice was barely audible.

I heard a pecking at the window around the corner from the kitchen. Three pecks—loud pecks. I froze.

Finally, I got up the courage to peek around the corner. A cardinal was clinging to the windowsill and had started to peck at it again. When I walked over to the window, the bird flew away. I relaxed and headed back around to the kitchen to retrieve my coffee.

Then a toilet flushed. My hair was standing at attention again. I was trying to decide if I should turn and run out the front door. The bathroom door down the hall opened. Thorne walked out.

"Hey Mom," he said so casually.

"Thorne, you scared me half to death!"

"Sorry."

"What on earth are you doing here? I thought you were with Brandon. Aren't you supposed to be back in school tomorrow?"

"Nope, I put my classes on hold for now."

"You mean you dropped out!" Disappointment gave way to anger for me. "What are you thinking, Thorne!"

"Don't worry, it's just temporary, Mom. Right now, I need some time to think some things through. The best way for me to do that is to pick up my brushes and paint."

"So just like that, you're dropping out of college because you need some time to think!" I was livid.

Without another word, he walked in to his room and slammed the door. I stood there with my arms crossed, trying to figure out what my next move should be. We'd never had to face anything like this with Brandon. He was always up front with us. Thorne is such an enigma. Just when I think I've got him figured out, he throws me a curve ball.

With my arms still crossed, I stood there thinking. *What are my responsibilities now as a parent, a parent of an eighteen-year-old? The guy's got enough money to pay for his entire college career—room, board, any extra expenses—and he drops out, because he needs to think some things through.* Maybe I should take him to the stables like Kirk used to do and give him a piece of my mind. Then I laughed at the thought.

Bursting into Thorne's room with a sermon about the value of an education just didn't seem like the thing to do, so I went back to the kitchen and was finishing off my now-lukewarm coffee, when Thorne came in and sat down beside me.

"I'm sorry for ignoring you like that," he said.

"Well, you must know you've got me worried."

"You shouldn't be. I've just got some things to think through. It seems like I'm being pulled in different directions."

"Who's pulling you?"

He looked at me a few seconds and let out a big extended breath. "There are just so many things going on right now. I don't know. That's why I need to take a break."

"A break! What are you talking about—you just started!" I felt my better judgment kick in and backed off with any further tirade. "Honey, you wanna talk about what it is that's pulling you in different directions?"

"No."

"Okay…Well, if you decide you do, my ears will be waiting."

He grinned. "And your mouth won't be."

I was so shocked I just sat there blinking my eyes.

A few seconds later, he took my hand and said, "You wanna see what I've been workin' on?"

"Well, sure. If you think I can keep my mouth shut." I turned my palm over inside his hand and squeezed it. "Come on, show me."

When he opened the door to his room, the painting of Dandy turning toward that outstretched hand was no longer on the easel. I was disappointed. I thought maybe he'd given up on that too.

What I did see on the easel was another of his typical ranch scenes—nicely done, but it didn't grab me like the other one did. "Hey buddy, did you finish the painting of Dandy? You know, the one with him turning toward that outstretched hand?"

"I worked some on it, but I had to put it aside for now. I'll finish it someday, but I need to get some more pieces ready to take into the gallery. That one won't earn me any money, 'cause it's never gonna see the walls of a gallery. It's not for sale."

I'll admit, I was a bit confused. He's never put any painting aside unfinished and started on another one. That's just not him. He was pouring his soul into the painting. It had the emotional signature of Thorne Barrow in every brushstroke. And to put it away in the closet is not like him. Something was wrong.

Thorne sometimes—no often—is quiet. But this time his silence smacked at trouble. I could feel it. What kind of trouble, I didn't know. But something was definitely wrong.

He brought out two other paintings and stood them on the floor, leaning them against the wall. They were both nice, and I knew they would sell in the gallery, but the passion was gone in those brushstrokes. Anyone would be proud to display them in their home, but the story was lacking. Or maybe it wasn't— at least to me. Could I be staring at an invisible story? A story of trouble.

23

I KEPT MYSELF BUSY around the house. I paid bills, cleaned house, and helped Brandon with the chores. We were both walking back from the barn after the ATV refused to come to life. "Brandon, why didn't you tell me Thorne wasn't going to ride back with you the other day? I thought you two were together. I heard a noise in the house and then freaked out when I heard a toilet flush."

Brandon laughed. "I don't know, Mom, I just figured you'd find out. I thought he was coming too. Then all of a sudden, he changes course, becomes somewhat cantankerous, and tells me to go on without him."

"Did he tell you he dropped out of school?"

"Yeah."

"When? When did he tell you?"

"Mom, I knew it before we even got home for that long weekend."

"And you didn't tell me?"

He stopped walking, turned to me, and said, "Look, Thorne is not my responsibility. If he wanted you to know earlier, he would have told you. Anyways, I've about had it with the turkey. I never know what to expect out of him. Well, maybe I do—nothing."

"Okay, well, in the past, you have always snitched on him to me when he's done something wrong. I would have thought—

"That's in the past, Mom. I'm through covering for him and through telling you and Dad what he's up to. I just don't care anymore."

I gave my hair an exasperated blow out of my face. "Yeah, well, maybe I don't care either. I've got enough troubles of my own to be trying to fix his and everyone else's. We've done our part—Dad and me—now it's up to Thorne to follow up on what we've taught him."

I saw an "I told you so smirk emerging from Brandon's face. "Mom, could it be you are starting to take our advice?"

"About what?"

"Chill."

I pretended to be surprised at his answer. But I wasn't. "You wanna drive me in to see Dad this evening?"

"Sure, just give me time to get a shower and find some boots that don't smell like—"

"Like a by-product of Angus cows?"

"Yeah, something like that. You mind if Amy comes too?"

"Amy? Don't tell me she dropped out of college too?"

"No, she's doing her student teaching at Wellston—I thought I told you—so she's back living with her parents for now."

"Oh yes, I guess maybe you did. No, she's welcome to come too if she wants."

"Mom, Amy asks about Dad almost every day. It's obvious she cares. She's like that."

"Yes, I think I can see that in her. I really like her. I think she is good for you."

"Funny thing…Just yesterday, she said, 'Brandon, you and your dad are so much alike—even look alike—I can't believe you are adopted.'"

When we got back to the house I asked Thorne if he wanted to go too. He had a distant look in those haunting eyes. "No," he finally said, "I think I'll stay here and get back to work on Dad's painting."

"Oh, so you plan to give that to Kirk?"

I got no answer. He walked away.

Dr. Brockman was making his evening rounds when we came in. "Katie, our funny guy over there in the bed is ready to vacate this room and move on to rehab."

"Funny guy?"

He grinned and looked over at Kirk. "Yeah, this guy's turned this hospital into one big party—keeps us all laughing. I think the nurses are going to hate to see him go."

I shook my head and mouthed the word *amazing*.

"I'm signing orders for him to be transferred to the Jim Thorpe Rehab Center Hospital over on Northwest Expressway. I'm also making sure Kirk will have a private room." He looked over at Kirk. "I think you're gonna really like your room over there. They have voice-activated TVs and lights. Even the window blinds are voice activated."

Kirk grinned. "That's nothin'. I've been voice-activated ever since I got married. I hear Katie's voice, and I jump into action."

Dr. Brockman looked at me and pointed his finger at Kirk. "See, what did I tell you, we've got Mr. Funny Guy here."

The doctor picked up a brochure that had been placed on Kirk's table, handed it to me, and looked over at Kirk. "This is an Integris hospital. It's world-class technology. They will be working to prevent muscle atrophy, keeping you cowboy-strong. They have a bionic-assisted treadmill—"

"I'll be walking? On a treadmill?"

"Yeah, Kirk, the machine will do all the work, but yes, you will *walk* on a treadmill. Jim Thorpe Rehab is one of only a handful of facilities in the country that has Ekso Bionics."

I found it hard to believe what I was hearing.

"Kirk has done so well here, I'm hoping he'll qualify for this special treadmill. If he does qualify, he'll have a special suit that can facilitate walking. They claim it is for individuals with up to C7 complete, or any level of incomplete spinal cord injury. I know one patient with C5 like Kirk who has qualified and was able to use the machine.

"Kirk is one determined man. I think we'll see him walk on that treadmill."

"Doctor," I said, "is this something he can do at home also?"

"No, unfortunately, it's only available in a supervised facility that has Ekso Bionics, like the Jim Thorpe facility."

"Then what's the point?"

"The point is the machine will be one of the tools to keep his muscles from wasting away. He'll be revisiting the facility as an outpatient for the rest of his life."

The rest of his life. That part in his statement was sinking in, and I'm sure the disappointment showed on my face, but not Kirk's.

"Hallelujah!" he shouted. "You hear that, Kate? I'm gonna walk!"

"Honey, the doctor said it will just be for rehab. He didn't mean you'll be walking up to the barn to feed the animals."

With his glaring eyes, he bit back at my skepticism. "Look, any step I take—no matter what it looks like—is a miracle for me. I'll take it whatever way it comes, even if a robot has to hold me up and force my legs into action."

"Yep," Dr. Brockman said, "that's the kind of talk I like. Kirk, you are the man!"

Guilt had already shrouded me for having such a negative attitude. How dare I take away hope from him? Sometimes we can be so heartless to the ones we love the most. I sat down in the chair, pulled at my collar, and quickly glanced over at him. How could a big, robust man in his predicament have such a positive attitude? I've got a lot to learn.

On the drive back home that evening, I was sitting in the back seat. Amy was up front with Brandon. He was quiet and had the radio tuned in to his favorite station. I liked the music, even though I struggled to understand the words. Amy was also quiet. She was a beautiful girl. Her sun-frosted long blonde hair trailed to one side and over her shoulder. Several times I caught them glancing at each other in an unspoken language of their own. I was caught up in my own world, thinking about Amy Phillips. I'd liked her from the first time we'd met. *Yes,* I thought, *maybe I'm looking at my future daughter-in-law.*

Brandon touched the Mute button on the steering wheel and glanced in the mirror at me. "You know, Dad has always been my idol, but tonight he blew the meaning of *superman* right off the charts. No one else—and I do mean no one—could ever be so positive in the face of total disaster like he's been harnessed with. He is writing the book on positive thinking."

"Yes, son, he is. The whole world needs to read his book." I thought for a minute, and then whispered, "Maybe I can make that happen."

24

Thorne wasn't in his room. His Miata wasn't parked outside. I wish he would tell me where he's going. I never know when he'll be present for dinner—most of the time, he's holed up in his room and won't come out. His pants look to be two sizes too big, and his face is shrunken in. He rarely shaves anymore. Looks like a dried-up peach. Something is really wrong. I wish I could read his mind.

The phone rang. "Katie, this is Lena Throckmorton. I just wanted to touch base with you. Thorne was in the gallery this afternoon—brought in a couple more paintings. Both are beautiful. I don't see the passion in either, but still, they should sell for a pretty good price."

"Lena, I had missed him. He never tells me where he's going anymore. He's become such an acrostic rascal. I'm only getting one piece of the puzzle at a time, and when I try reading the final outcome, I'm afraid it spells trouble."

"That's one reason for this phone call. I know Thorne is considered an adult now, so I may be out of line in telling you this…"

"No, go ahead. I need any information I can get. I'm worried about him."

"Well…please don't let him know I told you this."

"Okay"

"Thorne has asked me to change the bank account we have on file here to deposit the money from his sales."

"Really?"

"I think the deposit account was a savings account in both his name and yours, right?"

"Yes, I wasn't aware he even had another account."

"Oh gosh, I may be getting myself in deep mud here, but I still think you should know. Katie, the account is a bank in Santa Fe, New Mexico."

"No way! What on earth is going on?"

"Hon, I don't know. He seemed somewhat vague. I questioned him about the account, but he dismissed it, shrugged his shoulders, and said, 'Aww, I just don't need all my eggs in one basket.'"

"But why Santa Fe? There's plenty of banks right here in our area. This is like a puzzle with all the pieces turned upside down. How can I possibly put them in place? I'm clueless, and I can't get him to talk."

"You know, he looked awfully thin. Is he sick?"

"No. At least I don't think so. I just can't get him to eat. He stays in his room and paints, even well into the night. When he was younger, Kirk and I always went to his room at bedtime and said prayers. Now he keeps his door shut—even locked—and won't come out. I'm worried, but I don't know what to do."

"I've got a lady looking at those paintings of his now, so I better go. Please don't let him know I told you this."

Kirk was transferred to the Jim Thorpe Rehab Center Hospital. What a beautiful room he was placed in. His bed was next to a large window looking out onto a perfectly manicured lawn. A pond with a lovely spray of water jetting up from the center was in the distance, with a paved walking trail circling it and meandering back to an ornately dressed white gazebo. I saw a young man—probably in his early twenties—leisurely guiding his electric wheelchair toward the pond. A second look told me the guy had no legs, both amputated above the knees. A gorgeous golden retriever was following him, leashed to the chair.

Kirk's headgear was history now, and he was able to turn his head some. "Kirk, look at that guy with his dog. You think they'd allow you to keep Noah up here with you?"

"Katie, border collies aren't meant to be cooped up like this. He'd go nuts."

Wow, I thought, I could say the same thing about Kirk. But it was only a thought. I didn't say it.

What I said instead was, "Well, maybe I could bring him up just for visits."

"Yeah," he said, "okay. So tell me, babe, what's up with our Thorny boy? I haven't seen him in a long time. He hasn't even darkened the doorway of this room."

"I don't know, Kirk. Something's wrong. He won't eat. Just stays in his room with the door locked. He's losing weight. Soon his pants will be on the ground if he doesn't start wearing a belt."

"He still got his cell phone?"

"Yes, why?"

"Dial him, and put the phone up to my face."

I hesitated. "I'm not sure that's a good idea." But I dialed anyway and held the phone for him.

Kirk waited, letting it ring, and then tipped his head for me to take the phone away. "He's not answering. See if you can get him to pull away from those brushes long enough to come over and say hello. I miss him. Maybe I can get him talking."

Questions were galloping through my head. Should I tell him what Lena told me about the bank accounts? Would it just serve as another source of depression in Kirk's cavity of bleakness? What am I thinking? I'm the one who is in such a melancholy state of mind. Kirk sees his quadriplegia as just another episode in life's palmy path between the briars. How does he do it? Mom can't believe how he's handling this whole new static life. Dad, on the other hand said, "I know my son-in-law pretty well. He'll have that motorized chair running in high gear in no time. He'll probably figure out a way to milk those cows himself. He's a champ, no doubt about that."

I drove up, opened the big ranch gate, and started to make my way toward the house. I don't know why I did it, but I slowed the pickup truck down to a crawl. Then something caught my eye. I rolled the window down and saw it. A beer bottle lay in the grass beside the dirt road. *That's odd*, I thought. *No one comes to this ranch drinking. How would they have gotten in? Something's not right.*

I drove on to the house and saw it. Thorne's Miata was there in its usual spot, the front left fender bashed in. Full-blown panic would have set in, but I realized any accident he'd been in probably wasn't bad enough for him to be hurt. The car was a mess, but it looked like it might be drivable.

I jumped out and ran to the door. It was unlocked. "Thorne… Thorne, are you okay?" I got no answer, so I walked back to his room. The door was also unlocked. "Thorne, are you in there?" The house was eerily quiet. "Thorne! Talk to me. I know you're in there." I turned the knob and peeked in.

There he was, lying on his stomach on his bed. I stepped in close to him, and then I knew. The beer bottle I saw up by the front pasture had been his. How many had he had? Who or what did he hit? Any injuries? Then he blew out a pungent lungful I thought could have easily been flammable. I touched his shoulder. "Thorne, are you okay? Come on, talk to me." A slight grunt was his only response.

I walked out and closed the door. *Dear Jesus*, I prayed, *I don't know how to deal with this. I've led a sheltered life—never seen anyone crashed-out drunk. I need some wisdom here.*

How do I handle this? I wish Kirk was here. He'd know what to do. He's told me his dad would often come home drunk.

My thoughts went back to Kirk lying there in bed at the rehab center. What would he think about this? How would he handle it? Should I tell him?

I bowed my head. *God, this is not the way I had our life pictured. Kirk was healthy, loved his family, his horse. Thorne was on the right track and full of unprecedented potential. Now look at us. We're broken, Lord. Kirk will never walk again, his beloved horse is gone, and now, dear God, Thorne is lying in his room, liquefied by the very evil we've so despised. How could this all happen? Where did we go wrong? Lord, you know I've done my best—so has Kirk.*

The silver-leaf maples in the front yard slowly began to hide the evening sun. I ran my finger around the rim of my still-full glass of tea for the hundredth time. The light we'd all shared was now hidden, just like the sun. I continued to stare out the window. *Lord, if you can fix this mess we're in—*

The sun suddenly dipped between the branches of the tree, and a blinding light erupted through the window. As soon as it did, I heard a voice in my head, scolding me. "*If* I can?" That was all I heard, but it was there, and the emphasis was on the first word.

I was so stunned I knocked over my glass of tea. I don't know what transpired after that.

I must have wiped up the spill, but I don't remember doing so. I kept thinking about that "*If* I can." *If!* How dare I question God's ability? I looked up to the towering cathedral ceiling. Lord, I know you can. Maybe it's me who's not on board.

Then suddenly, the oddest thing happened. I remembered a friend in college. I think his name was Parker—Parker something or other. I knew he'd wanted to date me—had asked me out several times—but I had my eyes set on another guy by the name of Kirk Childers. Anyway, Parker approached me one day, so excited. "Katie," he said, "I finally got my pilot's license." I knew he had wanted that badly and had worked hard to get there. "Yeah," he said. "Got it just today. You wanna go up with me for a ride? I'll take you wherever you want to go. You'll love it. I promise."

"Parker, there is no way I'm gonna let you fly me."

"Why, Katie? Don't you believe me? Here, I'll show you my license."

"Look, Parker," I said, "I believe you are now officially a pilot, okay? I'm just not ready to get on board with you."

That flashback in time ended abruptly, and it became clear why I had remembered it. I bowed my head and wept. *Lord, forgive me. I guess I haven't been on board with you—never have been, really. Yes, I believe you are God. And yes, I believe you've always held that title. But see, it's a matter of trust. I guess I just don't really trust you. I've always tried to fix things myself. I've trusted myself, just not you. Forgive me.*

Right then, I knew it was not my responsibility to fix Thorne. I'd done my part. Now it was out of my hands—and in the hands of the Master Fix-It Man. I got ready for bed, but first, I checked in on Thorne to make sure he was okay. He was still sleeping. I didn't check his bathroom to see if he'd thrown up. If he did, that was his problem, not mine.

Brandon had been picking up Amy and taking her to church with him since he'd been living at home again. He had asked me if I would mind if he brought her home with him for Sunday lunch and then go over to see Kirk. "Of course not," I said. "Amy is a sweet girl. You have any special menu request?"

"No. She doesn't eat much meat, and she hates barbeque."

"Okay. That pretty much eliminates most of our diet in this house. Maybe you should go down to the pond and catch a nice bass for our lunch. That would impress her, for sure."

He stuck his hands in his pockets and grinned. "Mom, I'm way past that stage."

"What stage?"

"Impressing her. She knows I am who I am. No need to put on airs with her."

"Maybe not, but it never hurts to show a girl your best side."

He punched me lightly on the arm. "I don't have any other side."

"Okay, Mr. Perfect, go catch a big bass for your sweetie. I'll bake some potatoes and make a big salad. She does eat salad, doesn't she?"

"Yeah, she does. I take her out for pizza, and all she orders is a salad."

I heard the ATV pull up out front. The door opened, and Brandon walked in, holding his catch.

I put my hands on my waist and said, "You better have something bigger than that still out there." He was holding a scrawny sunfish, no more than four inches long.

"Nope, nothin' else was biting. I guess Amy will have to be satisfied with the salad alone."

I looked at my watch. "You've got time to run into town and bring back something more substantial from the market—catfish, a nice big bass. We don't have to tell her you bought it at the store."

"Mom!" He glared at me. "You and Dad taught me better than that. I can't believe you would suggest such a thing."

"I'm not suggesting you lie about it, Brandon. Just don't tell her, unless she asks."

"That ain't right, Mom, and you know it. I remember you once said, 'A half-truth is always a whole lie'. Total honesty is the only way to go, especially with someone you're hoping to be your spouse one day."

"Okay, it looks like it'll be hamburgers for lunch."

After lunch, Amy helped me clear the dishes, and then Brandon drove us over to the rehab center to see Kirk. Amy spent quite a bit of time talking to him. She sat down, Indian-style, beside his chair. "So tell me, what was Brandon like when he first came to live with you and Katie on the ranch?"

Kirk held nothing back. "At first, he was shy—seemed like he had really been traumatized by his past—but it didn't take him long to warm up to us. He loved the ranch and asked more questions than I could answer at the time."

"Has he ever been disrespectful to you guys?"

"No, never! Brandon has been the type of kid any parent could ever hope for."

"Does he ever lose his temper?"

I was eavesdropping and was pretty sure she wanted to know all about Brandon before their relationship progressed further. I jumped in at that point. "Amy, Brandon and Kirk are like two peanuts from the same shell. Neither of them ever loses their temper. I wish I could say the same about myself."

"Oh, come now, Katie," she said. "I've never heard you lose your temper."

"Hang around me long enough, Amy, and you'll eventually see this red hair bristle. But it's never about family. It's usually about the mistreatment of a child. I've been known to go ballistic then."

The conversation didn't last long. Brandon grabbed her, and they headed out toward the fountain. I watched them through the window, hand in hand. I was pretty sure I was looking at my future daughter-in-law.

25

Once again I had the bed all to myself. No long legs sprawling over to my side. No more flailing arm over my face in the middle of the night. But I don't think I'll ever complain about that again. Just to have Kirk here with me now would be wonderful. I'll gladly occupy the remaining 20 percent of the queen-sized bed. And that flailing arm of his? I'd gladly welcome it now.

Morning came way too soon, and I knew I should pull myself out of bed and go do the milking for Brandon. He would be back later today. His symposium wasn't going to be over until late last night, so he had told me he'd spend the night with a couple of his friends who had recently rented an apartment off-campus.

I grabbed a bagel, spread some cream cheese on it, and headed for the milk barn. Milking was the easy part. Our cows know to come into the barn as soon as they hear the truck pull up. They each know their places in the stanchion and know they'll soon be fed. Separating the cream and cleaning the equipment properly takes a bit longer, but it gave me time to think about the recent events in our life here on this gorgeous piece of real estate.

I jumped back in the truck and drove to the house, wondering if Thorne was still in bed. As soon as I walked in the door, I saw him sitting at the breakfast table with his head between his hands. I sat down beside him and said, "You want to talk about it?"

"First off," he said, "you got any aspirins in your bathroom?"

"Yes, sweetie, I'll go get you some."

I came back, got him a glass of water, sat down beside him, and put my hand on his knee. He quickly swallowed the two aspirins I handed him, drank the whole glass of water, and set it down with a bit of a thud. "You know, don't you?"

I stood up, went over to the coffeepot, and started making coffee. "Yes," I finally said, "I know you wrecked your pretty little car, and I know you were sloshed. All I want to know is, was anyone hurt?"

He only shook his head and then closed his eyes, looked down, and said nothing.

I put my hand on his. "Honey, you want to talk about it?"

He covered my hand with his. "Katie—Mom, I'm sorry. I was such a fool."

I pulled my hand from under his and wrapped my arm around him. In barely a whisper, I said, "Sometimes we have to learn things the hard way."

He tipped his head over to mine. "Yeah, Mom, but I knew better." Then he pulled away and looked into my eyes. "But no, I don't wanna talk about it. I wanna forget it ever happened—and never find myself in that place again."

I squeezed his hand. "That's exactly what God wants too."

"Please don't tell Dad." I could see the hurt in his eyes. "Dad would never forgive me."

"Oh, Thorne, I think I know your dad better than that. Sure, he'd be disappointed, but never forgive you? No, that's not Dad."

He stood up, started back toward his room. I barely heard his next words. "Not sure I believe that."

I followed him, and before he had a chance to close the door, I pushed my way in. "Honey, let me get you some breakfast. You must be famished."

"Naw, I can't eat anything right now."

"Then how about if I put together a really good lunch for us? Just the two of us."

"Where's Brandon?"

"He spent the night with his buds in Stillwater. I guess they recently rented an apartment off campus."

"Brandon and his buds rented an apartment? Who's gonna work the ranch?"

"No, I just meant his buds rented the apartment. Brandon just spent the night with them."

"So when'll he be back?"

"I don't know. He said he had a few things to wrap up on campus this morning."

"You gonna tell him?"

"Tell him what?"

"You know, how stupid his bro was."

"No, I think I'll leave that up to you."

"Mom?"

"What?"

"You're the greatest. Thanks."

I went back to the kitchen and poured myself a belated cup of coffee. I looked out the west window where the evening sun had suddenly streamed in through the tree. "God," I said out loud, "I'm on board now. You're the pilot, I'm the passenger."

As soon as Brandon walked in the door, he blurted out, "What the heck happened to Thorne's car?"

"Looks like it got smashed. You'll have to ask him."

"Geez! He drives like a maniac—always has."

"So how was your symposium?"

"Boring."

"You want to talk about it?"

He grinned. "Why do I get the feeling you asked Thorne the same thing about that smashed-up fender? So did he wanna talk about it? By the way, where is the scrawny little addict?"

"Addict?" My heart sank. *Does he know more than I do?*

"Yeah, addict. He's addicted to them paints—"

"*Those*, Brandon. *Those*."

"Okay, *those*. Those paints and *those* brushes."

"Brandon, I think we've been over this before. Those paints are going to see him through life—in style."

<hr />

It was my birthday. Thorne came in to the house and handed me a gift, unwrapped as usual, but in a large and thick plastic bag from an electronics store I was familiar with. "Set it down gently," he said. "It might break."

I sat down at the dining table, opened the bag, and slid out a large box labeled Apple. I looked up at him. "You didn't!" I tried pulling out those end flaps that keep the lid from popping open. "Thorne, is this what I think it is?"

He grinned. "Only one way to find out."

I still couldn't get my fingernails under those stiff flaps to open it. He took the box from me, pulled out his pocketknife, and popped the flaps out.

I opened the lid and found a 15" MacBook Pro laptop. "Okay," I said, "are you trying to bribe me? I told you I wouldn't say anything to Dad about your…you know."

"About my what?" I was sure he knew exactly what I was talking about.

"Your day of stupidity."

"Aww, that? Nope, I think I told you I didn't want to remember. And I don't think you do either."

"You're right about that, buddy. Now, why did you go out and spend a ton of money on this thing?"

"'Cause I'm gettin' tired of hearing you clacking out your story on that big black dinosaur. Mom, this is the twenty-first century! Get on board."

"Thorne, I don't know anything about computers. What am I supposed to do with it?"

"Me and Brandon will teach you."

I glared at him. "Oh yeah? Apparently, I've not been successful in teaching you good English."

He grinned. "Maybe not, but you taught me a few other important things in life."

"Okay, buddy, I'll take that. Thank you."

26

Brandon was assisting with a young heifer that was having some trouble birthing. Thorne was locked in his room again. He hadn't eaten in two days that I knew about. The few times I'd seen him, I could tell his despondence had returned. I asked him if he wanted to ride over with me to see Kirk. "This is the day Dad is supposed to be put on the special treadmill."

"Naw," he said, "I want to finish his piece." He stuck both hands in the side loops of his jeans and pulled them up a bit. "I'll wait and take it to him then." I could see an unexplainable sadness in his eyes.

"So are you getting close to the final brushstrokes?"

Devoid of any emotion, he mumbled, "Yeah, you wanna see?"

"Well, sure, I do. Come on and show me."

He opened the door, and I walked in. The last time I'd seen it, I could tell it would be a melodramatic piece. And I was right.

"Oh, Thorne! Dad will flip out. This is awesome!" Dandy's head and neck dominated the canvas. His head was turned a bit, reaching over a white fence. He was nudging the wilted hand I easily recognized as Kirk's left hand.

The detail in it was incredible. The typical dirt under the nails, the blackened thumbnail colored by a hammer after missing its intended target, and those big roadmap veins on the top of the hand—all were so obviously those of Kirk's. But the hand drooped, unable to reach out and pet his cherished friend. Dandy was undeterred by his master's inability, and he was stretching out to the hand.

Thorne had remarkably shown Dandy's warm expression with the bond between the two I'd seen so many times before. I looked over at Thorne. "How can one picture say so much?"

"You like it?"

"As I said, Dad is going to flip out."

"I've got some more work to do with the shadowing on the fence. Then I'm gonna frame it. I've got an idea for that."

"I'm so proud of you, Thorne. Do you remember the first pencil drawing you did on the big sketchpad Kirk bought for you? I knew right then you had a talent worth refining."

Without another word, he took my arm and escorted me out of the room. He then sauntered out of the house. I stood there, aghast, thinking, *What did I say wrong?* This puzzle is becoming even more complicated. I'm not seeing any definable picture to help me piece it together.

I watched as Kirk slowly took his first step on the Ekso Bionics treadmill. The big contraption held him vertical, while the electronics around his legs pushed each one individually. He let out a hoot for the whole room to hear.

"Kate, look at this!" Those cowboy-blue eyes were dancing like a young boy's would on his first solo bike ride. I stood back with my arms crossed, knowing this would be only a fleeting slice of freedom for Kirk.

I managed to smile and said, "Lookin' good, cowboy!"

As the machine slowly extended one leg in front of the other, I could see pure bliss enveloping Kirk. With each embarrassingly slow step he took—or, rather, each step the machine took for him—I realized how important this was for him. Kirk has always been an active man, never staying in one place for any length of time. If there is nothing for him to do, he will create something. He was constantly on the move.

I wish the boys could have been here. It would have meant so much to Kirk.

The boys hooked up my laptop, and Brandon showed me the basics of Microsoft Word. I don't need any of those silly games that came preprogrammed, nor did I need to learn how to watch videos. I suppose the Internet could be useful at times with my writing, but I have no intention of wasting my time on chat lines, e-mails, or Facebook.

I sat there, alone, tapping out two more chapters in my novel. *Should I try to get it published?* I took a few creative writing courses in college, so I'm familiar with the mechanics of acts 1, 2, and 3 of a typical novel. I know about the proper way to punctuate dialogue, and common sense will tell me what will keep a reader interested. What I don't know is the secrets they've hidden in this Word program. How do I find a word or phrase I've written previously in the document? I shouldn't have to scroll back through the whole manuscript to find what I'm looking for. I mean, this machine is all electronic, digital. There has to be a secret key to find what I need. The bar up at the top is helpful in many ways, but I don't understand the box labeled Styles. I've got to get Brandon to sit down long enough with me to teach me more. Thorne promised he'd show me how to use the Internet. Did I really need that? He said I do.

Brandon walked in and pulled up a chair beside me. "Lost it."

"The calf or the mother?"

"Yeah, the heifer's gonna be okay. I guess it took me too long to pull the calf. It was dead by the time I got it out. If I'd had some help, maybe two of us could have saved it. Man! I feel so bad."

"Brandon, your dad's had that happen before. You shouldn't feel bad. Maybe Uncle Carl will hire you a helper. Ronnie was a big help to Kirk. I'm proud of him for serving in the military, but I wish he could be here now to help you. I'm afraid I'd be of no help to you with pulling a calf."

Brandon looked over at the screen on my laptop. "So, looks like you're doing pretty well with Microsoft Word."

I told him a couple of my concerns, and he showed me what to do.

"Control F—well, I knew there had to be some secret to finding a previously typed word or phrase.

"So tell me, how'd Dad do on the new machine?"

"I wish you could have been there to see the expression on his face when he took his first step—with the assistance of the machine, of course. You should have heard him. He let out a whoop, loud enough to be heard in the next room."

"They got the machine in his room?"

"No, there is only one machine. Kirk's not the only one using it. They have all kinds of equipment for the patients. He's getting some movement in his shoulders and upper arms, enough to force his lower arms into some limited action. They think he'll soon be able to operate an electric wheelchair."

"Wow! He'll like that."

"Yes, he sure will. Hey, I think Thorne is planning on riding over with me to see Dad tomorrow evening. I'll help you with the afternoon milking if you'll come too."

"Sure. Thanks, Mom. I was planning on going over anyway."

27

With Kirk now at the rehab hospital and out of danger, I'd been able to spend more time at home. Several visitors had called, including Pastor Lindall. I got a call from a sweet lady from church. "Katie," she said, "Doris and I would like to come see you. I know you haven't been able to come to church while Kirk's been in the hospital."

"Sure," I said, "that would be nice. I'll meet you up at the gate to open it for you."

She laughed. "Oh, you don't need to do that. I may be past eighty, but I can still manage to open a ranch gate."

"Not this one, Kathleen, it's electronic. What time can you be here?"

We agreed on the time, and I drove up to meet them. I could have just given her the code, but we had decided when it was first installed to keep it secret, except to family and closest friends.

I thought I was probably early, so I took my time driving the quarter mile or so up to the gate. As I drove past, I noticed the beer bottle I'd seen there before, so I stopped, got out, and picked it up. I tossed it over the side of the pickup bed.

The ladies were right on time. I punched in the gate code and had them follow me up to the house. I stopped, got out of the truck, and waited for them to slowly get out of Kathleen's Cadillac. They started to follow me, and just as I turned to say something to them, Kathleen was peering into the bed of my truck. The look on her face was priceless. I thought about explaining that I had just picked up the bottle from the side of the road and tossed it in there, but then I decided I didn't owe them an explanation. It might lead to more questions than I was prepared to deal with.

I opened the door and invited them in. "Would you ladies like something to drink?"

Kathleen glared at me like I'd offered them a gin and tonic or a Scotch. Doris finally said, "No, thank you. We can't stay long."

Both were asking about Kirk, and Doris poured on an abundant load of sympathy. "Katie," she said, "what are you going to do? You can't run this big ranch by yourself."

I started to explain how Brandon was stepping in for Kirk, but she didn't let me get the first two words out. "Oh, you poor dear. I just can't imagine what you are going through. Kirk was such a nice man."

My blood started to boil. *Was?* I wanted to sound off—*Lady, he's not dead*—but I kept my mouth shut.

Kathleen had been sitting stone still, probably thinking about the beer bottle she'd seen in the bed of my truck. She finally came to life. "Katie, you know God can heal that man. You just have to believe."

I squirmed a bit in my chair and thought, *How do I reply to that? I've been attending church all my life, and I've heard that before.* "Yes," I said, "He certainly can…"

"Well, you need to have more faith!" she said boldly.

I sat up straighter. "Kathleen, I'm going to leave that up to God. He is the one in control here. I'm not in the habit of telling Him what to do."

That shut her up but earned me a prolonged disapproving stare. I was successful in changing the subject, and we chatted about nothing in particular for a while. Suddenly, Doris changed the subject. "Has Pastor Lindall been over to see Kirk?" Her lips were pursed, and I could tell she had every intention of pursuing some inflammatory remarks about our good pastor.

"Yes, Doris, Pastor's been checking on Kirk on a regular basis. He and Kirk are best of buds. They enjoy exchanging—"

"Well," she huffed, "a pastor should be more than a buddy!"

These old biddies had succeeded in raising my blood pressure several points. I'd had enough. "Look, ladies, I hate to be rude, but I have to help my son with the chores." Then I felt guilt wash over me. It's true I often help Brandon with the chores, but today he had already told me he didn't need me. I thought of what Pastor Lindall had said in one of his sermons: half-truths are nothing but whole lies.

I thought about walking them to Kathleen's Cadillac, but remembered the look Kathleen had when she saw the beer bottle. So I decided to just watch them from the kitchen window. Sure enough, as they approached my pickup, Kathleen pointed her finger toward the inside of the bed, and the chattering lips started.

Brandon came in to grab a Coke out of the fridge. "What's with the two old ladies in the Caddy?"

"Oh, those dear women just came by to offer me some… cheer."

He laughed. "I think I hear some sarcasm in your answer."

"Are you sure you don't need me to help with the chores?"

"Hey, I already told you I was gonna start early so we could go see Dad."

"Oh, come on, let me help you. Otherwise, I've just made myself out to be a big liar."

"You were just trying to get rid of those ladies, weren't you?"

I thumped him on the head. "I'm pleading the fifth on that one."

28

Pastor Lindall called. "Katie, you had mentioned you would need a van with a power lift for Kirk when he comes home."

"Yes, I did say that. I just don't see how I can afford it. Those things are expensive."

"Well, that's why I'm calling. Several in the community are putting together an auction to raise money, hoping we can get enough to buy one."

I was surprised. "Oh, that would be wonderful. You really think an auction way out here in the country would be successful?"

"We're going all out to try to make it happen. Several—no, all of the churches in the area are coming together to help. I've arranged it with Mr. Johnson to secure the high school gymnasium for the auction. People will be bringing donated items for the week before the auction."

"But won't that tie up the gym? The kids will need it."

"No, I've got that covered too. The bus barn will hold all the donated items up until the night of the auction."

"Pastor, how can I ever thank you? I didn't see any way for me to purchase a van for Kirk. Even if a portion of the cost can be raised, maybe our trade-in would make up the difference."

He gave me the date that had been agreed on and made sure it was okay with me. "Oh, by the way," he said, "if you've got any items there at your house or on the ranch you want to get rid of, I'll come by and get them for you. We're hoping to fill up the basketball court with stuff to be bid on."

I laughed. "You don't know what you're agreeing to. I could probably fill up the gym myself with stuff we no longer need. Kirk's accident has changed a lot of things around this ranch. I'm trying to get the house wheelchair ready, which means some furniture has to go."

"We've put up flyers all over town, even in the surrounding towns. One of your rancher neighbors has contacted others in the area to make sure they participate. This is going to be a really big event."

I thought about the date he'd set for the auction. "You know, Kirk should be released to go home by then."

"That would be fantastic if he could be at the auction. You think it might be possible?"

"Yes. We might have to put him in the horse trailer to get him there."

"Oh, that's funny. No, I think we can do better than that."

"Pastor, you have made my day. That will be an answer to my prayer."

I said good-bye and hung up the phone, hoping Brandon would come in soon so I could tell him.

Monday evening, the boys and I made a final trip over to the rehab center hospital. Kirk was scheduled to be released on Wednesday. Brandon drove, Thorne was in the front passenger seat, and I sat in the back seat with Thorne's painting. He had wrapped it in a sheet and gave me strict instructions to leave it covered. I tapped Thorne on the shoulder and whispered, "Hey, can't I just take a peek in one corner?"

"He turned around, gave me an evil eye, and said, "Don't you even think of it. Dad will be the first to see it."

Thorne walked in ahead of us, carrying the 20"x20" piece. At least that was the size of the canvas. The framed piece appeared to be much larger under the sheet. I hadn't seen it since he'd framed it. I know he had asked to use some of Kirk's tools to build the frame.

I was trailing behind a bit, as usual. As soon as the guys walked through the door, I heard Kirk's baritone voice. "There's my boys! I walked in behind them, and he said, "Hey, Thorny, what you got there?"

I stared at Kirk and twisted my mouth in an unspoken *Don't say that* expression. Kirk knows Thorne hates that.

Brandon walked over and tapped Kirk on the shoulder. "Hey, Dad, I hear you're comin' home Wednesday."

"Yep." He lifted his shoulder enough to force the arm up toward the window. "I'm ready to trade that fancy little pond out there for the big pond back home."

"Cool."

"You guys been catching any fish lately?"

Thorne stood back. Didn't say anything. I detected a major fault line about to break loose in his thoughts. The conversation wasn't going as expected.

Brandon jumped in. "No time to fish, Dad. I'm trying to keep up the work you did and my studies too. It's not easy."

Kirk looked at Brandon. "I'm proud of you, son. The ranch is a full-time job. I don't know how you can even have time for your studies. But I'm glad you do. Keep it up, son."

I saw Thorne start to hold up the painting and say something when Brandon cut in. "Dad, I'm loving the ag classes I'm taking. I'm gonna come out with an A in them, for sure, and I think my other subjects will be As too."

"I never had any doubts they'd be anything but…"

"Mom tell you about Amy?"

"No, I guess not. What about her?"

"She's doing her student teaching at Wellston—

I cut in, "Kirk, I think Thorne's got something for you." Thorne moved in closer to Kirk. "Come on," I said, "pull that sheet off so we can all see."

Thorne moved up next to Kirk's bed, held the piece up, and snapped the sheet off in one quick motion like a magician would. Kirk's eyes froze in place, and he was speechless.

I was looking at the frame Thorne had made. It was crude, maybe made from old barn wood. He held the piece up higher and pointed to a section at the bottom of the frame that looked to be chewed up a bit. "You know that old board in Dandy's stall that he'd gnawed on? You said you needed to replace it."

Kirk hadn't moved. I'd seen him do this before, and I knew he was really touched by what he was seeing.

Thorne slung his silky mop of straight black hair to one side. "Well, I got your hammer, took the chewed-up board off—don't worry, I replaced it with a new one. But it's got to be painted. I couldn't find any white paint. Anyways, I took the board to your wood shop, and—what's the power tool you use to make forty-five-degree angles?"

Kirk took his eyes off the painting. "Miter saw?"

"Yeah, that's it. I used it to cut the board for this frame. And you see the horsehair trailing down this one side of the frame?" Kirk was silent. "That's Dandy's. I found it in his stall. I think he must have snagged it on a nail, so I thought it would finish off the frame nicely."

I stared at the title plate: *It Was a Good Ride*. I thought, what an appropriate title. Under the title was the artist's name. This was all engraved in an elegant bronze plate with a barbed-wire design around the edge and affixed to the lower portion of the ablated old rail Dandy had chewed on. I was still thinking about the title he'd given the piece.

My mind fast-forwarded to the story I had been plunking out on the old Remington and now tapping out on my new laptop. That title Thorne had given the piece would be perfect for my story. *It Was a Good Ride.*

The room was quiet. Kirk stared at the painting for at least a minute, and then he closed his eyes tightly, as if the memory of his beloved horse was overtaking all other thoughts. Thorne continued to hold the piece up, but Kirk seemed to still be overwhelmed, almost in a trance.

Brandon touched the frame. "That's cool, Thorne. I didn't know you knew how to use a tool of any kind."

I stepped up and looked at Thorne. "Well, he certainly knows how to use those artist's tools." I thought I noticed a bit of disappointment in those walnut-brown eyes of his. Without a word, he set the piece down, turning the front of it to the wall. I watched him close his eyes for a second. The hum of the air-conditioning was the only sound in the room. Then he reached up with both hands and twisted his head to crack his neck. I held my breath. I noticed him twist his mouth to one side, obviously upset by the turn of events.

The silence was impenetrable in the room. I held my breath, knowing something awful was taking place.

Thorne turned and slowly walked out of the room.

Brandon looked at me and whispered, "What was that all about?"

I shrugged my shoulder. I thought I knew, but I didn't want to say it.

Kirk finally broke his silence. "Hold the painting up here again. That is amazing! Honey, just look—

"Kirk!"

"What? What, Katie?"

"Kirk, don't you think your comment is just a tad too late?"

"But—

"No buts to it, Kirk Childers!" I felt my hair bristle. "You said absolutely nothing to him. He probably thinks you hated it. I can't believe you were so unresponsive—so insensitive."

I turned and watched Brandon as he walked out of the room.

What had come over my guys? First, Kirk pretty much ignores Thorne's beautiful painting. Thorne suddenly walked out of the room, and then Brandon left the scene. Where is the love in this family?

I managed to unclench my teeth. "Kirk, I said, "when Thorne showed you his painting, and you said nothing, you just snuffed out all bonding with him that you've been so proud of." I stomped my foot, something I've never done before. "That was just so wrong!"

"Honey, simmer down a bit. I was totally stunned by seeing Dandy again, even if it was just in paint. The image of that horse flew straight at me, just like he was actually reaching out to me, nudging me. It was then I knew my worst fears had come true."

Kirk's eyes closed again, this time even tighter than before. "Dandy's gone, isn't he?"

Ten or fifteen minutes later, Brandon came back in the room. "I can't find Thorne."

"Maybe he went back to the truck."

"Nope, I already checked there."

"How about the vending machines? You check there?"

"Mom, I'm one ahead of you. I've looked everywhere. It's like he has vanished."

"He's got his cell. I'll give him a call."

Brandon leered at me. "He always walks out when the heat is on. You know that."

"Look," I said, "he had already walked out when Dad and I were fussing. So just cool your jets. I think he was hurt when Kirk acted like he didn't even like the painting."

"Honey…"

"No, Kirk, you should have put your feelings aside about Dandy and told Thorne how you loved his painting."

"Come on, Brandon," I said. "Let's go find your brother. He's got to be hanging around here somewhere."

But he wasn't.

29

Brandon and I searched the grounds for over an hour. "Mom, doesn't Thorne have a friend here in the city? I think I've heard him talking on the phone to him. He's like an artist friend. Thorne met him at the gallery one time, remember?"

"I think I do, but I wouldn't know how to get hold of him. I don't even know his name."

"Well, that's all I can figure, 'cause he's sure not around here, and I don't think he knows anyone else in this city."

We waited around for another hour. Thorne never showed, so we headed back home. "I'm glad you're driving, Brandon, because I'm pretty shaken up right now."

"Why? He does this kind of thing all the time. I never know what to expect out of yo-yo man. He's up one day and down the next."

When we pulled up to the house, Thorne's Miata was not there. "Now that is odd," I said. "How'd he get someone to give him a ride back home and take off before we got here?"

"Mom, that's not impossible. We looked for him and then waited for him for well over an hour. Did he have any money on him?"

"Maybe. I don't know. Why?"

"He could have called for a cab."

"A cab! All the way from northwest Oklahoma City? That'd cost a fortune."

"Either that, or he grew wings."

I grinned. "Thorne's not exactly the type for wings or halos."

"Yeah, more like—

"Okay, okay, I get it. No, Brandon, I'm really worried. Something's bad wrong. You think we should call the cops? Maybe he's met with foul play."

"Look, in the first place, Thorne is an adult. And secondly, he somehow managed to come get his car and take off. That's not exactly what I'd call foul play. He'll show up. He always does."

Kirk was released to come home on Wednesday before the Saturday night auction. Two men with big muscles lifted him into the pickup, and I had arranged for our neighbor to come and help Brandon get him out and into his wheelchair. This would be a twice-weekly task. The rehab center wanted him there three times a week. Even twice a week seemed to me to be an impossibility. I didn't know how I'd do it.

When the men got him out of the truck and into the wheelchair, I told them I wanted to push him into the house. The flagstone path to our front door squelched that idea. The wheels stuck on every rock, and I couldn't budge it.

Kirk laughed. "Give it up, Kate. Let the guys push me."

The rehab center had delivered a hospital-type bed and one of those lift chairs with specially made bars to wrap around his body to prevent him from tumbling out when in the up position. They taught me how to maneuver him into his wheelchair from that. I donated our seven-foot leather sofa and matching chair to the auction so his bed could go in the big room, where all the action would be.

After our good neighbor left, I asked Kirk what he thought about his new digs. "This room isn't quite as glamorous as it was at one time. I wish I could make it as pretty as the room you had at the rehab center."

"Honey," he said, "home is where you are. I don't care about the décor, as long as you are part of it."

I stooped down and kissed him. "That's my man. *Unselfish* would be a good middle name for you."

There was so much I had to learn in caring for a quadriplegic. I hate that term! A specially trained home health nurse was knocking on our door almost as soon as we got Kirk inside. The guy spent several hours with me. I was taught the proper way to transfer Kirk from the bed to his chair and vice-versa—not an easy task. He went over the procedure for intermittent catheterization. I learned high blood pressure is often a sign of a full bladder. Of course, I'd already been told about the importance of pressure relief and warned about the consequences if he developed bed sores, which are difficult to clear up.

Kirk's diet was going to have to change. The good old farm-cooked meals he'd loved in the past would not work on a daily basis. I would have to rethink my menus.

We talked about the emotional aspect of being a caregiver for a quadriplegic and how it could be overwhelming and at times much more difficult than the physical aspect. He had been looking over the big room and then walked over and faced me. "Watching someone you love in this situation is upsetting, to say the least. You need to be both physically and emotionally strong to handle it. Have you arranged to have a PCA here with you at least part time?"

"What's a PCA?"

"Personal care assistant. You can't do this by yourself."

"I've got to do it. There is no one else—I can't afford to hire help."

"Look, Katie, being his only caregiver will be an emotional and physical strain on you. Most caregivers need to call in help—friends, neighbors, other family members can help."

"My mother has said she would help out, and I know Dad would."

"But even then, with help from your parents, if you find you're unable to provide what is needed, try not to feel guilty. Support groups might be helpful."

"Are you kidding? Where will I find a support group of this nature way out here in rural America?"

"You might have to go into Oklahoma City. There is one there I'm familiar with. I'll leave the contact name and number for you."

Yeah, right! How was I going to leave Kirk here and drive thirty-five miles to a support group?

The guy also worked with Kirk, showing him how to use a slider to move himself from the bed to the chair. He showed him how to use a specially designed stick to get his pants on. "You know," he told Kirk, "shorts would be much easier to manage. I know you're a rancher and probably used to wearing jeans, but trust me, shorts are better." He included Kirk in the discussion on diet. "Look, buddy, some of the food you're probably used to will have to go." He explained how certain foods would create problems for a person with limited activity.

"No problem, there," Kirk said, "I've gotten used to the grub they've been feeding me in the hospital. I'm starting to like it."

"Kirk," he said, "I can tell you're going to do just fine. I like your attitude." He handed me his card. "Katie, if you need anything, just give me a call. I can usually walk you through about any situation. Of course, if it's a serious medical situation, you'll need to call 911."

"Yes," I said, "I have a friend who's an RN, and she's told me to call her anytime if we have questions."

Brandon had hung around for a while after they got Kirk inside the house, but told Kirk he needed to separate some young steers to get ready for sale. I had placed Kirk's bed in the big room so he could see the whole room, the kitchen area, and down the hall to the bedrooms. He looked all around the room, then down the hallway. "Thorne back in his room working on another painting?"

I didn't have the heart to tell him we hadn't seen him since the Dandy painting incident at the rehab hospital. "No, I don't know where he is."

If I allowed myself to worry like I used to, I'd be sick to my stomach, but still, someone needed to be searching for him. I'd wanted to call our sheriff, but Brandon told me it would be useless. He was probably right.

I knew caring for Kirk would help keep my mind off Thorne, and did it ever. The first night was quite an experience for this gal. I tried to remember everything the guy had told me, but that test resulted in a big fat F for me. Kirk was so patient with me, but I felt like a total failure as his caregiver.

After the morning routine of transferring him from the bed to his chair, bathing and toileting and then dressing, I wheeled him into the kitchen and up to the table.

He looked on as I sliced up fresh fruit and placed it on top of a bowl of pumpkin flax granola cereal. The doctor had already warned me about unpasteurized whole milk, so I grabbed a carton of store-bought low-fat milk and poured it over the cereal. He frowned. "Guess I can say good-bye to the good stuff straight from our cows, huh?"

"I'm afraid so." I picked up the spoon and started to feed him.

"Put the spoon down," he said. "I've got this."

I watched as Kirk attempted to eat using the spoon. His hands were permanently balled up in a loose fist, the fingers curled back toward his palms. He was able to move his shoulder around, which allowed for the arm and hands to follow. He maneuvered his right arm toward the spoon and positioned it so those curled-back fingers wrapped around the handle of the spoon. It was a struggle for him, but he seemed to make a game of it. Grabbing the spoon between two lifeless fingers proved to be a skill that would need a lot of improvement.

"Honey, you want me to do it for you?"

"Nope. I've got to do this myself."

"Kirk, when you get the handle of the spoon between your fingers, see if you can turn your arm a bit. Maybe that will wedge the spoon in between the fingers."

"Yeah, sounds easy. Maybe that would work."

And it did. Slowly he brought the spoon up toward his face, and then he missed his mouth. The food dropped to his lap. He tried again and missed. And then finally, he was able to get the spoon and food up to his face. "Now, get in there," he growled. "Center, right under the nose, dang it!"

I had to laugh. "You're about to get it…"

"Now straight in," he said.

"Hey! You got it!"

Kirk's determination was amazing. I think more food ended up on his lap than ever entered his mouth. But he didn't seem to mind. But for me, that meant changing him out of the milk-soaked shirt and shorts.

30

It was Saturday, the day of the auction. Mr. Johnson and two of the high school teachers had called Brandon to come open the ranch gate. "Katie," Mr. Johnson said, "we're here to load up Kirk and take him to the auction. Is he ready to go?"

"Guys, I am so thankful you came. I had no idea how I would accomplish that. I knew I wouldn't be much help to Brandon. I've learned how to get him from the bed to his chair, but getting him up in the pickup is another thing."

We arrived early at the high school gym. The parking lot was already packed, and there were cars and pickups parked for several blocks, almost to Main Street in one direction. I looked back at Mr. Johnson sitting in the back seat with Kirk. "Where did all these people come from? This must be half the population of the entire county."

"Uh, Katie, there will be people from other counties as well. We've been working hard to get the word out to everyone we can think of."

The guys unloaded Kirk, got him in his wheelchair, and I walked in behind them. Mr. Johnson suggested I push Kirk inside. As soon as I saw the crowd, my jaw dropped. All the bleachers were full, and they had put up folding chairs all around the mountain of donated items. I looked at Mr. Johnson and said, "This is amazing. Look at all those donations to be auctioned."

"Katie, you haven't seen it all. Back behind the gym, there is a boat, trailer, and even two vehicles—all donated."

Everyone was chattering. The noise was deafening. I was wondering where we'd sit when Mom came bouncing over to greet me. Her eyes were sparkling, and she was saying something, but I couldn't understand a word of it. She hurried up ahead of us.

Suddenly a band started playing. The chattering stopped, and everyone began to stand. Mr. Johnson escorted us to an area up front where five wingback chairs had been placed. Brandon was already seated there with my dad. I pushed Kirk up next to one of those velvety chairs where Brandon was pointing. I sat down next to him, with Mom and Dad on the other side of Brandon. The fifth chair was conspicuously empty. I had mixed feelings—sad, and a bit angry. I was sure Kirk was feeling the same.

Mr. Johnston stepped forward, took a microphone, and motioned to the band to stop. "Friends and neighbors, thank you all for coming out this evening. As you know, we are here for an auction, the proceeds of which will go toward the purchase of a vehicle with an electronic ramp for our friend Kirk Childers."

I looked over at Kirk. "Isn't this amazing? I said." His face was shining.

"Most people here know Kirk and Katie Childers. Kirk is a rancher. Katie has taught elementary here in Luther, both as a full-time teacher and as a substitute. Kirk and Katie have devoted their entire lives to children. They have fostered several and adopted two.

"Not many know this, but Kirk Childers is the reason Luther has a Boy Scout troop. Kirk started mentoring boys several years ago with the idea of eventually forming a Boy Scouts troop. Kirk never had the opportunity to join the Scouts as a boy, but that didn't deter him. He didn't have much support at first. But as many people know, Kirk Childers does not give up easily. He searched till he found a qualified man to start up a troop. But he didn't stop there. For years, Kirk attended the meetings, offered to host the boys for fishing trips to the pond on his ranch, and shuttled boys who didn't have rides to and from the meetings.

"Folks, I could talk all evening about Kirk, but we are here to have an auction, and if I don't shut up soon, I'll have to order breakfast in for all of us." That brought a roar of laughter. "One of our local auctioneers, Mr. Ben Jenson of Jenson and Jenson Auctioneers, has agreed to volunteer tonight for this event.

"So let's all pitch in. When you see something you like, start bidding. I don't want any of these items left unsold. Our Luther Lions have a game in here Monday evening, so this all has to be gone, but before we start, I've asked Reverend Lindall to open with a word of prayer."

Pastor Lindall's prayer was brief and to the point. "Lord, we've come this evening to bless our friend in a way so typical of this community. Now I ask that you would bless each of these generous people in return. Amen."

Ben Jenson wasted no time in getting the bidding started. First up was a brand-new Giant Rincon bicycle, donated by our local hardware, followed by a ladies' Giant Flourish bike. Both went quickly.

There was such a variety of items—from clothing, cakes and pies, to sports equipment, even farm equipment. And of course, the boat and trailer and two pickup trucks out back.

The bidding was fast and continued escalating the price of each item. The auctioneer stopped briefly to give everyone a break. Before he resumed, he asked Kirk if he'd like to say a few words.

Brandon held the microphone for him. "I'm in awe," Kirk said, "of what's happening here. I can't even begin to thank everyone for the kindness and support I'm witnessing here tonight. There is one important thing, though, that Mr. Johnson failed to mention. Those Boy Scouts fished my big pond completely out of bass. Now all I've got left is a bunch of stinkin' crawdads."

Jenson took the microphone from Kirk. "Folks, if I know Kirk, he'll have that pond restocked with largemouth bass before the next Boy Scouts can get their tackle together and get back out there to the pond."

So many times during the evening, I saw items bid up far beyond what they were worth. The one that really caught me by surprise was a pecan pie made by my previous visitor Kathleen Vonagan. Her friend Doris started the bidding on the pie, others joined in; but Kathleen would immediately outbid them. I heard her holler out, "My husband got mad at me for bringing that pie to this auction. I've got to get back home with it." The bidding price kept escalating. Jenson played along with the two women. Doris would bid, Jenson would ask for more, and Kathleen's hand would pop up quickly. Finally, I think Jenson was just tired of it all and closed Kathleen's winning bid at $6,500.

I looked over at Kirk and saw he was grinning, and Brandon said, "Holy cow!" Somehow their chattering last week about that beer bottle in the bed of my pickup didn't seem to matter. At the time, I had called them a couple of old biddies. Now, I'm thinking that term has a new meaning.

I knew Kirk was exhausted, so I asked for some help in getting him back home. Brandon stayed with him so I could go back to the auction. Household items, farm supplies, toys, clothing—all went at unbelievable prices. I think any item there could have been purchased at retail for less than the final bid was.

As I continued to sit there in the comfortable wingback chair, friends started coming around to visit as the auction continued. I'm pretty sure every teacher, janitor, cafeteria worker, and bus driver attended the auction. Most of them took the time to stop by my chair and visit. At twelve thirty, Mom and Dad said they were too tired to stay any longer. I was really tired too, but I felt it was my duty to remain until the auctioneer closed the shop.

I was so busy visiting with friends I didn't know when those big items outside sold. It was Pastor Lindall who told me about it. He stooped down in front of me. "Katie, one of those pickup trucks out back was just three years old. It went for eighteen thousand dollars!"

"Eighteen thousand!" I said. "Who would have donated such an expensive item?"

"I recognized the truck," he said. It belonged to the late husband of Doris Cantrell."

I just about choked. "You mean, Doris—Kathleen Vonagan's friend?"

"That's right. I know it was her who brought it to the auction, because I recognized the bumper sticker."

"Bumper sticker?"

"Yes, I'd seen it on the green F-150 just last week."

"What did the bumper sticker say?"

"Forgiven."

31

For the first time, Kirk had managed to transfer himself from the bed to the chair. I watched as he used his shoulder muscles to prop his arms on the arms of the wheelchair, push up a bit, and adjust his seating position. "Now that is the Kirk Childers I know." I brought his morning coffee to him. "You've never given up on anything you set out to do."

"True," he said, "but sometimes I think others have given up on me."

"What's that supposed to mean? No one is giving up on you."

I detected a sadness blanketing his face. He sat there in the chair with his head thrown back. "That looks uncomfortable. You want a pillow for your head?"

He'd taken up my habit of not answering immediately—and I found it a bit annoying.

"No, I'm okay. Just get my cell phone and dial Thorne's number."

I was beginning to see what this dampening of spirits was about. "Honey," I said, "he'll call us when he's ready to. You know Thorne—it's always been in his timing, not ours."

"Dial it, Kate."

How many times had I dialed the number with no answer? I picked up his phone and dialed. This time there was a recorded message, "You have reached a number that has been disconnected." My heart sank.

I flipped the phone closed. "It's been disconnected."

Kirk looked up. "That's good news!"

"Why would you say that?"

"Well," he drawled, "at least we know he's okay."

"How do you figure?"

"If he'd met with foul play, his phone wouldn't have been disconnected. He's done that himself. And we know the cell phone company didn't cut him off for non-payment. That's taken out on an automatic draft, right?"

"Yes, but why would he have dropped his cell phone service?"

"Maybe he didn't. Could be he switched to a service in another area. Maybe he's in Paris now, starting to live his dream."

I remembered Lena Throckmorton's comments about him switching bank accounts to a bank in Santa Fe. "Yeah," I said, "or New Mexico."

"New Mexico? Kate, what are you withholding from me?"

"It's just what Lena told me. She said Thorne had come into the gallery and asked her to change the bank account she'd been depositing the money from his sales. It was a bank in Santa Fe, New Mexico."

"And you didn't bother to tell me? Just let me hang here on a huge question mark, dangling—"

"Honey, I didn't want to add to your list of worries."

"Well, you failed in that mission. I've been worried sick over him. She give you the name of the bank?"

"No, why?"

He grinned. "Babe, you'd never make a detective. Think about it. If we knew the name of the bank, we could call and get an address, maybe a new phone number for him."

"Joe Friday, you're the one who's not thinking. The bank wouldn't give us that information. It's against the law."

"Call Lena," he said. "Ask her what bank."

"Kirk Childers! You're thinking about calling and telling the bank you are Thorne, aren't you? I've already got your plan figured out. You plan to tell the bank you think they have your address wrong and you just want to correct it. Right?"

He tipped his head upward. "Aww, come on, Kate, why would I do a thing like that?" Then he nodded toward the phone. "Just make the call for me—please."

"No, I won't. That would be a lie. I'm not having any part of it. Besides, what would you do if you could get his address? Jump in your truck and go chase after him?"

"If I had legs, yes, I probably would."

My cell phone vibrated in my pocket. I'd forgotten to take it off silent last night after the auction. "Hello, this is Katie."

"Katie, I've got some good news." It was Pastor Lindall. "Are you sitting down?"

"No, but if it's good news, I'll take it standing up."

"Just got the figures from the auction last night."

"Oh, that's exciting. So tell me."

"You won't need to worry about having enough money to buy that van for Kirk. You won't even have to trade in his pickup if you don't want to."

"Really?"

He related the final figure to me. "That's enough to buy a brand-new specially equipped van with an electronic lift. There's even enough money to buy him the Storm Ranger power chair you'd hoped for."

I had to sit down now. "This is an answer to prayer—one I'll have to admit, I just really didn't believe would ever happen."

"Well, believe it, Katie. I'll bring the check out to you later today if you're going to be home."

As soon as I hung up the phone, it rang again. "Katie, this is Doris Cantrell."

32

Doris Cantrell! Oh my gosh, what can I possibly say to the woman?
"Katie, are you there?"

"Yes, Doris, I'm here. Thank you for calling."

"I was calling," she said, "to see how you and Kirk are doing after the big night. I know you didn't get home till quite late."

"Yes, I think it was around three o'clock. Kathleen, I want to thank—"

"Katie, I just called to offer my services. I don't know if you know, but I am a registered nurse. My training and experience is in quadriplegia. I know you're going to need some respite, all caregivers do.

"Of course, I'm retired now—I'm sure you guessed that." She giggled. "So I would be able to come most anytime you need me."

"Oh, Doris! That would be wonderful. I know there will be times when I have to run errands, and Brandon won't be here to stay with his dad."

"Honey, errands are not really what we call respite. I'm also talking about times when you need to get away, go visit your parents, go see a movie, go shopping for yourself. You will have to do this. Caregivers must take time for themselves. If you don't, you're going to burn out."

"Doris, that is so sweet of you, but you may not understand our financial situation. I won't be able to pay—

"Stop it, girl! I don't want pay. I just want to be able to help. You and Kirk are such sweet people. How could I not?"

I thanked her, and we hung up. I sat there holding the disconnected phone in my hand. And to think I almost blew it that day she and Kathleen came for a visit. I had quickly—and embarrassingly—escorted them to the front door. That was just plain rude on my part.

I hadn't had time to tell Kirk about the auction results. I sat down beside his chair, took his limp hand, and said, "Kirk, last night's auction brought in enough to buy a brand-new van, equipped with an electronic lift."

"Wow! You sure?"

"That's not all. Pastor Lindall says it should also be enough to buy you the Storm Ranger power chair we talked about."

"Man! If I had my legs back, I'd be walking on air right now. I'm blown away by that. How'd that happen? I mean, I know there was a ton of stuff donated, but that's just unbelievable."

"Kirk, Pastor Lindall told me, I think in confidence, that the pickup parked out behind the gym was donated by Doris Cantrell. It belonged to her late husband. Pastor said it went for eighteen thousand dollars! And think about it, there was that boat and trailer someone else donated."

"Boggles my mind."

"And remember, Kathleen's sixty-five-hundred-dollar pie."

Kirk shook his head. "You know, Kate, these people in our part of the world are the most generous people I know. Okies are the best!"

"Remember, I told you about the pickup that was donated by Doris Cantrell? Well, she called just now. This lady has offered to stay with you while I run errands. And—get this—she is a retired RN, trained in caring for spinal cord injury patients."

"So when's she coming over?"

"No, Kirk, the lady has offered to come about anytime I need her. She's retired, so she has no set schedule."

"That's cool." In the same breath, he said, "You sure you don't want to ask Lena Throckmorton for the name of Thorne's bank in New Mexico?"

"Kirk!"

When Brandon came in from his chores, I relayed the same information to him. He went over to Kirk, gave him a thumbs-up, and said, "Dad, you're gonna be under the wheel, driving that van in no time."

I shook my head at him and mouthed the word *no*.

"Mom, I've been watching the videos on the Internet. They show guys with C5 incomplete using EMCs to literally drive a van all by themselves."

"What's an EMC?"

"Electronic mobility control. They use a joystick to steer and voice commands for most other things. It's amazing. This one guy navigated his power chair up the ramp and inside the van. He maneuvered it in place in front of the steering wheel, pushed a button, and locked the chair in place. He was careful—went through all the precautionary procedures. He backed the van out of his garage and drove himself to his destination and back."

"I don't know," I said. "Sounds pretty risky to me, if not impossible."

We were standing behind Kirk. He threw his head back toward us and yelled, "I will do it. You guys just sit back and watch."

I looked at Brandon. "If I know your dad, he will do just what he sets out to do."

"Yep," he said. "I'll drive to some of the cattle auctions around here, buy and sell cattle just like I've done in the past. I'll drive myself back to rehab. And I'll drive to New Mexico. Kate, you can come along if you want."

Brandon looked at me with question marks in his eyes. I shrugged and pretended I didn't know what he was talking about.

Kirk turned his head a bit toward us. His face was reddening. "I will find my son!"

"Okay," Brandon said, "you guys are holding out on me. What's going on?"

"Don't listen to him. He's just hoping for another impossible dream."

Brandon glared at me. "Look, I thought we were a family! Families don't keep secrets from each other, so, Mom, you just need to come clean with me."

I put my hand on his shoulder. "You're right, Brandon. I've left you out of some things, and that's not fair. It wasn't intentional. It's just that you weren't in the house when I told Kirk about it."

"Well, I am now! Start talkin'."

I relayed the conversation I'd had with Lena Throckmorton about the Santa Fe bank account.

"So you think he's there?"

"It's only an assumption on our part, but we believe Thorne may have picked up and moved to New Mexico. Most of his clothes are still here, but his easel, paints, brushes, and everything is gone."

"Makes sense," Brandon said. "I saw this magazine he was reading before he left. It was one of those art-type magazines from Santa Fe. It was filled with Western art. He saw me looking through it, grabbed it out of my hands, and shoved it in a drawer."

"You think it might still be in that drawer?"

We looked. The drawer was empty, as were most of the other drawers in his room.

Brandon left to finish up feeding the animals, but was back in the house twenty minutes later. "Mom," he said, "I just got a phone call. It's bad news."

33

"Uncle Carl just called, said he couldn't get hold of you. Aunt Wilma died this morning. He said she was having chest pains. He called 911, but she died on the way to the hospital."

"Oh, that poor man! Wilma was his soul mate. I think he told me recently they'd celebrated their sixty-first anniversary. You should go tell your dad."

"Why aren't you answering your phone? I tried to call you too. It just goes to voice mail immediately."

I pulled my cell phone out of my jeans pocket, flipped it open, and saw I still had it on silent. "Sorry."

The next week was a bit of a nightmare for me. I had to call for someone to help Brandon load Kirk in the pickup to go to rehab—twice. And then again for Wilma's funeral. On the way back from the funeral, Brandon was driving. "Mom, when are we gonna go shopping for that van for Dad?"

I agreed, this was getting to be a real hassle. "Let me call Doris. See if she can come over Saturday and stay with Kirk while you and I hit the road to the dealerships."

"Yeah," Kirk said, "I'll do the milking. You guys just go."

"Funny, Dad. Real funny. That's like saying we could have Thorne do the milking. He couldn't even do it when he was here."

Doris agreed to come and stay with Kirk while Brandon and I went shopping for Kirk a van.

I soon learned you don't just walk in to a car dealership and pick out a specially equipped van with a power lift right off the showroom floor. We first looked at full-sized Ford E-250 vans, but after driving one of those big lunkers, I settled on a minivan with a raised roof. The power lift had to be ordered, but just having those wide sliding side doors was a big help. The van was set lower to the ground than our pickup which would make it easier to get Kirk's chair inside.

"Mom," Brandon said, "I'll build a wooden ramp to use while we're waiting on the power lift to be delivered and installed."

Both middle captain chairs were removed, making room to maneuver his chair around and be locked into position.

"Mom, you think you'll have enough money left to buy his power chair and equip the van with those EMCs so he can drive it himself?"

"I don't know, Brandon. That kind of equipment must be expensive. I'll first buy Kirk the power chair he wants, and then we'll see what's left. I'm still skeptical about your dad actually being able to drive a van himself."

I knew Kirk had asked me not to trade in the pickup. "Brandon will need it here on the ranch," he had said before we left. "That fancy Dodge of his doesn't need to be banged up with the treatment it would get here."

I wrote out a check for the minivan. What an awesome feeling, being able to pay cash for a new vehicle. It was a first for us. The salesman spent a good deal of time showing me how the equipment worked—the fancy stereo system, the navigation system. It even had a retractable sun roof. He handed me the keys and said, "Congratulations, Mrs. Childers, on your new van. I think it will be perfect for your husband, especially when the power lift comes in. I'll give you a call for you to come back over for it to be installed."

Brandon was smiling. "Come on, I said, let's go buy Kirk that fancy power chair he's been dreaming of."

So Brandon drove the old pickup and followed me in the new minivan to a medical equipment store he had searched out on the Internet. We bought the Storm Ranger power chair, and the salesman taught us how to use the controls.

I knew Kirk would be ecstatic when we got home with it. It would be one more step to freedom for him. But for me, I was just thrilled to be able to write out a check for it, after writing an even bigger one for the van. I thought back about the auction for Kirk. What generous people we were surrounded by. Kirk was right—Okies are the best!

Brandon followed me in the pickup back to the ranch. I quickly came to love the minivan. It was much easier to get in and out of parking spaces, and all the fancy options were fun to operate. Those power sliding doors on the sides would be wonderful. I would make sure Kirk had one of the electronic key fobs so he could operate the door himself.

When we got home, I helped Brandon lift the 215-pound power chair to the ground. I asked him to go push Kirk to the front door. "Leave the door open so he can see," I said. I sat down in the chair, waited till I saw Kirk at the door, and then I touched the forward button. I was watching Kirk as I rode up to the door.

I've never heard a bigger shout come from my husband. He threw both his arms up as high as he could get them—which weren't but six inches or so. "Holy moley!" he yelled. "A whole quarter! Shazam!"

Brandon looked confused. "What's all that nonsense about?"

I said, "It's a phrase used by the comic book character Captain Marvel."

"Never heard of it."

"Well, your dad has used the expression before. But he's never been so loud with it."

I continued to bounce over those flagstones and up to Kirk. I watched those denim-blue eyes of his dance, like twinkling stars on a pitch-dark night. "Wanna take these new shiny wheels for a ride, big guy?"

"Does a pig squeal when taken away from its mama at lunchtime?"

Brandon shook his eyes and grinned. "Dad, where do you come up with all these corny aphorisms?"

"Aphor-whatems?"

"Aphorisms. Sayings, Dad, sayings."

Kirk was leaning forward, like he was anxious to get out of the old chair. "Probably the same place you came up with that fancy word—*asporisms!*"

"*Aphorism*, Dad!"

"Whatever! Just get me out of this old pusher model. I wanna see how fast them hot wheels will go. I'm ready for a sprint."

Brandon stepped up to help Kirk out of his chair and into the new one. "The salesman said the maximum speed for it would be about three and a half miles per hour." He lifted Kirk out and set him in the other one. "It's the Ranger II—the most expensive one—so it will have a range of about fourteen miles."

"Three and a half miles per hour, huh?" Kirk said, "Bet I can get it to do five for me."

Kirk's attitude still amazes me. I don't think he's ever considered complaining. And that's been his approach to problems ever since I've known him. How can this new lifestyle not make him complain? Most people in his condition would be asking, *Why me, God?* I don't think I'll ever understand how he does it.

"The turning radius on it is twenty-three inches. Pretty good, huh? Maximum weight of the occupant is two hundred fifty pounds." He laughed. "So, Dad, you can't gain a lot of weight."

He pointed toward the wheels. "This is rear-wheel drive. That's the traditional configuration for power chairs. Rear-wheel–drive chairs give you a stable ride over lots of types of terrain. The Ranger II is supposed to be the best rear-wheel drive choice available."

Brandon's recall of all of the technical specs surprised me. "Brandon," I said, "how do you remember all that stuff?"

He gave me a funny look. "I knew Dad would be interested."

We said thank you and good-bye to Doris. Kirk was eager to get outside with his chair. He was already fast-wheeling out the front door when he hollered back at me, "Kate, you wanna come too?"

"Just tell me where you think we both would fit on that?"

"Naw," he said, "I ride, you walk."

"Okay, well, maybe. Where are you headed?"

"Up to the milk barn and then to the stables."

"I'm not walking. But I don't want you going alone the first time out with your new toy. I'll follow you on the ATV."

"Suit yourself, Katydid."

There it was again—*Katydid*. I'm starting to like that silly nickname. When he calls me that, I know he's happy.

But the happiness didn't last.

34

My job had always been to keep track of ranch expenditures and income. I'd furnish Uncle Carl with those figures in a monthly report that I created. Uncle Carl would usually take a quick look at it and hand it over to Kirk, "Lookin' good, Kirk," he'd say. I could never understand why he'd be so disinterested in the figures. This is a big ranch, with a lot of expenses.

Brandon had taken over the job from me recently. He sat at the big dining table with a calculator. "Mom, this don't look good."

"What *doesn't* look good?"

"I don't understand how this ranch is supposed to make a profit." He shoved the page with his figures on it to me. "Look at this. Expenses this month are way more than income."

Kirk was listening to the conversation. "Probably right," he said. "You can't just look at one month and get a good picture of the end results. You gotta look at several months, maybe even annual figures."

"Yeah, Dad, I know. And I've gone back over the past year and studied the figures. This ranch hasn't made a profit for the entire year."

Kirk looked over at me. "You're the bookkeeper, Kate. What'd it do last year?"

I knew the past year's figures, and I'd tried to get Uncle Carl to take notice. "Kirk, I think we talked about this. You know as well as I do this ranch hasn't been profitable for the past four years. We've brought it up to your uncle several times. He seems to not be concerned. The mortgage he's got on this is eating up all of the profits, and he's been paying interest only for the past year."

"Well, it's even worse now," Brandon said. "Now that Uncle Carl is paying me a salary too, the red ink is starting to get even redder."

"Brandon, when your father had his accident, I talked to Uncle Carl about that. I was concerned we would have no home and no way to make a living, but he told me not to worry, that your father's salary will continue, and that you will paid too, and that I should leave it up to him."

Brandon pushed the calculator back and exhaled loudly. "I hope Uncle Carl is a rich man, 'cause this ranch is in a heap o' trouble!"

I looked over at Kirk. I could tell his worry wheel was gaining speed. "Brandon," he said, "I'll talk to him about it and see what we can work out."

"Okay, Dad, Mom, I've got work to do."

After Brandon was out of the house, I could see Kirk's demeanor was changing. "Kate," he said, "we both knew this was coming. My uncle's generosity can only go so far. What are you and I going to do?"

"Kirk, we're in a fix. We have no options. I can't go back to teaching and still take care of you, and I can't take care of you anywhere but here on this ranch and have money to pay the bills."

"We filed for my Social Security disability. Won't that help?"

"Help, yes, but enough to allow us to rent a place of our own in town? No, it wouldn't be enough. You haven't been able to show enough income over the years to get your disability amount up. We've lived okay on your salary, but it was because this house, utilities, and most of our food was furnished."

"Yeah," he said, "we're penalized for living frugally. That really sucks."

"And you know, Brandon will be in the same boat. Thank goodness he is still single, living here with—"

"Uh, Kate…that's something I haven't had a chance to tell you. Brandon came in and talked to me last night. He's about to ask Amy to marry him."

I heard a car drive up. My heart skipped a beat or two. I knew only a small handful of people had the combination to the ranch gate—my parents, my friend and caseworker Betty Sawyer, and Uncle Carl. Thorne! Could it be? I ran to the kitchen window. The Miata I was hoping for was a Cadillac. Doris Cantrell slowly exited the big car. I went out to greet her. "Good morning, lady. What brings you out today?"

"Katie," she said, "your mother called me last evening and wanted to know if I could sit with Kirk. She said she wanted you to come over and visit."

"Well, sure, I guess." I wondered what that was all about. Mom knows she can come out here anytime she wants. I filled Doris in on what I'd already done for Kirk—bath, breakfast, cath change.

"Katie, I think your mom is planning on you spending most of the day there with her. She told me she had a nice lunch planned, and your dad was going to grill something for dinner."

"Oh, Doris, I can't ask you to stay that long."

She put both her hands on my shoulders. "I've got nothing else to do. You need this time with your mother."

I still found it hard to believe this woman would devote her time—oh gosh, and her truck she donated to the auction—for us, especially after I'd rudely ushered her and Kathleen out the door that day.

The minute I walked in the door, I knew Mom had something serious on her mind. She tried to hide it, but I knew. Only after we'd had lunch did she open up to me. "Katie," she said,

"Brandon called and talked to Lynn last night. He was worried about the ranch. He said it was in trouble financially.

"Mom, is that why you wanted me to come over?"

"Yes, I'm concerned for you and Kirk. If the ranch were to go under, where would you and Kirk live? How can you survive on Kirk's disability income? It's not like you can just go back to teaching. You've got your hands full right there with Kirk."

I had been helping her clear the table. I sat down in the nearest kitchen chair and ducked my head. "Mom, this is one time I just don't have the answers."

"Well, I do!"

I almost laughed. This was sounding just like me before Kirk's accident. I'd fret and fume till I came up with a viable option for everything, from the most minor problem to the big ones even God struggled with—or so I thought. "Mom," I said, "we'll be okay. I'm not going to worry about—"

"Look, you don't need to. I've got it all figured out."

I looked up at her, and this time I couldn't help it. I laughed.

She sat down beside me. "Katie, girl, you just sit there and listen to me." She tapped the table with a stiff index finger. "I've talked it over with Lynn. We're going to put this house up for sale and buy a nice duplex. One side for us and the other for you and Kirk."

"Mom!"

"No, don't you 'Mom' me! It's already decided. Lynn is out with a realtor right now looking at a couple of nice duplexes not far from here. He said this house would sell the first week we have it on the market. We've kept it up, even upgraded this kitchen and both bathrooms. The curb appeal can't be beat; it's the best-looking house on the block. It'll sell quickly, and we're going to already have a duplex under contract."

I knew better than to try to interrupt her. She and I are both cut from the same piece of fabric. The only difference is Kirk's accident has weaved a new thread in for me. Maybe I'm just too busy taking care of him, or could it be God has taught me a lesson?

Mom ran her fingers through her hair. "Katie, this will work."

"Why don't we wait and see what Uncle Carl can do. He's told me we could stay there as long as we want, and he's continued to pay Kirk's salary."

Mom ducked her head and peeked out over the top of her glasses. "Okay, daughter, you can't fool me. Brandon told us what shape the ranch is in. He said Carl has been paying interest only on the mortgage. He said the ranch hasn't made a profit in four years because of the huge loan on it. It's simple, Katie: you are going to have to move. Look, if you don't have rent to pay or a mortgage, you'd probably be okay with Kirk's disability."

Just then, something Thorne had said one time popped in my head, and I said, "I'll think about it."

35

WHEN I WALKED in the door, I could see Doris was troubled. "Katie," she said, "come out to my car with me."

The silver-leaf maples in the front yard were hiding the fading sun. "Doris, watch your step. This flagstone walk will trip you up." I opened the gate for her, and we walked out to her car. "What's wrong, hon?"

The short woman opened the door to her Cadillac but stood there with her head cradled in her hands on the top of the door. "I've watched Kirk, even before his accident. He has always been upbeat. Nothing ever seemed to affect him. Even after his horse threw him violently to the ground, his physical condition had never once stifled his spirits. Until today. Something is wrong. The joking was gone. He barely spoke to me."

"Doris, you're right. Kirk had turned this catastrophe into a cake walk. I don't know how he did it, but I think I might know what is bothering him now."

She took my hand in hers. "Is there some way I can help?"

"Honey, you already have—in more than one way. No, this problem is out of our control. It's got God's name all over it. I know He has a plan. And this time, I'm not about to tell Him how to handle it."

"Well, if my name is written in that plan, you let me know, because I want to help in any way I can." She walked around her big Cadillac door, hugged me, and patted my back.

I went back in the house and found Kirk slumped over in his chair. "Kirk! What is wrong? Are you okay?"

I got no response for a minute, and I had the same feeling I'd had when he was lying out there on the damp ground, lifeless. I touched his chin. There was no movement, but eventually, he raised his head a bit. I thought I detected the track of a tiny tear. He touched the controls on the right arm of his chair, turned it away from me, and looked out the window. "Kate, I was thinking—no, praying."

"Good. You worried me for a minute. You want to share with me what's on your mind?"

"Naw, babe, we've already talked about it."

I reached down and kissed his cheek. "If it's this ranch you're worried about, I'm following your past lead—I'm not worrying about it. It's in God's hands."

The Storm Ranger power chair turned out to be Kirk's ticket to freedom. He rode it up to the barn every evening to watch Brandon do the milking. He would like to have made the morning rounds as well, but it was way too early for me to get him ready. It always took me a minimum of four hours to move him from the bed, bath him, clothe him, feed him, administer his medications, not to even mention the toileting routines. I barely had time to finish before it was time to start lunch.

Brandon loved having his dad up at the milk barn with him in the evenings. They talked, joked with each other, and Kirk said Brandon shared his deepest thoughts with him.

"Katie," he once told me, "he thought Amy was the best thing that ever happened to him."

I frowned. "I'm not so sure of that. Kirk Childers, you have got to be the best thing...that ever happened to the guy."

"Probably. But sometimes it just takes a female to ride the range with a guy for more than a day." He grinned. "The guy is melting like a Snickers bar on a hot car dash. He can't stop talking about her. And you know, I like that. I think he needed something, or someone, to move him away from the brotherly squabbles he had with Thorne."

"So has he asked her yet?"

"To marry him?"

"Yes. You said he talked to you about it."

"That's what we talked about today up at the barn. He's already bought her a ring and plans on giving it to her tomorrow night."

"That's exciting."

"Get this, babe—he wants me to be his best man."

"Now that's sweet. I could have expected that." It did my heart good to see my man back to his old self—talking, laughing and pitching his worries overhead, out of sight.

I had hoped the wedding would have been in our little country church, but Brandon and Amy both insisted it be held here in our house. "Don't you see," he said, "this is the perfect place. It's where I got a new life, back when I was just seven. Now it's gonna be where I get a new life again—with the one I love."

Mom came over and helped me get the house ready for the wedding. Doris came and tended to Kirk while I prepared a few invitations and decorated the big room. It would be a small wedding, with family and a few close friends. Only twelve invitations were mailed, and Amy had made those on her computer. She is such a talented young lady.

With a western theme, the front of the invitation showed a branding iron in the shape of double connected hearts. "Branded for Life" was printed above in an Old West font. The inside gave the usual information, the names of the bride and the groom, the names of the parents, and the date and time. An inset picture of the two riding together on Brandon's horse, Puzzle, was done in sepia, making the picture look aged. A separate card was enclosed with a map to the ranch, but again, even this was made to look like a timeworn map, with the edges worn and parts of the map a bit faded.

"Katie," Mom said, "I can't believe Amy designed these cards. They are beautiful—and so fitting for this wedding. I would have thought her major in college would have been in graphic arts."

"No, Mom, Amy is dedicated to the teaching profession. She'll be one of the best teachers Luther's ever had."

"What? She got a job at Luther?"

"Didn't I tell you? The day she turned in her application, I called Mr. Johnson and was going to put in a good word for her. But apparently, there was no need. 'Katie, he said, 'Amy Phillips was one of our best students. Of course I hired her. I was just hoping she hadn't applied at any other school.'"

Mom picked up one of those pictures of the two on Brandon's horse. "Well, she certainly is a beautiful girl."

"Mom, you're right. She is so good for Brandon—bubbly, thoughtful, and totally devoted to him. I can't wait for you to meet her."

36

Brandon and Amy's wedding was to be at three o'clock Saturday afternoon. At ten that morning, I got a call from FedEx asking to speak to Brandon. "Brandon isn't here at the moment, could I take a message?"

"Yes," the man said, "I have a package for Brandon Childers. The sender gave this phone number with instructions to call prior to an attempted delivery."

Brandon was still in town doing some last-minute errands. One of his buddies had agreed to come and do the milking for him the day of the wedding, as well as for the next three days. I tried calling Brandon but just got his voice mail, so I drove up to the ranch gate to meet the FedEx truck at the agreed-upon time.

The driver pulled up to the gate, got out, and walked back behind the driver's seat. When he came out, I thought I recognized him. "Aren't you…"

He grinned, and immediately, I recognized the big dimple he'd had as a child. Back then, it was the biggest dimple I'd ever seen on a kid his age, and time hadn't diminished it a bit. "Yeah, Trent Garrison," he said. "You were my third grade teacher at Luther."

"Oh my gosh! And here you are, all grown up and driving a FedEx truck!"

He was pulling a large package out of the truck. I tried to see a sender's address, but it appeared to have been ripped off. "That's odd," I said to Trent. "How do I know who sent this?"

He grinned. "Mrs. Childers, the sender requested it be removed prior to delivery."

"Well, for heaven's sake! Why would they do that?"

"You got me."

I looked at the size of the package and frowned. Trent was kind enough to carry it and place it inside my van. I thanked him and said, "Trent, it's good to see one of my former students doing well in the world. How long have you been driving?"

"I'm going on my third year now with FedEx." He did a funny two-finger salute. "Had a good teacher. You was the one that made math easy for me."

"Now, Trent"—I laughed—"it sounds like I did a really poor job teaching you grammar."

He looked confused. So I knew I really had done a poor job at teaching him grammar. Before he closed the van door, I slid the big box back out a bit. "Are you sure there is no indication of where this package originated?"

"No"—he grinned—"you won't find it."

I was still searching for some clue. The box was huge. "Should I be careful getting this in the house? Looks like it might be valuable."

And there it was again—the enormous dimple spreading halfway back to his left ear. "Might be," he said. "Boss told me to be careful with it. He said the sender insured it for ten grand."

"Ten grand! You've got to be kid—" Just then, it hit me. My heart did a flip right then in my chest.

Could this be one of Thorne's paintings?

He closed the side door to my van. "Gotta run, Mrs. Childers. They keep us drivers hoppin'."

He drove away, and I searched every square inch of that big package. The packing slip evidently had been ripped off just like

Trent said. I wondered if that was even legal. Had Trent still been there beside me, I think I would have grabbed him by the shirt and demanded he tell me where he'd tossed that packing slip.

If this package was from Thorne, it would have his address on the label. I found myself angry that a former student of mine would do that. Then I found my anger directed right at Thorne. "Thorne Barrow!" I said out loud. Only those five Angus heifers standing next to the fence could hear me. "If I find out this package is from you, and you refused to disclose an address for yourself, I think I'll…" I stomped my foot. "I don't know what I'll do!" The heifers stared at me, not the least bit afraid.

I drove back to the house, hoping Brandon would come home soon. Curiosity was killing this mama cat.

The package sat there in the big room up until two thirty, right before the wedding was to start. I'd asked Brandon to open it as soon as he got back from town. He tipped it to one side and then leaned it back against the wall.

My impetuous mouth was stammering. "And…you're gonna just leave it there? Not open it?"

"Yeah, I'll open it, but just not now."

I was about to bite my nail till I remembered Doris had just polished them nicely for the wedding.

Pastor Lindall stood before Brandon and Amy in front of our massive fireplace. Kirk sat in his power chair next to Brandon. I tried to focus on what was taking place at the moment, but my curiosity with the FedEx package leaning against the east wall of the big room was still running rampant. I wondered if Brandon had had the same thoughts as I did about who might have sent it. Probably, but it's just like him to act disinterested. He's so much like his dad. It takes a lot to get his fire ignited. That, actually, is a quality to be admired. It's served Kirk well for as long as I've known him. It's sometimes frustrating for me, but I know Kirk always waits, analyzes the situation, and then waits again before jumping to conclusions. I wish I could be more like that.

"Brandon Childers," the pastor was saying, "do you take Amy Phillips to be your…"

I shut my eyes tightly and thought, *I am missing half of this beautiful ceremony, sitting here captivated by the unopened FedEx box.*

If Thorne had sent it, wouldn't that be a good sign? Maybe he's not angry with Kirk for not showing any emotion when he presented his beautiful painting of Dandy to him there in the rehab hospital. That would also mean he is okay. No harm has come to him. I whispered under my breath, "Thank you, God."

"Brandon," Pastor Lindall said, "you may kiss the bride."

I bit my lip. I hadn't even been aware of Kirk handing Brandon the ring—and as far as I was concerned, that would have been the highlight of the ceremony. I knew Kirk was proud. I just wish I hadn't been off somewhere on planet Pluto, disconnected from my own surroundings.

I knew he had practiced raising his arm as much as he could, with the ring slightly taped between his limp fingers. How could I have missed that? Maybe someone took a picture.

If the package was from Thorne, maybe he would have put his phone number inside. Maybe a business card? Then I thought, how ridiculous. Why would he have asked FedEx to remove the shipping label if he was going to do that?

I looked up and saw Amy was bending down and kissing Kirk on the cheek. Brandon had his hand on her shoulder. "Dad," she said, "I'm honored to be your new daughter-in-law."

Kirk touched her forehead with his own. "And I'm honored that you are my daughter-in—no, *daughter*. I like the sound of that better."

I sat there addle-headed. I knew I should get up and act my part, give my sweet Amy a big hug and tell her how proud I was of her. But my brain hadn't communicated any movement to my butt. A myriad of miniature images from the past were marching across my mind.

Kirk sitting on top of that magnificent Morgan.

Brandon, the shy seven-year old, standing at our door with his caseworker, back when he was afraid to take the cookie I'd offered him when we first met.

My sweet Lana Lou, holding her Folgers coffee can out to a stranger passing by.

Thorne, with his gorgeous walnut-brown eyes, tossing his head to the side to shake the long black hair out of his eyes.

Then the huge FedEx package leaning against the wall, not three feet from me.

"Katie…Mom," Amy was saying, "you've made this one of the most beautiful wedding settings ever. This house is perfect. I wouldn't have wanted it to be anywhere else."

I managed to pull myself out of the trance I was in and stood up. "Amy, sweetie, you have made me quite a happy mother today. I'm so proud of you."

I realized Doris was starting to serve the guests. "Brandon," she said, "you and Amy need to come on over and cut the cake."

Brandon's big baritone voice rang out over the small crowd. "Doris, give us a few minutes. I've got something over here that my mom is flouncing at the bit for me to open."

I blushed.

He grabbed Amy's hand and started toward the package. I just knew it had to be from Thorne. Who else would send something to Brandon in a box that size? With Amy at his side, Brandon ripped the box open. It was a painting, just as I thought.

Amy held her hand to her chest. "Oh my gosh! Brandon, look."

Brandon looked at me. "Well, if it's not my long-lost brother sending us a wedding present."

I was standing on the wrong side to see it, so I blurted out, "Turn it around, Brandon, so I can see."

Brandon and Amy were riding on Puzzle. The wind was blowing Amy's hair straight back, mimicking Puzzle's mane and tail being blown by the wind. Brandon's shirt was one I'd seen him wear for years. It was a western-cut shirt, black and khaki with a running horses border near the top of his chest. Amy was wearing a similar western-cut shirt in black with turquoise embroidery on the sleeve. I looked at Brandon. "Did he ever see Amy? How did he know how to paint her?"

"Mom, he's seen Amy. Remember, he went with us to that Skillet concert. And we've all hung out together at OSU."

"Oh, sure...sure."

"Mom, your age is catching up with you. Maybe you should take some kind of vitamins to help your memory."

I knew he was saying something else derogatory, but my curiosity was still running rampant. "Turn the painting around. See if there's anything on the back."

He turned the back toward me. "Yeah, Mom"—he shot a condescending glare at me—"it's the back of the canvas." That brought a giggle from a few of the people watching on.

He set the painting down and leaned it against the wall. I grabbed the box and did a thorough search inside and out. I saw no name, address, or phone number. I got down on my knees and looked at the signature: *Thorne Barrow*. "Wait!" I screamed. "What's this under his signature?" There was some writing, but it was too small for me to read.

Brandon knelt down next to me. "Five five six Aspenglow... no, maybe that's an *8*." He got closer. "I think it says 558... Alpenglow. Yeah, Alpenglow. That's right."

I bounced up from my kneeling position. "Kirk, here it is! Now we know where our boy is."

The front door flew open, and the late-afternoon sun pierced the big room. I was still shouting at Kirk. It's 558 Alpenglow, Santa Fe, New Mexico!"

That heavy front door closed with a thud. "Nope, I've moved."

"Thorne!" My scream echoed in the big room. I froze. *Am I dreaming?*

He walked over, hugged me, and then immediately knelt down next to Kirk, put his arms around him, and gave him a kiss on the cheek. "Dad, I've missed you."

"Well, we've missed you too, buddy. Where've you been?"

The room was Christmas Eve quiet. No one was making a sound. I glanced over at Mom. Her jaw was locked in a downward position, her eyes bugged.

Thorne held up his right index finger. "Just a minute." He walked over to Brandon and hugged him. "Sorry, bro. I didn't mean to interrupt your special day."

"Hey, you didn't interrupt nothin'. Wedding's over with." He held up his hand with the shiny new gold band.

"Sorry I was late, Brandon. My plane got diverted to DFW, and that made getting here two hours late."

"No worries, man," Brandon said.

I think Mom and I were both in shock. Her jaw was still open, and I was at a loss for words—not like me at all.

Thorne turned back to Kirk. "I'm living in Santa Fe, New Mexico, now, Dad. I thought you knew that."

I jumped in: "How would we know that?"

"I just figured Rhena Throckmorton would've told you. I called and gave her my new address. I told her not to tell you, but I figured she would anyway."

"Thorne Barrow! You have no idea how many nights' sleep I have lost because of your disappearance."

"Sorry, Mom."

"I've cried buckets of tears, burned with anger, and about gone crazy with worry."

"Sorry."

"Thorne, we didn't know if you'd been abducted, died in an accident, or…or maybe you just were just ticked off at your dad because of that night at the rehab hospital."

"Well"—he was choosing his words carefully—"I wasn't ticked off, just confused. Maybe disappointed."

"Thorne, son, come here." Kirk was holding his arms up, as much as he could. "You see the painting over there behind the TV, turned around backward?"

"Yeah…"

"I haven't been able to look at it since you left. Katie said she'd cried a bucket of tears. Buddy, I've cried fifty-five gallon drums of tears.

"It was my fault that you left like that. When I saw that painting, I was stunned! But I had no idea you would take my silence the way you did—that I didn't care, that I hated it." Kirk swallowed hard. "See, no one had ever told me what happened to Dandy. I thought I knew, but no one would talk. So when I saw my horse on that canvas—so lifelike, so majestic—buddy, I just lost it. Any possible words were locked deep inside me. Can you forgive me?"

Thorne knelt down next to Kirk, touched his head to Kirk's. "Dad, forgiving you isn't even necessary. I wasn't mad at you, just confused." He grinned. "Okay, you taught me not to lie. Maybe I was hurt—just a little." He took Kirk's limp hand in his. "But I'm not now. It's all good, Dad."

From the other side of the room, Doris belted out, "Okay, people, this cake's getting stale with each passing minute. Brandon, grab your bride and get over here and cut this cake before I decide to do it myself."

37

Thorne told us he could only spend one night; he had to catch his plane the next day. I was still wondering how he knew about Brandon's wedding. When he wandered into the kitchen for breakfast I questioned him about it. Breakfast had turned cold an hour ago. He picked up his favorite mug I'd filled with coffee and dumped a ton of sugar in it. "I have the local paper sent to me," he said. "The announcement was in there."

"And another thing," I said. "When I saw the shape of that big package coming out of the FedEx truck, I thought it might be a painting from you. So why on earth did you have them remove the shipping label?"

He laughed. "I wanted it to be a surprise for Brandon—didn't want him to see my name on it until he opened it and saw the painting."

I reached over and messed up that silky black hair of his. "I looked all over for a name or address—"

"Yeah, you probably went over the box from top to bottom. I'm surprised you didn't rip it open right there."

"I thought about it. I guess you know my curiosity caused me to miss half of the wedding. You are to blame for that. I was so interested in the box and the contents my brain developed a dead zone as to what was taking place right in front of me."

He grinned. "Nope, you're not gonna lay the blame on me. You just shouldn't be so nosy."

"Thorne! We hadn't seen or heard from you since you disappeared over a year ago! Of course I was nosy—no, buddy, the word is *concerned*. That's my job as a mother!"

"Yeah," he said, "I should've left you a note or something."

I glared at him and said, "Well, duh!"

"Sorry, Mom."

"You say good morning yet to your dad? You know, he's been just as worried about you as I have been."

"Yeah, I was just in there with him. We had a good talk. He was hoping you'd get back there to him soon and get him out of bed. He said he could do it himself, but it'd take him three times as long."

"I probably should have just left his bed here in the big room, but he insisted on being back there in our bedroom for more privacy. I mean, he's got that nice power chair now, and he goes about anywhere he wants."

Thorne gulped down the last of his sugary coffee. "Mom, I've gotta run. My plane leaves in an hour. I'll barely get to the airport on time."

"Thorne, you still haven't given me your address or new phone number."

"I'll e-mail it to you when I get home."

I thought about that for a second. "How do you know I even have my e-mail set up now?"

He grinned. "I've got my ways." Then he jumped up and started toward the door.

"Go tell your dad good-bye."

"I already did. See ya."

I watched him as he walked out to his rental car. The guy is such an enigma. I still had a hundred questions, but at least I knew he was safe.

Mom came back over the next day to clean the house for me. I don't know what I'd do without her. Brandon and Amy made a quick honeymoon trip to Branson. They were excited to go there during the Ozark Mountain Christmas season. I would love to do that too. I'd said to Kirk, "Honey, I guess we're just going to have to get married again so you and I can go to Branson."

He looked at me in the strangest way and said nothing. I was about to question his silence when the phone rang. It was Uncle Carl. "Katie, is Brandon around where I can talk to him?"

"No, Uncle, he and Amy are in Branson. He'll be back in a couple of days."

"Anything I need to do to fill in while he's gone?"

"I don't think so. He had one of his buddies come over and do the milking for him and check on the water for the horses. The cattle will be okay too. They've got that creek running through all four pastures, and Brandon's buddy's going to pitch out a few bales of hay for them."

"He tell you I gave him permission for him and Amy to move into the white house up on the corner?"

"No, he didn't. It seems no one tells me anything anymore. He's getting more like Thorne in that respect."

"Thorne still there?"

"No, he had to catch his plane back to Santa Fe. I barely got to talk to him. I still don't have most of my questions answered, but it was good to see him again and know he is safe."

"Katie, I've got a plan I want to talk to Brandon about. I'm hoping it will put this ranch back in the black. Have him call me when he gets back."

I told Kirk about the call from his uncle. He dipped his head a bit, and I could tell he wasn't on board with what he thought Uncle Carl's plan might be. "I think I know what he's thinking about."

"So what do you think Uncle Carl's got up his sleeve?"

"I think he's planning on putting the back half of the ranch up for sale. He asked me about it quite a while back, over a year ago. I told him it would really limit the size of the herd, because the back half has some of the best pasture."

"Selling it makes sense to me," I said, "because Brandon would have no problem managing it all then."

"Honey, he has no problem managing it now, so I don't see your point."

"Finances, Kirk. Think about it. I'm sure your uncle could get a nice sum for that acreage back there. It's got road access, a year-round running creek. And like you said, it has some of the best pastures around. That big mortgage is hovering over Carl's head now. Maybe he could sell the acreage for enough to pay off this ranch."

"I know, I know, Kate. It's just that I feel like part of me is being stripped away, and I'll never get it back."

I put my hand on his. "Sweetie, it already has." I took a deep breath and looked at his legs, which had already lost muscles. "And you won't get that back either." As soon as those words rolled out of my mouth I regretted saying them. I saw Kirk nod his head ever so slightly, and his mouth contorted to a one-sided sneer.

"Oh, honey, I'm sorry I said that. Now I feel awful."

He turned his head, looked out the window, and waited a minute before replying. "Yeah, life's like that. Some of the best things—and people—are yanked out from under us."

"Kirk, we just have to take what's left and move on." I thought about that. Probably wasn't the best thing to say either, because

I know moving on with what is left wouldn't have been in Kirk's plans. Living anywhere but here on this ranch for Kirk would be demoralizing. I didn't want to think about it anymore, so I made plans to go up and clean the house Amy and Brandon would be moving into. I wanted to get it cleaned before they returned from Branson. But when would I have the time to do that? I knew I'd find the time somehow.

Mom was on the front porch, putting a Welcome Home sign on the front door. I was in the kitchen putting up dishes and extra kitchen utensils I'd had for years and seldom used. Brandon's buddy had helped move a few items from his own house, which he and his wife had donated to the newlyweds.

"Hey, what are y'all doin' in my house?" It was unmistakably Brandon's big, booming baritone. I ran into the living room and got there just in time to see Brandon carrying Amy through the door.

He put her down, and I said, "Brandon, that custom was way before your time. I'm surprised you even knew about such a thing."

He didn't respond, so I said, "How was your trip?"

He still was silent, and I thought I detected a problem. "You and Amy already have your first spat?"

"Mom!" he said. "Quit trying to outguess everyone. No, we have not had a *spat*." That last word was emphasized with a hefty dose of sarcasm, and I knew there had to be a problem somewhere.

I got up close to his face. "Well, what is it, then?"

He shook his head and grimaced. "Uncle Carl wants to sell off—get this—half of this ranch!"

"How do you know that?"

"He came through the ranch gate just ahead of me. We stopped and talked."

"Well, maybe it would be a good thing."

He turned and headed back out the front door. "Mom, I don't wanna discuss it now!"

Amy came to me and put her hand on my shoulder. "Katie, come on in the kitchen and show me what you girls have done. It looks like you've been working really hard on this place. I never dreamed I'd come home to this. It's looking so nice."

I looked back out the open front door and saw Brandon sitting on the porch steps, deep in thought.

38

THE SMALL WHITE bungalow that had sat abandoned for so long was looking loved once again. Amy worked most of her spare minutes after school and on weekends decorating, organizing, and finding garage sale bargains to transform the four-room cottage into a comfortable and cozy home for the two of them.

Brandon spent most of his time with the ranch duties—milking, mending fences, feeding the cattle since the pastures had gone pretty dormant for the season, and caring for the large herd, now more than five hundred. In the evenings, he divided his time between his OSU online studies and keeping the ranch books.

The joy had evaporated from his handsome face. "Kirk," I had said, "I'm afraid this is all too much for Brandon."

"Aww, that just sounds like a mama talking."

"No, really, I can see it in his eyes. He's always tired. Sometimes even grouchy. He can't keep up with his studies and keep this big ranch running. It's just that simple. Amy says he usually spends an hour or so each evening, paying ranch bills, searching online for the best prices for feed and supplies, not to mention updating the reports for Uncle Carl."

I didn't like the look I was getting from Kirk. "Look," he said, "Brandon's doing fine. I kept up with it. Brandon can too."

"You didn't have college classes, and I kept the books for you—paid the bills, placed the orders. The herd has grown. This is the most head of cattle this ranch has ever seen. Brandon can't do it all. Something's going to give."

Kirk touched the controls on his chair and spun around, away from me. I hate it when he does that. I walked around and faced him. "You know, ignoring this won't make it go away."

He glared at me, eyes squinted almost shut, and his lips squeezed tightly. A *Shut up, Kate* was written all over his angry face. He touched the chair controls again and spun back around. It was his attempt to sequester the words gathering on the back of his tongue. I walked outside, more than a little annoyed. Noah came up and put his paws on me—something he doesn't do much anymore. His tail wags more like a near run-down grandfather clock pendulum now. I reached down and rubbed his ears. "Yeah, Noah, old boy, I guess time changes a lot of things."

Saturday afternoon, Brandon brought in a basket of eggs, handed them to me, and started back toward the door. "Hey," I said, "why don't you take these to your house? I've got enough to last a few days."

"No, we've got enough."

"Look, Brandon, we haven't seen you all week. At least come in and say hello to your dad."

"Gotta run, Mom. Got a heifer down. I need to help her if I can."

He opened the door and ran straight into Uncle Carl. The older man grinned. "I started to knock—guess there was no need."

Brandon placed his hand on Carl's shoulder. "Come on, Uncle. give me a hand with this little heifer. I'm thinking she's gonna need some help."

The two of them jumped in Brandon's Dodge, and I watched as the tires spun gravel. Brandon still hasn't heard from his birth mother, several years now after she'd given him the Dodge as a birthday gift. A stranger woman I don't think I've ever known.

She fought for years to regain her parental rights, then turned around and asked us to adopt him, which we gladly did.

Brandon had always followed Kirk's steps here on the ranch. They were the best of buds. And now…now, things have changed. Brandon still loves his dad, and Kirk thinks Brandon can do no wrong. But I can see it all unfolding. Brandon knows he has all but lost his dad—the dad who taught him everything about cattle, horses, and ranching in general. Taught him how to be a man. Taught him to honor God in all he does.

Kirk still wheels his way up to the barn in the evenings to watch as Brandon does the milking, but the days they used to spend together working the ranch are gone. The love is still there. The best-of-buds affair they enjoyed is lost…lost one early foggy morning in a two-second tumble from a legendary horse.

And Kirk…Kirk not only lost his best-of-buds relationship with his son, he lost the use of his legs, his hands, and—most disturbing to him—the ability to work. He felt he was no longer needed. Just last night he said essentially the same thing to me. "Kate, I'm no good to anyone now," he said in a barely audible tone.

I jumped on that negative remark like a cat pouncing on a mouse. "What are you jacking your jaws about, Kirk Childers!" This was not like him. "You are the one who's kept me going through this whole ordeal. You're the one who declared war on sympathy. You've refused the pity party anyone ever tried to organize for you." I shook a friendly fist in his face. "Don't you dare talk like that!"

The phone rang. "Mom, Uncle Carl is down. I've called 911. I think he's had a heart attack."

"Oh dear God! Should I go up and open the gate?"

"No, I just went ahead and gave them the code. I didn't know if I'd be able to reach you."

"Brandon, I can't leave Kirk right now. I'm giving him his ba—"

"No worries, Mom. The paramedics will be here any minute now."

"Where are you?"

"We're just on the east side of the barn. I told them where to find us."

As soon as I hung up, I could hear the sirens up on Hogback Road, even a half mile away. I was debating whether to tell Kirk about his uncle. He was already in a funk. I thought he didn't need any more bad news.

But Kirk had heard enough of the one-sided conversation. "What was that all about? Is Brandon okay?"

I still didn't think he should hear any bad news. I turned around from him, pretending to be busy. He saw right through that. "Come on, Kate, I asked you a question. I deserve an answer."

Those anger-laced remarks reminded me how Kirk was changing. What had happened to the mild-mannered man I had always known? Nothing used to bother him. I was always the one blurting out remarks I was later sorry for. Our roles were definitely changing.

"Kate, quit playing your wait games with me. You've been doing this your whole life, and I'm tired of it."

"Okay, I'm sorry. I just didn't think you needed any more bad news. It seems like everything seems to upset you nowadays."

"Spill it, Kate! Out with it."

"It was Brandon. He said Uncle Carl is down. He's called for an ambulance, thinks Carl's maybe had a heart attack."

"Get me in my clothes. Let's go."

"Honey, what could we do? Brandon's doing what he can, and I just heard sirens up on Hogback. I think the ambulance is already on the ranch."

39

"'The ranch goes to your dad.' Mom, those were Uncle Carl's last words to me."

"He said that? The ranch goes to Kirk?"

"Yeah. Mom, he didn't even appear to be in any pain. I thought he'd be okay. They had gotten him in a room, and he'd even joked with one of the nurses."

Kirk was in his chair, next to Brandon. He hadn't said a word. I tried to read him; usually I can, but this time his face was a mystery. Brandon went on to tell us each detail of the incident when they were helping the heifer with the birthing.

My mind was whirling. The ranch goes to Kirk. What did that mean? I knew there was a huge mortgage, but I also knew Uncle Carl hadn't been taking any income from the ranch for several years, and it was still in the red. Without Uncle Carl, how could we even afford to keep the ranch?

Mom and Dad had sold their home and bought the duplex. Would Kirk ever agree to live there? What if Dad had already leased the other unit of the duplex? What about Brandon and Amy? What if there still wasn't enough ranch income to make it work for them?

I was jolted from my what-ifs by Kirk's statement. "Well, Kate, there goes my idea of how to make this all work for me and you."

"What are you talking about?"

"Honey, I had it all planned out. It was going to work."

"What was going to work? What was your plan?"

"Well, I guess it doesn't matter now." Kirk ducked his head and his shoulders slumped. "Our life here on this ranch is over."

"Kirk Childers! Quit playing games with me. What are you talking about?"

"It's over, Kate. Just like the title Thorne gave to my painting of Dandy, *It Was a Good Ride*. Well, it was a good ride, but it's over."

"Get to your point, Kirk. What was your plan?"

"You know I love you, Kate. I do. This will sound like I don't, but I do. I really do."

"Yes, I love you too, but right now I'm about to kill you! Get to your point."

"See, before Uncle Carl died and willed this ranch to me, I had a plan—a good plan." Kirk touched the controls on his chair and turned himself around to face the window. "We would divorce—"

"We would what!" I reached over and touched the chair control to turn him back around to me. "Kirk Childers, have you lost your mind? Divorce! We would do no such thing."

"Just hear me out, babe. We could have divorced. I'd have no income—own no property, so I'd qualify for assistance. I'd go to a nursing home. Get all the rehab I needed—"

"Kirk! I don't want to hear this nonsense."

He turned his chair back toward the window. "Then you could go back to teaching. You wouldn't have to care for me then. You'd have a life again, and Brandon and Amy could get on with their life."

My blood was boiling. I was so mad at him I felt like slapping him in the face. Then just as quickly, the anger left, and the hurt set in. How could he even think such a thing? I was stunned. For the first time in my life, I could think of no fitting words.

I didn't have to. Brandon walked around the table to his dad, touched the controls on the chair, spun him back around, and thundered out a string of angry words, the tone of which sounded remarkably like a chain of curse words. "Dad, that is the stupidest thing I've ever heard you say! We don't wanna hear any more crap like that! You need to pull yourself out of the pile of manure you've allowed yourself to fall into."

He knelt down to the side of Kirk, his tone mellowing, "Dad! Loosen your grip on the reins. Let God lead us all through this thing."

Kirk ducked his head. "Yeah, Brandon, I know you're right. In fact, I think I've used that same phrase with Katie in the past." He tipped his head to one side as if to ask Brandon to come closer.

Brandon moved in and touched his forehead to Kirk's shoulder. "Dad, you're not done yet." The faucet broke, and tears gushed out of Brandon's eyes. "Just because you're unable to move most of your body doesn't mean your life is useless." He gently beat his dad's shoulder. "All my life you've given me advice—good advice. Don't stop now—please. I need you. We all do. I need you to share your experience with this big cattle operation. I need you to keep me on the right track toward being the kind of husband and dad you've been. Mom needs you to comfort her, like you always have. Even Thorne—

"Oh, come on now, Brandon. Don't you think that's going a little too far? Thorne needs me like he needs a sting from a scorpion." He grinned. "What Thorne needs is a wife to keep him in line."

"Well, yeah, that too. But he needs your love. Dad, he's told me sometimes he wonders if he's a disappointment to you. You know…you were the big rancher guy, muscled up and ready for any chore here on the ranch. And he's the artist type. Won't even go to the gym. Doesn't even have a wife, much less working on grandkids for you."

"No, he's sure not a disappointment to me. Look what he's made out of himself. He's doing quite well. Without me."

"Maybe so, but he needs to know you're proud of him. Did you tell him so while he was here?" Brandon reached up and turned Kirk's face back toward him. "Did you?"

Kirk touched the controls on his chair and turned toward the window and whispered, "No, I don't think I did." He sobbed. "What's wrong with me?" He ducked his head so far his chin was touching his chest."

Brandon reached over and touched the controls on the chair again, turning him back around. "Look, Dad…" He placed his finger under Kirk's chin, forcing his head back up." You're about to get me amped up here. Pull yourself out of the funk you're in. Get back to being the dad I used to know. I'm waiting—so is Thorne."

I stepped in, put my arms around Kirk, and whispered, "Honey, we'll get through this. I know we will. You don't know what our future looks like. Neither do I. But I know we'll be okay. So Brandon's right. Hold your head up high. Smile. Show me those gorgeous cowboy-blue eyes. Let's just see what God's got planned for us."

Kirk looked straight at me; his face was still wet with tears. He grinned, and the special twinkle in his eyes got my attention. "Sounds good, Katydid, but right now, I just want to see what you've got planned for lunch."

I looked over at Brandon. He raised his eyebrows, smiled, and walked toward the door.

40

For the next two weeks, I found myself a bit out of focus. There were so many things to consider. The memorial service for Uncle Carl—I guess it would pretty much be left up to me to arrange. Then there was the lingering question of the outcome of this ranch. Could we all survive? And I guess if I'm truthful, I was still ticked at Kirk for his ridiculous idea of divorce as a way to solve our problems. And that's what had clouded my thinking. Anger had crept into my mind—no, it had blasted me with a chill, and disrupted any logic I once had. Common sense would tell me I should get with Brandon and take another look at the ranch books. Maybe there would be ways we could maximize income and reduce expenses. But somehow I found myself not even caring anymore.

The mental fog enveloped me with a sensation distantly familiar. I felt lost, even though I was familiar with every square inch of the house. My kitchen window needed cleaning, but I didn't care. A white-breasted nuthatch was making its way down our tree outside the window, oblivious to the trouble brewing inside. An ominous quiet penetrated the big room, from the huge fireplace on the north to the dirty dishes asleep in the kitchen sink.

I placed both my arms on the kitchen table and lowered my head into them. As soon as I did, I heard the gentle hum of Kirk's chair moving into the room. A few seconds later, I felt his head touching mine. "Babe, are you really that tired? My snoring keep you up again last night?"

I turned and kissed him. "No, sweetie, I don't think you even snored. Are you ready for some breakfast?"

"Naw, just coffee will do. Coffee and talk, that's all."

I got up and retrieved his favorite plastic insulated mug, poured it and handed it to him. It's amazing how he has learned to grasp the lightweight mug between his wrists. His limp fingers didn't work at all, but he managed to guide his hands together from his upper arm muscles. I always fill the plastic mug, but only half full to lessen the weight and to help prevent him from sloshing the hot liquid out.

He drank, and then he motioned for me to take the mug. "Kate, I'm sorry I upset you about the divorce thing. You know I love you. Always will."

"I know you do. It's just the fact that you actually considered it as an option."

"I'm sorry I mentioned it to you. I knew neither of us could actually go through with such a scheme. Just forget I ever said it—please."

"Okay, I forgive you. Just don't ever mouth that nasty word again. Neither of us has ever uttered the d-word in all the years we've been married."

He grinned. "Deal, Katydid."

I was getting to where I didn't even mind my silly little nickname. In fact, it was even becoming a bit calming to me. There was a time, not too long ago, when I wasn't sure if I'd ever hear him say that again. Each day I thank God He spared Kirk's life. Broken as he is, Kirk's kisses are as good as they ever were. Soul mate? Oh, no question.

I looked up at him, and those cowboy-blue eyes pulled me right smack into his inner world. "Okay, what's on your mind, big guy? I can see you've got a plan."

"Yep, I do. Wanna hear it?"

"Well, duh!"

"Katie, you're picking up the boys' slang. Not like you, Miss Perfect English."

"Like, I don't think you care, dude." I winked. "Get on with it, Kirk. What's your plan this time? And it better be a better one than your last one, because I'm armed with hot coffee in my mug this time."

He grinned. "Okay, babe, I'd like for us to go back to the museum today. You know, the National Cowboy & Western Heritage…"

"Are you sure you're up to it?"

Without cracking a smile, he said, "Yep, but maybe you ought to drive."

Four hours later, we were finally ready to go. Morning caregiver chores with a quadriplegic take time. A lot of time. And then, after getting him ready, I had to get myself ready. I've never been one to wear makeup. Now, that comes in handy with all my other morning duties.

When I take Kirk anywhere, I thank God for our new minivan with the automatic side door and ramp for his chair. I don't know how I could manage without it. We'd hoped to catch lunch at the Blueberry Hill restaurant in the museum, but they had just closed as we were getting there.

Kirk didn't seem a bit disappointed. "Let's head to the art gallery."

"What, you don't want to go see the rodeo exhibit first?"

"Nope, that's in the past."

I stared at him, not believing his lack of interest in the rodeo life now. It was a stare I must have held a bit too long, not even blinking.

"Yeah, it was a good ride," he said, "but it's over."

We made our way back to the gallery, with room after room showcasing some of the top Western artists. Remington, Russell, Catlin. Then some of the more recent artists. Frank McCarthy, Bill Anton, David Mann. I was still finding it hard to believe

Kirk would want to spend time in the art gallery. The American Rodeo Gallery was where his heart was when we'd visited the museum before.

"Katie! Follow me. Isn't this the name of the gallery Thorne mentioned?" He was already motoring that way. The sign indicated the entire next room was works from the Lambert/Zapsin Gallery in Santa Fe. My eyes wandered from wall to wall, each filled with amazing Western art. I was staring at one titled A*lmost There* by Gerald Cassidy. It was a small 12"x18" oil on canvas. It showed a horse stretching out over a high cliff with his Native American ride perched high atop, and obviously no feasible trail to take. That brought a slight giggle from me. I was thinking that was the kind of piece our Thorne would paint. There is always more to Thorne's art than is readily obvious. He likes to make sure there is a hidden story to his art.

The next piece had gotten my attention when I heard Kirk shout, "Katie! Look!"

I turned to look, and Kirk was wheeling his way up close to a large piece screaming with big bold color. "Look," he said. "This is Thorne's piece!"

"No way." I moved in closer and saw the familiar signature: *Thorne Barrow*. "Oh my gosh! Kirk, that's our boy!" I felt a tear starting to ooze from my eye.

Kirk stretched his head forward like a chicken reaching for a drink of water. He whistled, loud enough for anyone in the gallery to hear. "Holy…"

"What?" I was a bit embarrassed.

"Kate, look at the price on this!"

I moved my new bifocals up a bit. The gold lettering on the card below the piece read, "*Carry-On*, by Thorne Barrow, $85,000." My jaw dropped. "You have got to be kidding!"

"Nope, Kate, the card definitely reads eighty-five thousand. Can you believe that?"

Carry-On showed a young man, probably just out of his teens, riding a little paint horse, which looked remarkably like Brandon's horse, Puzzle. A border collie was tucked under his arm like a football. The trek up the side of the mountain was a bit steep, rocky; and the undergrowth concealed any trail that might have once been. The entire painting was shrouded in a haze so typical of Thorne's artistic technique. In the sky above, a barely visible jet stream streaked the steel blue sky.

"Kirk, I think I would have recognized this as our boy, even if there was no name. Everything about this painting shouts Thorne Barrow—the amazing haze he's added, the colors he's used, even the title of the piece."

"Yeah, *Carry-on*. That's pretty fitting with the jet stream in the sky and the little dog stashed under his arm."

I felt someone walk up behind us. "Sorry, this one just sold."

I turned and saw a lady in a long black dress with a card in her hand. She taped the card marked Sold to the bottom of the frame. Turning back to me, she said, "Do you know this artist?"

"Oh my, yes. This is our son."

I'm not sure she believed me. "Really?" she said.

My mouth then went into overdrive. "Yes, he was our foster son for several years until his mother died, and we adopted him just as he was turning eighteen."

"Well, from what I've been told, this artist is quite the sensation in Santa Fe. His art is demanding prices right up there with the best of them."

"Really?"

"Honey," she said, "the Lambert/Zapsin Gallery is showcased here for this month. I understand the reason they are here is due to the insistence of this artist you say is your son."

"Yes, he's our son."

"Well, did you see his other pieces? They are occupying the east wall over here." She pointed us over to that wall. "Just look at these pieces. They all tell a story."

"Yes," I said, "that's what he does. One gallery owner told him 'If your painting doesn't tell a story, it's nothing more than a pretty picture.'"

"Well, honey, his *pictures* are bringing a *pretty* price—each of them."

Kirk had wheeled his way over and was whispering the price of each—sixty-eight thousand, fifty-five, eighty-five—Then he stopped, whistled loudly, and shouted, "Ninety-five thousand dollars! Holy crap!"

I blushed.

The lady grinned. "And you must be the father of this artist?"

Kirk beamed. "Yes, ma'am, I am."

I looked at her and said, "I'm sorry. Introductions would have been in order. I'm Katie, and this is my husband, Kirk Childers."

"Childers?"

I could see her confusion about the difference in names. "Yes, when we adopted Thorne, his art was already selling quite well, so he elected to keep the birth name of *Barrow* for his art."

"Oh, I see. Well, have you had a chance to greet your son today?"

I felt myself reeling and incapable of any intelligent answer. Kirk came to my rescue. "Thorne is here? Today?"

41

THE LADY POINTED toward the door behind us. I turned, and there he stood, looking amazing. Black dress pants, a heavily starched beet-red-and-gray-striped button-up shirt with a large silver arrowhead necklace. A handsome asymmetric turquoise was set in the center. His black patent leather shoes mirrored the man he had become.

I ran the thirty feet over to him. He immediately hugged me, and I breathed in his light aroma—Clive Christian No. 1. My fist beat his back. "Why didn't you tell us you were going to be here?"

He broke away and looked at me. "Well, I didn't know you were gonna be here either. How'd that happen?"

Kirk had rolled up beside him. Thorne reached down and hugged him, and then he knelt down beside his dad. "I was gonna call you today and see if you guys could come over. But how'd you know about my exhibition here?"

"We didn't. I just had a wild idea this morning and told Katie I'd like for us to go over to the museum."

Thorne touched Kirk's hand, massaged it gently. "Wow! Just like that? So this is quite the coincidence."

The lady we'd been talking to came over. "Thorne, I just got a message from front desk, instructing me to put a Sold card on your *Navajo Buddy*.

"That sold? I figured it'd be the last one to go."

She whispered to him, but I could hear "Seventy-five thousand."

"Thanks, Mrs. Coltrane. I hope whoever bought it was local. I love my native Oklahomans."

"Well, it wasn't exactly a person. It was a gallery owner. I took the call earlier this morning, and I guess she just now called back and gave the front desk her credit card information. I knew she planned to resell it in her gallery."

"Wow! Thorne said. "That's cool. What gallery was it?"

A lady from Throckmor—

"Lena Throckmorton?" he blurted. "Where is she? I've gotta see her!"

"No, she just called in and purchased it without having ever seen the actual painting."

"How'd she—

"She had seen it on our website. Wanted you to know she'd be in later to see you."

Thorne was still kneeling down beside Kirk, massaging his hand. "Dad"—his eyes were dancing—"this is only the first day of the exhibition. Five more to go—and I've got six more paintings on display." The excitement in those beautiful walnut-brown eyes brought back memories of a much younger Thorne Barrow after winning that school art contest.

We were now alone in the room. "Son," Kirk said, "you've definitely made the big time. What're you gonna do with all that money?"

"I'll think of something, Dad." Thorne's cryptographic grin told me he already had plans for it.

"Buy yourself a nice house up in the hills. Then invite some friends over."

Thorne grinned. "I'll think about it."

"Okay," I said. "I want to know when you got in town."

"Plane got in late last night."

"Why didn't you call? I'd have come and picked you up."

"Well, the Sheraton is right there in the airport complex. I was tired, so I just got a room there."

"Well, you just check out of that room, buddy. I'm taking you home with us and give you some decent meals. You look like you've skipped way too many."

He grinned at me. "Why did I know you'd say that?"

"You know me pretty well, don't you? But right now, I need to get Kirk something to eat. It's really important he keep on schedule."

"The Blueberry Hill restaurant just closed," he said, "but I could ask around and see where some good restaurants are in the area."

"Will you come with us?"

"No, I need to stay here. You know… meet and greet the visitors. It's worked well for me in the past. I get to talking with them, pull out my charm card, and they pull out their credit card."

"Well, we'll be back in about an hour. I know where a good Italian restaurant is, not far from here. Now go spit-shine that charm card. "

When the museum closed for the evening, we took Thorne back to the Sheraton to check out. On the way home, I called Brandon. "You'll never guess who we've got here in the van with us."

"Yeah," he said, "I think I can. Must be Thorne."

"How did you know?"

"I saw it on Channel 5. I guess my brother's name is big news around town. You bringin' him out to the ranch?"

"Yes, we're on our way. Should be there in about fifteen minutes. I just wanted to make sure we could catch you. Thorne's looking forward to seeing you again. You and Amy plan on coming up and have supper with us. I'll grill up something. Thorne is saying 'Make it burgers.'"

"Yeah, sure. We can do that. I've got some really bad news. I'll tell you about it when you get here."

"What? Give me a clue now—

All I got was a click. He'd hung up.

42

I was dying to hear Brandon's bad news. Could Amy have been pregnant and miscarried? But rather than stop on the way at their farmhouse, I decided to go on to the big house and tend to Kirk. He was tired and needed a change from the chair. Transferring a quadriplegic from the chair to the bed isn't an easy chore. Then there was the catheter collection bag that needed to be changed, the blood pressure and temperature check.

Thorne volunteered to grill the burgers. Brandon and Amy came on up to the house. I watched out my kitchen window and saw Thorne and Brandon hugging, slapping each other on the back.

Amy came in to the house, and I could tell the bad news Brandon had mentioned to me earlier was affecting her as well. Were my suspicions right? "Amy," I said, "tell me what the bad news is."

"Oh, Mom, I think I'd better let Brandon tell you." She quickly changed the subject.

I noticed Brandon stayed out with Thorne, and I watched through the window as the two talked nonstop. Brandon's face spelled trouble. Thorne seemed to be offering support between flipping of the burgers. What was this all about?

With dinner on the table, Brandon offered to transfer his dad from the bed back to the chair. Kirk rolled up, taking his place at the head of the table.

The five of us bowed our heads for the usual prayer before the meal. No one started. It was a bit awkward. Kirk usually starts, but he was quiet this time. I was at a loss as to how to begin, because I didn't know what kind of trouble Brandon was facing. Finally, Thorne whispered a quick and perfunctory prayer. "Thank you, God, for your blessings. Guide this family and bless this food."

We ate pretty much in silence. I kept waiting for Brandon to fill us in on the bad news. I brought to the table a pecan pie I'd picked up at Cracker Barrel. "Okay, Brandon, I can't wait any longer. Let's hear the bad news."

"Mom, Dad, they've hit us."

"Who's hit us?" I said.

"Cattle rustlers! While Amy and I were at the doctor's office in the city, someone came in and loaded up—from what I can figure—thirty-five head of Angus cows and another twenty-seven of their calves. A potload."

"How'd they get in?" Kirk said.

"It's simple. They cut the barbed-wire fence over on the east side of the ranch. They probably caught the cows and calves all in one area there by the fence. I could see their tracks on the dirt road running alongside the property. That road is so narrow the tractor trailer would have blocked it on both sides. They pulled out their ramps, and it would have been easy to prod them into the trailer."

"Well, at least insurance will cover it," Kirk said, "minus our deductible."

"Wrong, Dad. I found out Uncle Carl cancelled the policy three days before he died. I talked to the insurance agent.

Apparently, Uncle Carl had gone in and told the agent he just couldn't afford it anymore."

Kirk whistled. "Man! That's gotta be a good fifty-thousand-dollar loss—at least."

"Yeah, Dad, we can't stand this kind of loss. We're barely making it as it is. I haven't taken any pay for the last three months. We've been living on Amy's teaching salary."

I looked into Brandon's eyes—eyes that were once bright blue but now seemed a bit gray. "Have you called the sheriff and reported this?"

"Yeah, Mom. He said we aren't the first to be hit. He said they had been hitting at night, but now they're loading 'em up in broad daylight."

"They'll get caught."

"Yeah, they will," he said, "but it'll be too late for us. I was counting on taking those calves to the auction Saturday—just so I'd have some money to pay the feed bill. Electric bill's due too, and there's no money."

"What about the mortgage payment?" Kirk said. "That been paid this month?"

"Dad, Uncle Carl quit paying monthly payments six months ago. He talked the banker into interest only—and another interest payment is due next month."

"Guys," I said, "this ranch has been in trouble for the last three years. Even if it wasn't for the theft, we wouldn't make it anyway." No one had touched their pie. "I think it's time we all think about ways to get out of this mess. Kirk and I can move in the other side of Mom and Dad's duplex. They've been holding it for us. Brandon, you know cattle ranching as well as anyone. Maybe some of our neighbors would hire you."

Brandon closed his eyes, "Problem is, most of the other ranches are in trouble too. The hay hasn't been good this year. Not enough rain. Prices in our area are off. What I hear is people are not eating much beef anymore."

Kirk grinned. "Maybe we should become chicken farmers."

"Hey," I said, "that's not a bad idea. It wouldn't take eighteen hundred acres for chickens. We could sell off half of this ranch."

Thorne had been quiet, sitting there listening. Then he stood up, turned his chair around, sat back down, and rested his arms on the back. "I've got a better idea."

We all stared at him.

"Turn this ranch into a dude ranch," he said. "Make it a guest ranch for Christian singles."

I looked around at the others, staring in disbelief at Thorne. "That's a nice thought, but how do we go about doing that? And do we really want a bunch of city folk traipsing all over the ranch, getting in the way?"

Kirk touched the controls on his chair, moving back from the table. "City slickers don't belong on this ranch. They know nothing about our lifestyle. Probably would be telling us how to better do our job. No, I don't want a bunch of greenhorns running loose, spooking the cattle."

Without moving, his head still ducked into his arms on the back of the chair, Thorne said softly, "Sounds familiar. I was one of those *city slickers*. You probably didn't want me either."

Silence shrouded the room for an embarrassing several seconds. Brandon stood up. "Yeah, Dad, I too was one of those city slickers. So how'd that work out for you?"

Kirk ducked his head. "I'm sorry, guys."

I felt sorry for Kirk. I saw him twist his tight-lipped mouth around in a manner that I knew he was aggravated he'd said such a thing. I wish he'd think before he opens his mouth, because some things can't be taken back.

No one moved. I finally said, "Okay, guys, you've made your point. You know Dad didn't mean it like that. So, Thorne, why don't you tell us more about your guest ranch idea?"

"Naw, Dad don't wanna hear it. I mean…what do I know? I'm just an outsider with a few paintbrushes, slapping color on a canvas."

I looked over at Kirk. He was backing farther away from the table. He turned and wheeled his way over next to Thorne. He tipped his head toward Thorne's. Thorne bent his over and met Kirk's. To use T. S. Eliot's term, a moment of lucid stillness overtook the two. Kirk moved his upper arm, his limp hand dropping on top of Thorne's. "Buddy," he said, "I'm the one without any creativity whatsoever. All I ever knew to do with a brush was to curry a horse—no skill required there."

Thorne took Kirk's limp hand, "Dad, I'm sorry I said what I did. I love you."

Kirk's face began to flood with tears. "I love you too, buddy. We've had some good times together—you and me." Thorne took his napkin and wiped his dad's face. Kirk's eyes drilled into Thorne's. "Come on, man, let's hear your idea. It's probably a good idea. I'm just too dumb to know how to accomplish it."

Thorne looked into Kirk's eyes and winked. "Naw, Dad, you're not dumb—maybe just a bit stubborn."

43

Rather than have me drive him back over to the museum the next morning, Thorne had called for a rental car to be delivered out to the ranch. I didn't see any way I could have gotten Kirk up, taken care of him, and got Thorne back to the city in time for opening.

Kirk was quiet most of the day. I could tell he was doing some serious thinking. I heard Brandon tell his dad he was going to take some of the steers to the auction to get money to pay the feed bill and the electric bill. "I don't know what else to do," he said. "It's just a tiny Band-Aid on a big, gaping wound. We're not gonna be able to make the interest payment on the ranch next month."

"I wish I had an answer for you," Kirk said. "Maybe Uncle Carl was right. Maybe we should put the back nine hundred acres up for sale. I'll call a realtor, see what it'd bring."

"Dad…I don't want to do that, and I know you don't either."

I heard Thorne's car drive up, and I walked out to meet him. "How'd it go today? I wish I could have been there again."

He ran his fingers through that gorgeous silky black hair of his and said, "Sold a few."

"You sold a few? Tell me about—"

"How's Dad?" Clearly he didn't want to discuss any details. Is he up in his chair now?"

"Yes, he'd been resting for a couple of hours, but I'd just gotten him up now. Dinner will be ready in a few minutes."

"So what's for dinner?"

"Your dad just wanted sandwiches and chips. One of my friends brought over a feast of a lunch—lasagna, garlic bread, and a big tossed salad. So we're not hungry. But I can throw something together for you if you'd rather not have a sandwich."

"No, a sandwich is fine. Are you planning on going anywhere this evening?"

"No, why?"

"I was hoping I could borrow your van."

"The van? What's wrong with the rental car?"

"Uh, I was hoping to take Dad out for a ride. Think he'd be up to it?"

"Well, sure, Thorne. But I can never figure you out. What do you have planned?"

"I just wanna talk. You think you could make those sandwiches to go?"

"Sure, I can do that, but let me see if it's okay with Kirk."

Thorne got Kirk loaded into the van. Ten minutes later, the phone rang. It was a realtor asking for Kirk.

"He just left. I'm not sure how long he'll be out."

"Okay," the guy said, "Kirk said you'd probably be the one to answer my call anyway. So just tell him I have a figure for him on the acreage out there on Hogback Road."

"Why not just tell me? That way, he wouldn't have to call you back unless he had questions."

"You understand, I just had an appraiser give me a rough estimate, based on the number of acres. I told him there would be no improvements—you know, houses, barns, and the like. Kirk did say the entire acreage was fenced. Is that right?"

"Yes, that half of the ranch is fenced separately from the front half. So what's it worth?"

"I hope Kirk will understand, an appraiser would have to come out and do a full-blown market analysis. Kirk had indicated he wasn't ready to spend the money for that just yet."

"Yes, that's probably right. So what does your guy say it's worth?"

"He would have to see the land. He'd need to know the percentage of pasture and to treed area. Once we get the full analysis, I'd need to sit down with you and Kirk, draw up a listing agreement—

"Just give me a figure to work with. We're not even sure we would want to list it for sale."

"Well, should I wait and discuss this with Kirk?"

My impatience was taking over good manners. "Just give me the figure. I'll have Kirk call you back on it."

There was silence, and I wondered if he'd hung up. "We're thinking somewhere in the neighborhood of one point four. But you gotta understand—

"One point four million? Is that what you're saying?"

"Yes, ma'am, that's what we're thinking, but you need to under—

"Give me your name and number," I said, "and I'll have Kirk call you."

Without even thanking him, I hung up the phone. My analytical brain was doing overtime. The mortgage on the ranch was just over a half million. There would be a realtor's fee. The mathematical side of my brain calculated it to be eighty-four thousand, based on 6 percent. I knew Kirk would negotiate the percentage down a bit. He's good at that. Maybe this could work.

44

The sky was looking dark. I checked the evening news, and sure enough, rain was on the way. I hated to have Kirk out in a downpour, even if it was just to move from the van to the house. I wished Thorne would head on back. Maybe I should get an umbrella ready.

I'd just sat down with my latest Terri Blackstock novel. The sky lit up, and a huge clap of thunder shook the rafters in the big room. The lights blinked. I bookmarked my page and set it down. My unremitting brain was still trying to figure out what Thorne was up to.

Several years ago, while Thorne was still at home with us, he and Kirk enjoyed a camaraderie most fathers only hoped for with their son. But since the day Thorne walked out of Kirk's room at the rehab center, their relationship had been cold at best.

Something's up! I just knew it. Why was I the one who was left out of everything? Okay, I know—I should just chill, like I've been told numerous times by Kirk and the boys.

The rain had just started when I heard the van pull up out front. I jumped up, ran, and opened the door. Thorne had already bailed out of the driver's seat and was releasing the big OSU orange-and-black umbrella. He pulled the ramps out and held the umbrella for Kirk as he made his way down the ramp. Still, a bit of fear gripped me. What was the *talk* all about? I wish I could see their faces. I'm usually pretty good at zoning in on a problem, just by reading facial expressions. I hope Kirk chose his words well before allowing them to take flight.

Thorne continued to hold the big umbrella over Kirk as he wheeled his way to the front door. Kirk was dry, but Thorne was soaked.

Kirk rolled into the kitchen while Thorne removed his rain-soaked sweatshirt and threw it down on the rock floor of the barbican entry. "Looks like you survived the downpour," I said, "but Thorne may need several towels."

"Kate!" Kirk literally shouted at me. "Call Brandon and Amy and have them come up now."

"Are you crazy? They don't need to get out in this weather."

Thorne had already headed toward the bathroom for a towel. "Yeah," he hollered, "tell 'em to come on up. I'll meet 'em out front with the umbrella."

"Kirk, what's this all about? I hope it's as good as you seem to think it is."

"Babe, you've just got to hear Thorne's idea for this ranch. But Brandon and Amy have to be in on this too."

I wanted to tell him about the Realtor's call and the $1.4 million, but Kirk had other plans. "Put a pot of coffee on, Kate. This is gonna take a while."

Thorne came back into the room, still towel-drying his raven-black shoulder-length hair. Kirk motioned toward the phone. "Go ahead call 'em up."

"Well, what would you prefer I do? Call them up or put on a pot of coffee?"

Kirk winked. "Aww, Kate, you can do both."

"Here, Mom, I'll make the coffee. You make the call."

It only rang once. "Are you nuts, Mom?" Brandon was clearly irritated. "It's pouring out there!"

"I know, but your dad and Thorne both insist. They want Amy to come too."

"Okay, I don't know what this is all about, but it'd better be good."

The coffeemaker dripped its last drop just as the kids came in. Amy pulled off her plastic poncho, and Brandon walked in—dripping water as he came. "What's this all about? You pull us out of our nice, cozy recliners, right in the middle of Thunders' biggest game of the season." His eyes bore through each of us—first me, then Kirk, and then hanging on Thorne. "You guys are gonna owe me!"

I agreed with Brandon. This had better be good. I put another log on the fire and brought the coffeepot over.

Kirk started, "Okay, I know you guys sort of blew off Thorne's idea about the ranch last night—especially me—but, guys, you need to hear us out." I noticed Brandon sliding down in his chair, acting bored. Kirk pulled his chair up closer to the table. "I've been listening to Thorne for the last couple of hours. He's got some creative ideas as to how we can stay right here on this ranch and make it work for us."

Amy's smile was cordial, Brandon's nonexistent.

"I had no idea a Christian singles guest ranch could bring in the kind of money Thorne is describing. I'm sure you're asking yourself, how would he know? Tell them, son."

All eyes were on Thorne. He looked at each one of us and then said, "Okay, see…I've gone to this really cool one up near Glacier National Park in Montana—been there a couple of times. Lots of activities." He grinned. "And a lot of hot chicks."

"So where's your girl, Thorne?" Brandon smirked, "You find one to suit you?"

"Nope, not yet, but I'll be goin' back soon." The grin reappeared. "She's out there somewhere." Then it got quiet.

I sensed Thorne would like to move the conversation forward. "So, tell us how you think a guest ranch could bring in enough income to make this work for us."

"Have any of you ever looked at prices for vacation packages on a guest ranch?"

I laughed. "Well, no. I don't think we've had a need to do that. Our ranch vacations are right here, and free."

"Here's the deal, guys. A six-night, five-day stay cost me twenty-seven hundred bucks. The shorter version—three nights, two days—will run thirteen hundred."

Brandon slumped in his chair and stared at the sparks flying inside the big fireplace, boredom written in those blue eyes. I noticed Thorne glancing over at him. "Guys," he said, "take that twenty-seven hundred times an average occupancy of thirty singles, and you get a whopping eighty-one thousand bucks. And get this, people—that is every week! Five days of work, two days off, then we start all over again. Take that one-week income times, say, fifty weeks and you've got a gross income of over four million."

He certainly had my attention now, and I saw Amy's eyes bug.

Thorne circled the room with his outstretched finger. "Any of you think that might pull this ranch out of the hole?"

Brandon spoke first. "Aww, come on…you're talking gross income. What's it gonna take to get us down to a good reasonable net income?"

"Yes," I said, "and who's going to cook the meals for all those guests?"

"You hire it done."

"Where's this giant kitchen and dining room—and guest cottages?"

"There'll be a hundred-by-three-hundred-foot metal building, with a nice rustic façade to make it blend in with the barns and fences. It will house a big commercial-style kitchen, a dining hall with picnic-style tables and benches. See, the idea is to get these guests together. Let them get acquainted. Let some romances bloom."

"Hold on," I said. "That brings up the question of sleeping arrangements. How's that going to work?"

"Two big dorms. One for the guys and one for the girls. I'm talkin' really nice dorms, not your typical summer camp dorms we had as kids. The amenities are numerous—several TV sets, Wi-Fi available, desks, soda and snack vending machines, a kitchenette with fridge and microwave, and, of course, comfy beds—not the typical bunkhouse cots."

Brandon sat up in his chair. "All right, dreamer boy, where do we get the money to build these fancy dorms and big mess hall?"

Thorne looked over at Kirk, as if they'd already had that discussion, and then back toward Brandon. "I'm willing to help out on that."

My jaw dropped. Could he actually pull this off? I knew he'd been getting big money for his art. I'd seen those art magazines featuring "The Incredible Art of Thorne Barrow." And I knew what a couple of his pieces had just sold for. One that had caught my eye was priced at $165,000. But how much of that had he saved?

45

Thorne had told me he'd be back around seven. With bathing, seeing to Kirk, and preparing an evening meal, I hadn't been able to give much thought to the Realtor's remarks.

Now I was in a dilemma. Should I even mention it to Kirk? He had seemed so excited about Thorne's guest ranch idea. And Thorne had been adamant about keeping the whole acreage. But why would we need all eighteen hundred acres if it was just going to be a guest ranch? Surely, nine hundred would be plenty. One point four million dollars would pay off the mortgage and go a long way toward building guest facilities.

I decided to get on the Internet. Thorne had taught me how to use Google for about anything I'd want to know, so I first typed in "dude ranches." Many of them seemed to advertise fly fishing. As far as I know, trout doesn't exist in Oklahoma, certainly not on this ranch. Most of the dude ranches seemed to be big on chuck wagon dinners, and even spa treatments. I'm not up to cooking out on an open fire in our pasture. And doing massages on strangers doesn't appeal to me in the least.

Then I typed "Christian singles guest ranches" and found some in Texas and Tennessee that seemed to be more what Thorne had envisioned. Horseback riding, of course, was big, but the thing that interested me was the educational aspect. There were wranglers teaching the young singles all about typical ranch life. I could see our Brandon doing just that. I've always thought he should have been a teacher. There could be lessons on calf roping for the guys. We could hire Linda, my friend from our neighboring ranch, to teach barrel racing to the ladies. Linda was champion in the Better Barrel Races at the Oklahoma State Fair Park last year.

One ranch's website homepage featured a large common area, like Thorne had described. Massive rough-cut pine posts towered up to the tin roof. Young singles dined on rustic tables, eating smoked ribs, brisket, potato salad, and coleslaw. I could almost smell the fresh-out-of-the-oven sourdough bread with butter and honey. Yes, we'd have to serve sourdough bread.

Another attraction some of these ranches offered was hot tubs. I wasn't too sold on that idea. Maybe Pastor Lindall would come out and lead in brief devotions. I knew I wanted to keep the Christian aspect intact. Christian singles would be a lot less rowdy. No alcohol. Yes, it would be a much better group than if we opened it up to all singles.

Some of the websites mentioned various games, horseshoes, badminton, and Ping-Pong. One offered disc golf, and even zip-lining.

Our ranch would have hay rides, campfires, hiking, and cattle roundups. Target shooting for both men and women might be good. I could see the first sparks of romance coming from the guys teaching the girls about firearms safety and technique.

The more I searched these sites, the more excited I became about turning our piece of heaven into a guest ranch—a Christian singles guest ranch. But could we really expect the kind of income Thorne had believed from such an operation?

Then I thought about Kirk's role in such a plan. I could see him wheeling around in the big commons area, visiting with the guests. Yes, he could be quite an inspiration to those youngsters. And I know he'd be talking to them about his faith. People have always liked Kirk, but since his accident, he seemed to draw an audience anywhere he goes. That's just my Kirk—cowboy handsome and always Oklahoma friendly. Nothing shy about Kirk. I've told him he could make friends with an old weather-beaten fencepost.

There's something about that wheelchair, coupled with Kirk's friendly voice, that attracts a crowd. He's definitely a man's man, but the ladies are just as intrigued by his stories. When a man can get a group of women to be quiet and listen, that is quite remarkable. Kirk has a way of grabbing the attention of all within listening distance.

This could work.

I hit the Back button on the screen and jumped over to another guest ranch website. This ranch was out near the Oklahoma panhandle. There were no attractive pictures, and the print was almost too small and dull to read. Why didn't they hire a good web designer?

A putrid smell wafted my way. *The beans!* I'd been so wrapped up in those guest ranches I'd forgotten all about the pot of beans I had on the stove, now boiled dry and scorched beyond saving.

"Kate, what's that awful smell?" Kirk yelled from the bathroom.

Kirk! Oh gosh! I'd forgotten all about him. I ran to the kitchen stove and set the pot of beans in the sink, then ran back to the bathroom. "Honey, I'm so sorry."

He looked up at me with that sly grin of his. "Kate…"

I stared at him for a second, and then figured out what he was implicating. I grabbed a hand towel and slapped the back of his head with it. "Kirk Childers! What will I ever do with you?"

"I don't know, but just don't make me eat them burned beans."

"Yes," I said, "I burned the beans. And Thorne will be here any minute. I promised him a good meal tonight. I'm sure he didn't even have lunch. Now all I've got is the ham and some leftover scalloped potatoes from yesterday."

I started out the door to tend to the burned pot in the kitchen sink. Then I heard, "Uh, honey…

"Kirk, I'm sorry."

He grinned. "You already said that once."

What was wrong with me? I felt like Absentminded Abbie. First, I left Kirk alone in the bathroom, something you should never do with a quad. Then I scorched our evening meal. "Look," he said, "why don't you just open a can of those Bush's Grillin' Beans? Thorne'll never know the difference."

I finished sponge-bathing Kirk, got him dressed, and then moved to the big room, where the odor of the scorched beans drew out another wise-cracking grumble from him.

Thorne didn't get home until after eight thirty. "Why so late?" I asked.

"I sold my *Cashin' In*. The couple who bought it wanted to know all about me. When did I get started painting? Was I a native Oklahoman? I guess they thought I was American Indian because of this New Mexico tan." He laughed. "Dang, Mom, what's that smell in here?"

"You don't want to know." I saw him looking over toward the kitchen. "Did you stop for anything to eat on the way home?"

"No, I'm starved. Haven't eaten all day. Whatcha got?"

"There's ham and scalloped potatoes keeping warm in the oven, and I'll reheat the beans."

"Got any cornbread?"

"No," I said. *I'd probably burn that too.* "But I've got a question for you."

"Shoot, Katydid."

"Okay, I want to know just how serious you are about the guest ranch thing. What would be your part in this?"

He poured himself a glass of iced tea, sat down, and stuck his foot up on the next chair. "I'm serious." He took a swig of tea and stared at me. "And as for my part, I'd move back here and help out."

I gasped. "Oh, Thorne, would you? That would be awesome!"

"Yeah, Mom, I'm ready to come home. Santa Fe's been good to me, but it's time to come back, settle down, and find a good girl that'd have me."

"Thorne, there are plenty of girls that would *have* you. I mean, look at you. You're one handsome dude, and you're not hurting for money. You could have about any girl you choose."

"Don't know about that. But you know even better than I do, there's more to it than looks and money." He downed half the tea in his glass before continuing. "Yeah, I got some cash, but I want someone to love me even when I'm not so lovable."

"Well, I know it will happen. Your mama, Lana Lou, knew it too. She could see what we saw in you. You've got a heart of gold—"

"Uh, Mom, you're forgetting something."

"What?"

"I think them beans are burnin'."

46

THE NEXT MORNING, I got up early and made breakfast for my guys. Pecan pancakes with real maple syrup, crisp bacon, scrambled eggs, some fresh fruit, and I even ground the beans for our coffee. Most days I just grab the Folgers can. I'd already managed to get Kirk up and in his chair. I poured his half cup of coffee and waited for Thorne to make his appearance.

I knew he'd have to hurry if he had time to eat and get back over to the museum. He has said one reason his paintings sell so well is he tries to be on hand to greet any potential buyers. I've heard him say, "They like to know the story behind the artist." Thorne says he always shares the story he's hidden in the painting. He's right: there is always more to the painting than meets the eye. Some people get it right away, but some have to be told.

The eggs were getting cold, and I'd already filled his big OSU mug. "What's his hold-up?" I asked Kirk. "He's gonna be late for opening."

"Naw," Kirk said, "you seen him zigzagging through traffic in that Miata? The guy's a live comet on four wheels. Sometimes just two."

"More like a microchip on four wheels. Just the same, I'm gonna check on him. Maybe that supper made him sick."

When I walked into his room, the blinds were opened and the bed was made—something Thorne rarely does. His luggage was missing. I looked around the room for a note. There was none.

I went back to the kitchen. "Kirk! He has already left! He knew I planned to get up early and make breakfast for him." I sat down and pushed my own coffee mug away. "How could he be so inconsiderate?"

"Aww, Kate, don't get your knickers in a knot. He probably just didn't wanna be late gettin' back over for opening. Thorne never eats on a schedule anyway, you know that."

I waited anxiously all evening for him to come bouncing in and telling us about his art sales for the day.

He never showed up. And he never called.

47

I WANTED TO GO over to the museum to see him before he left to go back to Santa Fe, but Kirk's needs came first. I tried calling, only to get his usual voice mail: "I'm with a client. Leave a number." I hate that greeting. I wish he'd change it to something more cordial.

The following day, I got the same: "I'm with a client. Leave a number." A bit of anger began to crawl up my esophagus. *Inconsiderate little stinker!* Why couldn't he at least say good-bye?

Two weeks went by. "Leave a number" was really chapping me. Each day we were getting closer to being kicked off the ranch, and he didn't even have the courtesy to make contact with us. Foreclosure was looming, and I still didn't know what to do about trying to sell the acreage. Now we might not even have time to get it on the market and find a buyer.

The phone rang.

"Katie, what do you plan to do about moving over to the duplex with us?" Mom asked with a bit of impatience in her voice.

"Okay," I snapped, "I don't know what to do."

"What does Kirk say?"

"You know Coolhead Kirk, he just grinned and told me to sit down and take a chill pill. I've heard that from my boys, but never from him."

"Well," she said, "if time is running out, like you say it is, you've got to make a decision."

My extended breath sounded like a nasty Oklahoma wind. "Yeah, Mom. It looks like it's gonna be all up to me."

Kirk's voice roared from the big room. "Kate! My phone's ringin'. Can you get it?"

A chill ran up my spine. *Oh no!* Could that be our banker? Kirk never gets phone calls. I started mentally rehearsing how I would beg for more time before the inevitable foreclosure notice.

I picked up Kirk's phone. "Mom?"

"Thorne! Is that you? Where have you been? I've been worried sick."

"Aww," he said, "you're always worried sick about something. What is it now?"

"What is it! Look here, young man! You left here without saying a word!" My prescription had run out for those chill pills. "You haven't even had the courtesy to return any of my calls. Of course I'm worried sick! And I haven't only been worrying about you, I'm totally without a clue as to what I'm supposed to do about this ranch."

I could almost see that sly grin of his through the phone. "Mom," he said, "maybe you should go lie down and put a cold rag on your head. Sounds like your fever is about to bust through the top of the thermometer."

"Thorne Childers…Barrow—whatever you're calling yourself! You inconsiderate little—"

"Mom! Stop bashing me for a minute. I've got something I want to tell you."

I sat down in the recliner, next to Kirk, and an F5 tornado of wind was gusting out my nostrils. "Well, what?" I managed to say.

"Dang, Mom! That sounded like a dragon snorting."

"Okay, I'll admit I'm still a bit miffed. So what do you have to tell me?"

"Well, first of all, I've been back up to the Montana Christian singles guest ranch—

"Thorne! Here I am looking for a notice of foreclosure any day now, and you run off to your playground in the mountains, leaving me to figure out what I should do about selling this acreage. Have you forgotten that you asked us not to sell?"

"Don't sell, Mom!"

"Well, you tell me what I'm supposed—

"You put that cold rag on your forehead like I asked you to?"

I wanted to hand the phone to Kirk and tell him to handle this whole mess. But I knew he probably couldn't hold on to it and would drop it. And I can never remember where that little speaker button is. "Okay," I said, "the cold rag is on now. Start talking."

That goofy grin of his somehow filtered through the phone line again. "As I was saying... I've been back up to the guest ranch in Montana, and I've got some great ideas for our ranch. But I've also got some other news I wanna share with you."

I touched my forehead. Maybe I did have a fever. "I'm listening, buddy."

"Mom, while I was there, I met this girl who has really scotched my wheels. I mean, she is the most beautiful creation God has ever put together. She's got the most gorgeous long flowing sable hair, and her Hershey's chocolate eyes drill right into me. She's insanely in love with my art, and she has a degree in commercial art. Mom, we sit and talk for hours."

"I take it you like her a little—

"A little! Mom, I just got back from this specialized jeweler here in Santa Fe and bought this gorgeous engagement ring. She's gonna love it! It's a ring of sapphires encircling a perfect two-karat diamond. Only problem, I think it may be too big."

"Well," I said, teasing, "if it doesn't fit, you mustn't commit."

"Funny, Mom."

Two karats! I hope he didn't spend his whole life savings on a ring. "So when do you plan to give this to her?"

"That's just it. See, she lives in the UK. After our time was up at the guest ranch, she went back to Cardiff, where she works. Cardiff is the biggest city and capital of Wales."

"Okay, so what's her name? "Oh yeah. It's Arabella, but she just goes by Bella."

"So how are you planning on getting the ring on Bella's finger?"

"For real, Mom?" he said. "I'll ask her to hold out her hand, and I'll gently slip it—"

"Thorne, you toad! You know what I mean. How are you two going to get together again? I mean, with her being thousands of miles from you."

"No problem, they've invented airplanes. I thought you knew that."

"Well, I'm glad one of us has a sense of humor."

"Mom, her parents have invited me to come over and meet them. I'm flyin' out tomorrow. Bella is the sweetest thing. You're gonna love her. We share the same faith, and she is just as crazy about me as I am about her. Oh, and she's an inch or two shorter than me. Not that it matters or anything…"

I held the phone out from my ear for a few seconds.

"Mom, get this. Bella's folks own a big guest ranch in the UK. They call 'em horse-riding ranches there. Bella's dad knows horses as much as Dad does…uh, speaking of, how's Dad?"

"Dad's right here trying to eavesdrop. You wanna talk to him?"

"Sure, put him on."

I held the cell phone over to Kirk's ear. I wish I could remember where that speaker button hides so I could hear too. They chatted for a good twenty minutes, and I watched as Kirk's face began to light up more and more the longer they talked. I couldn't hear what Thorne was saying, but he obviously was telling Kirk about this Bella girl, and the camaraderie between the two guys was obvious.

I could tell the conversation was winding down, and it didn't seem there had been any talk of the situation we were facing here on the ranch. I tried to get Kirk's attention that I wanted to speak to Thorne again, but he ignored me.

The next I heard Kirk say was, "Okay, we'll look forward to meeting Bella." I waved my other arm wildly at Kirk but once again got ignored. "It sounds like you've picked a winner. Talk to you later, buddy." I grabbed the phone, but Thorne had already disconnected.

Kirk's eyes met mine. "Kirk!" I exploded. "You sat there and chit-chatted for twenty minutes. And you never got around to a discussion of the real issue we're facing here." I leaned back in the chair and blew my bangs out of my eyes. "I can't believe you guys! How can you be so lackadaisical about the real issue?"

Kirk grinned. "And what would the real issue be…Katydid?"

I jumped up and threw the cell phone down. It bounced off the chair onto the floor. "Kirk Childers! We are going to be looking at a foreclosure notice soon. And you just act like nothing of any importance is going on. I wanted to talk to him about selling the back acreage so we could avoid being thrown off this ranch." I knew my face must be matching the color of my flaming red hair. "I've told you, Mom and Dad have been holding half of the duplex for us if we have to move from here. If we could sell the nine hundred acres, we could pay off the mortgage and have some—

"Katie!" Kirk's face had turned rigid. "He told me not to sell it."

"But how can we—

"Katie, I told you, he said don't sell. Said it'd all work out."

"Fine!" I turned and stomped out the front door. *Men!* Someone in this house had to take some responsibility. I should have known it wouldn't be either of them.

48

It was a Thursday. I got a call from our banker. "Katie." I could tell by the way he drawled out my name it wasn't good news. "I'm afraid the board has told me to start foreclosure proceedings out there on Hogback Road." He hesitated, and I said nothing. "I know that comes as a real blow for you and Kirk, but I have no other choice."

"Gary," I said, "do what you've got to do." I closed my phone and stared at the ceiling. *This is really happening.* I guess I should make a phone call to Dad and ask if the other half of the duplex is still available.

"How much time we got, Katie?"

"Honey, I didn't even ask. My head was in a dark fog. I guess we'll find out when we're served with the notice." My eyes were starting to cloud from the onset of tears. I walked over to his chair, knelt down in front of him, and put my head in his lap.

"Whatcha thinkin' 'bout, babe?"

I looked up at him, with incredulous tear-tainted eyes. "I can't believe it's come down to this. How will I be able to manage in that small duplex? Your equipment won't even come close to fitting in those small rooms."

"Aww, Kate, just stick me out in the backyard with the dog. I'll bark when I'm hungry." He somehow managed to tip my head up with his elbow and winked at me.

"Kirk, do you never take anything serious anymore? Honey, we are in a fix, in case you haven't given time to think about it. If only you and Thorne would have discussed the situation and made a plan—"

"Come on, babe, we've got a plan. Thorne said don't sell the acreage. He said it'd all work out."

"Well, it's not worked out. Thorne's not answering his phone again, and we're going to be getting served formally with a foreclosure notice by the sheriff any day now. I don't know what else to do. This could have worked out. Now it's too late."

"Katie, I trust Thorne. If he said it'd work out, then it'll work out."

"How? Thorne can't pay off this mortgage. And here he is flying off to England to be with his sweetie—"

"Wales, not England."

"Same thing."

"No, Kate, it's not. Wales is part of the UK, and so is England. But they're not the same."

"Whatever!"

49

I FINALLY PICKED UP enough courage to call Dad and tell him we'd take him up on his offer for the duplex. At least I'd have Mom there to help me with Kirk. She'd already told me she could prepare most of the meals. Kirk loves her cooking, and she knows about his diet. So that would take a huge load off me.

I sat down at my laptop and booted it up. It'd been a while since I'd worked on my book. *But who would publish it?* Did it really matter? It was just good therapy for me. I could sit down and pour my heart out, without any backlash from anyone.

Friday morning, Kirk was served with the foreclosure notice. We were given thirty days to vacate the premises. "Kirk," I said, "what about the animals?" I'd been so worried about what I'd do with Kirk in the close quarters of the duplex that our dairy cows, the horses, and the few head of cattle we had left hadn't even entered my mind.

"They stay right here on the ranch. Honey, we've talked about this. We're not going anywhere. It'll all work out. You'll see."

"Kirk Childers, I am beyond exasperated! You and Thorne are both delusional."

I went back to work on my book—the book I'd been working on for two years now and still didn't have a title I could be satisfied with.

The foreclosure of Childers Ranch was scheduled on the steps of the Oklahoma County courthouse in downtown Oklahoma City in two days. Each time I'd started a conversation about how we were to get our household goods moved over to the duplex or what we were to do with the animals, Kirk blew me off and refused to discuss it.

Brandon was the only one in this family with any forethought. He and Amy had rented a small house in town, and Brandon had applied for a job at the creamery station—a job I knew he would hate.

Here we were, two days away from being forcefully removed from this ranch, and we hadn't even scheduled a moving van. And what about our horses? Brandon thought a friend of his might let us pasture them on his folk's farm, but he wasn't sure.

My heart was breaking. How could we even give up our three dairy cows? They'd been a part of this family for years. Would the new owner of the ranch treat them good?

Oh dear God! Or would he ship them off to market?

I snatched a tissue from the end table, swiped at my teary eyes, and picked up the phone. "Dad, it's Katie. I know I probably don't sound like myself much. I've been crying for the last hour. Dad, I don't know what to do. We've only got two days before we have to vacate the ranch, and I can't get Kirk to even discuss it. What is the matter with him?"

"Sweetheart—

"Dad, the guy is delusional! Thorne has told him not to worry about it. He's made it clear to both of us we shouldn't sell the acreage, and now it's too late anyway. Kirk won't even let me start packing! I am beyond exasperated—

Dad broke in and stopped my rant. "Katie, do you think he knows something you don't? Do you think he and Thorne are keeping something from you? Maybe they do have a plan. Ever think about that?"

"Why would they—

"Do you trust Kirk?" I could almost see Dad's eyebrows take a down turn. "And more importantly, do you trust God?"

"Trust God!" Now that really added helium to my anger balloon. "Of course I trust God, but I think God would want us to use some common sense! He wouldn't want us to just sit around and do nothing in the midst of disaster."

"You're right, to a point. I still think Kirk and Thorne know something, and they're not telling you."

"Well, if you are right, then I must say they are both being inconsiderate. You don't treat someone you love like that."

"Maybe Kirk is waiting for the sheriff to kick you off the premises—

"Dad! That's what a foreclosure notice is. Kirk was served notice already!"

"You want me to talk to him?"

"No, I don't think it would do any good. He is just a stubborn old mule."

"No," Dad slowly said, "that's not our Kirk. He doesn't roll that way."

I returned to my laptop. Could I even continue writing my book without spraying my anger on every page?

As soon as I opened the file, the title popped in my head: *Will You Love Me Too?* And, given that title, how could I even allow any anger to appear on the pages? My fingers began to fly over the keys in marathon timing. Nothing else mattered. I wasn't aware of my surroundings. Words propelled from my fingers to the keyboard at amazing speeds. Paragraph after paragraph, chapter after chapter, I poured my heart into this love story.

I say love story. Yes, it is a love story. It's a story of a mother's love for her son, a love that transcends normal thinking. It is the story of Lana Lou Barrow and her son, Thorne. I've changed the names, places, and many events to make it a novel. Only the closest friends of Lana Lou Barrow or Thorne might recognize the similarity.

Kirk had been reading my novel as it progressed over the years, and he had been supportive of my endeavor. On several occasions I'd seen tears in his eyes as he read from selected pages I'd printed off for him. "Kate," he had said, "this is really good. I think you're on to something here."

I've read a few craft books on creative writing. I'm a bit of a "seat-of-the-pants" writer, as is Stephen King. I have no formal outline. The story is simply embedded in my brain. I know exactly where I'm going with it, and I know how to get to that point without petering out in the middle.

I knew I could do nothing about our situation here on this ranch, so I allowed myself the luxury of writing. It was therapeutic. I forgot all about our troubles. The purest scenes of love—a mother's love for her child—in my story far outnumbered the hours and days of turmoil and anger surrounding the fate of this ranch and our family. Kirk was glad to see the change in me. His frequent kisses told me so. He'd sneak up behind me in his whisper-quiet chair and plant a kiss on my cheek and then say, "Kate, you are absolutely beautiful when you're sitting there typing on your laptop."

Yeah, I needed that. And it catapulted me on to dozens more pages.

Until I glanced at the calendar and reality hit me smack between the eyes.

50

It was the day I'd been dreading. Foreclosure day. I got Kirk up, bathed and dressed him, and had just placed him in his chair in front of the TV in the big room when Brandon walked in and pitched his hat on the sofa.

"Mom, I guess you know what day it is. I heard you say one time that you wanted to be there when they auctioned off the ranch. You still want to?"

"Yes, I do. But I can't take your dad out. He's running a bit of a fever. I don't want to take a chance of any infection. And I sure can't leave him here alone."

Brandon walked over to the kitchen, poured himself a cup of coffee, looked back at me, and grinned. "That's why I'm here. Get yourself dressed and get outta here. Dad's my responsibility today."

"You're getting no argument from me, son. Just make sure you keep watch on Dad's temperature. If it goes much higher, call his doctor. The number's here on the cork board at the end of the cabinet—

"Mom, I've got the number on my cell. I know the routine. You just get on over to the courthouse." He threw up both his hands. "Maybe there won't be any bidders show up."

"Well, I don't know how that works. I'm pretty sure the bank would kick us off anyway."

"Mom, I haven't told you—"

"What?"

"You know I'm good friends with Sheriff Turner's son, Lance. He knows about our situation, and he told me he knew his dad wouldn't kick us off immediately, especially if the ranch remained bank owned. But I'm guessing if it sells today, he won't have much choice but to force us off." So let's hope no one shows up and First State Bank becomes the sole owner of it."

"Great! That might buy us a little more time."

On the way over to the courthouse I had one of my favorite Mercy Me CDs playing in the van when a call came through. The music automatically muted, and Brandon's name popped up on the navigation screen. I managed to touch the right button on the steering wheel to answer the call. "Mom," Brandon said, "I've called Dr. Linn. Dad's temperature has gone to a hundred and two."

"Oh gosh, Brandon. I should turn around and come back."

"No worries, Mom. Doc told me which medication to give him, and it should start to come down. I'll call you if it doesn't."

"Okay," I said. "I'm about five blocks from the courthouse now. Call me back in fifteen minutes and update me."

"Yeah, Mom. I said I'd call you if his temp doesn't come down. But I know you, you gotta hear it yourself. I'll get back to you in fifteen. 'Love you."

The eleven-story concrete art deco courthouse loomed before me. I knew right where to find a parking spot. The parking garage around the corner was newly erected when we adopted Brandon. Then years later, we'd parked there again when we adopted Thorne.

I knew it was against the law to pull into a handicap spot without Kirk, but at this point in time, I just really didn't care.

My handicap license plate said I wouldn't get ticketed. I whipped into the spot, grabbed my purse, and headed for the courthouse.

I was ten minutes early, so I called Brandon. "Dad's temp coming down yet?"

"Mom, we agreed I'd call you back in fifteen minutes. It's only been about five. Now stop worrying. Dad's fine. You at the courthouse now?"

"Yes, I see a couple of suits standing just outside the door. Probably attorneys, but there's no one else in sight."

I kept glancing down at my watch. Five more minutes, and life as we'd known it for the last twenty-five years was about to implode. My nerves were frazzled. I felt weak, as though my sugar level was taking a dive.

I looked at my watch again—two minutes. The two men in suits had now been joined by two others. My vision was a bit blurred. One of the men was in uniform. Was that our sheriff? I looked around for something to hold on to. Now I knew my sugar level was dropping. Had I even eaten before leaving?

Then I heard one of the men start talking. I couldn't tell what he was saying. My ears had started ringing, and I felt as though I'd go down any minute. Rather than make a scene right there in front of everyone, I simply sat down on the nearest step. My vision cleared a bit, and I could hear better.

Several minutes later, after much legal jargon, I heard one man say something about starting the bidding. I ducked my head down toward my knees. I wasn't sure I wanted to hear what came next.

I could hear someone running toward me. Was that flip-flops they were wearing? I opened my eyes.

"Mom!"

Oh dear Jesus! I recognize that voice!

51

"Are you okay, Mom?"

"Thorne! I can't believe that's you. Yes, I'm okay. Just weak. I think I'm having a sugar drop."

"Here"—he reached in his pocket and handed me a piece of gum—"try this. It might help."

My brain was trying to process what was happening. Why was Thorne here? I thought he was still in the UK with that Bella girl. Why hadn't Brandon called me back? Had Kirk's temperature not come down? Shouldn't I try to stand up?

And then I heard Thorne's baritone voice shouting, "Half million!"

Someone on the steps said something, and Thorne repeated, "Half million cash—and I've got a certified check right here."

52

Thorne insisted on driving my van back home. "You're in no shape to be driving," he said.

I still couldn't believe what he had done. "Where did you get that kind of money, and why didn't you tell me what you were going to do?"

He glanced my way. "Been savin' it. You taught me well. And what was your other question?"

"Why didn't you tell me what you planned to do? I've worried myself sick."

"Aww, Mom, I wanted to surprise you."

"Well, what on earth do you plan to do with the ranch?"

"Mom, you okay? I'm thinkin' you're still a bit loopy" He ran his fingers through his mop of inky-black hair. "We've all discussed this before. Remember? The Christian singles guest ranch?"

"Thorne! I had no idea you could pull that off. Are you serious? You really think this can work? And did Dad know you planned to place a bid on the ranch?

"Not exactly. I just told him not to worry, it'd all work out."

"And just like that, he accepted that? Didn't question you further?"

"Why should he? Dad and I got this thing going—we trust each other."

"So he still doesn't know?"

Those walnut-brown eyes of his drilled into me. "Naw, I thought you might wanna tell him. How do you call on this car phone?"

"Thorne, I'm so rattled now. I'll just dial him on my cell."

While I was digging it out of my purse, he said, "Soon as I get the deed to the property, you and Dad are going back with me to the courthouse. I'm deeding the ranch back to both of you."

I was stunned! I looked upward. *Lana Lou, do you know what our son just did?*

I was still digging in my big purse for my cell phone. "Thorne," I said, "you just plopped down a half million dollars for the ranch, and you're going to deed it to us?"

He grinned. "Yeah, but you gotta let me build my house on it somewhere."

"Baby, you can build ten houses for yourself on it. I am speechless!"

He gave me a sarcastic look. "Naw! Katie Childers has never been speechless."

I finally dug out my cell phone and called Brandon.

"Hey Mom. I figured you'd be callin'. Dad's temp is down to ninety-nine. I got busy putting together a sandwich and chips for him and forgot to call you."

"Honey, is your dad there close by?"

"Yeah, hang on."

"No, just put me on speaker. I've got some big news for you both to hear."

"Hey babe," Kirk said, "you coming home to start packing?"

"No! We're not moving—ever! You guys will never guess who I have in the car with me. And he's listening in"—I giggled—"so watch what you say."

"Okay, Mom," Brandon said, "you gonna tell us or just give us a lecture on our English?"

"Guys, Thorne is driving my van. We just left the courthouse. Brandon, your brother just paid a half million—"

Thorne was trying to shush me, but I ignored him.

"Yeah, Thorne just paid a half million dollars to buy this ranch. Guys, we don't have to move!"

There was dead silence on the other end.

"Did you guys hear me?"

"Yeah, we heard," Brandon said. "*Stunned* is not even the word for it. We're both sitting here with our jaws hanging down. How—"

Thorne spoke up. "Brandon, I hope you won't spread that around. I'd rather no one else know."

"Okay, buddy," Kirk said, "when do we start those buildings?"

"Dad, I've already got some estimates and a commercial builder lined up. I can come up with about 90 percent of the money, but I'm gonna have to go to my banker for the rest."

Kirk let out a big "Woohoo! Way to go, man! You told me it would work out okay. Hey, I trusted you, but I'm afraid your mom didn't so much."

"Whoa!" I said. "It wasn't a matter of trust. I just wasn't clued in as to his plans, and I sure didn't know he could cough up that kind of cash."

"Dad, Brandon, I hate to cut you off, but I'm getting in some pretty heavy traffic—probably ought to get off here."

"Okay," Kirk said, "see you in a bit."

I heard Brandon's famous exclamation whistle, and he said, "Can you believe it! That little—

I snapped the little flip phone shut. I wasn't sure what was fixing to coming out of his mouth next.

The rest of the drive home, Thorne told me more about his plans for the guest ranch. He also started raving about Bella.

"So, did you ever get across the pond to see this Bella girl? I know we haven't heard a peep from you."

"Yes, I did. And Miss Bella will be here next month."

"You gave her the ring?"

"Yep, she's got it on. I'll show you the pic when we get home."

"Okay, Mr. Highpockets, I want to know. Does she know how much you paid for the ring?"

"Of course not! That would be so uncool!"

I had been dying to ask this next question. "How do you guys plan to make a marriage work? I mean, she lives in England, and you said you're going to live here."

"Wales, Mom. It's not England."

Technicalities! "Okay, so I've been told."

"Bella will be moving here with me after the wedding, which, by the way, will be in two months and in her hometown in Cardiff."

My jaw dropped. "You've got to be kidding! And we won't get to be there."

"Wrong. I've already bought your tickets—you, Dad, Brandon, and Amy."

"Oh, but Dad? How will that work?"

"No problem, Mom. The airlines make special arrangements for quads. There's a special place on the plane for his chair. I've got it all arranged. I've also hired an RN to travel on the plane with us. Over and back."

"Well, that sounds okay—I guess." Although I had several questions storming through my head, which I knew I needed to dismiss. "Tell me about Bella's parents. You did visit with them, right?"

Thorne gave me a brief synopsis of her parents. I just realized I didn't even know their last name.

"Mr. and Mrs. Morgan are super people. They are well known in the country. Mr. Morgan is also an author. He's published several books. He told me their name is somehow connected to the

Morgan horse. I've forgotten just how. They live in this humongous country home, a whole row of stables out back. And yes, they do have several Morgan horses."

I said, "So tell me more about Bella." Then I regretted having asked. It was nonstop Bella this and Bella that the rest of the way home. He painted a pretty good verbal picture of the girl. I felt as though I would recognize her when I saw her.

53

WE ALL FLEW over for the wedding. The airline accommodated Kirk quite well. The RN was sitting on the left side of Kirk, and I was next to him on the window side.

I've never seen such a beautiful wedding, and on such short notice. It was a garden wedding to the rear of their huge house on a beautiful rolling lawn. Mrs. Morgan told me they had invited five hundred guests, and almost all showed up. She is as lovely as her daughter. I asked her if she wasn't sad her daughter would be so far away, and her reply was, "Oh, we plan to come and visit as often as they'll allow us." Mr. Morgan made a point to sit down and chat with Kirk several times, Morgan horses being the subject of most of their conversations.

After the wedding, Thorne and Bella were off to an island resort in Fiji. He told me Bella and her mother had found a floor plan he also liked and would start building as soon as they arrived back in Oklahoma. "Mom," he had said, "I already know exactly where I want to build."

"Really?"

"Yeah, I want my house right in front of that big sycamore with the deer blind. I've already talked to Dad to get his permission."

"Why there? That's an ugly old thing someone built up in the tree years ago. It's definitely seen better days. In fact, I think the old wood in that shanty was rotten to start with."

He explained, "The place is special to me. I remember it well. It was just Dad and me that day. It was then I realized what an awesome man he is. Bella knows. I've described the place to her, and I've told her exactly how I feel about Dad."

54

Thorne had told me he and Bella would be back home in two weeks. We were expecting them any day now. Kirk and I were in the big room watching TV when we heard the news. An Airbus A380 had gone down in the Pacific, about seventy miles off the California coast. Parts of the plane had been spotted, but it was believed there could be no survivors.

"Katie," Kirk said, "what airline were the kids flying back to the US on?"

My heart did a flip and stopped.

"I don't know. He didn't give me an itinerary. I don't even know what they left the UK on. "How could we find out?"

"At some point," Kirk said, "they'll release a passenger list, but probably not until relatives have been notified."

"Kirk, I'm scared. I think we should pray right now."

"The time to have prayed would have been before, not after the crash. So how does it help to pray now?"

"Just the same, we're going to pray *now*." I knelt down in front of his chair, took his limp hands in mine, and poured my heart out. "God, at this point, we don't know how to pray, but we put our trust in you."

Several days passed, and we hadn't heard from Thorne. The passenger list had not been made public. Fear ran rampant through me. *God, this just can't be.* Then a thought hit me. We were assuming this ranch would still be our home, but Thorne hadn't had a chance to deed it to us yet. I wasn't even sure he had made a will. "Kirk, how will this work? I mean, if he doesn't have a will?"

When Kirk dips his head and peeks out under those big bushy eyebrows at me, I know I'm in for a reprimand. "Look," he said, "there you go jumping to conclusions, letting fear dictate what comes outta your mouth."

Both my fists were balled up against my cheeks. A waterfall of tears had started rolling down my face.

"Look, Kate, are you tracking what I'm saying?"

"I know, I do tend to jump to conclusions and fear the worst. But we haven't heard peep from him. What am I supposed to think?"

"Okay, babe, you know Thorne's record. He doesn't run on any schedule. He probably wanted to stay over. Or he may have decided to hop over to another island and spend another week or so. I mean, it's their honeymoon, for goodness' sake! Neither have a job they have to be back at a certain day for. So why wouldn't they want to spend more time in an island paradise?"

My balled hand felt my chest. The steady beat was there, but the alarm bells hadn't ceased.

Kirk's cowboy-blue eyes lasered straight through to me. "Why worry about something we know nothing about?"

"Okay," I said, "I know you are right. But I think I'll call Mrs. Morgan and see if they've heard from them."

"Look what you'd be doing, Kate! You'd only put fear in them. There's no need for that."

I knew he was right. I took a deep breath, walked outside, and thanked God for our many blessings. I thanked him for sparing Kirk's life, for my wonderful parents, for Brandon and Amy. What a blessing they've both been to us. And yes, I thanked God for Thorne and the total transformation we had seen in that obnoxious, know-it-all nine-year-old kid. I thanked Him for everything I could possibly think of, and especially for our sweet friend Doris Cantrell, who continues to come out to the ranch to care for Kirk while I run errands. And when I'd finished, my fear was gone. I felt refreshed. I went about my daily tasks—tending to Kirk, preparing meals, and even talking to friends with no mention of my previous fears.

Right then, I knew what my reaction would be anytime Old Man Fear jumps out and feeds me a lump of panic poison. Being thankful was the antidote, and it has been many times since.

The next day, I got a call from a commercial contractor. "Mrs. Childers," he said, "your son authorized me to get started on some buildings there on his ranch. We've been in touch and—

I screamed into the phone, "When! When did you talk to Thorne?" I think he thought I was angry. "Oh, please, sir, can you tell me the exact day you last talked to him?"

The man hesitated a few seconds. "Uh, well, it was yesterday. Why?"

I wanted to jump up and shout *Hallelujah!* In fact, I think I may have done just that. "Can you tell me where my son is now?"

"No, I don't know where he is today, but yesterday he and his wife came by my office here in Dallas. We drew up plans for a large building he's calling Kirk's Place, and also plans for a couple of extravagant dormitories, or *bunkhouses*, as he's calling them."

Okay, God. You taught me how to get rid of my fear. Now if you can teach me how to get rid of the anger I'm feeling right now.

I stood there holding the phone away from my ear. How could Thorne come back to the US and not call us? I thought back to the times he'd done just the same thing. One time he disappeared for more than a year, moved to New Mexico and never let us know, and wouldn't return my calls. The guy is—

God forgive me. Here I was, allowing myself to get angry at Thorne when he'd done so much for us.

By the time I realized I'd left this guy hanging on the phone, he'd hung up. I guess he'd had enough of this loony gal. I pulled up his number, called him back, and apologized. He said he was sending out a surveyor to show where the buildings would be built. I couldn't wait to go clear back to the bedroom to tell Kirk. I started yelling halfway down the hall. "Kirk! The kids were in Dallas yesterday! They're safe!"

55

Thorne and Bella showed up the following day. In the past, I would have yelled at him for not keeping me informed as to where he was, what he was doing, and when he would be back. This time, I ran to them, wrapped my arms around both of them, and said, "You guys are just in time for lunch. After they moved their luggage inside, Thorne and Kirk started talking nonstop. Bella started helping me by setting the table and pouring our drinks.

After school was out, Amy and Brandon came up. We grilled burgers for supper and then sat around the big table discussing plans for the guest ranch.

Now I have so many more things to add to my gratitude list. And I've found it interesting that each time I start using the fear antidote, by being thankful for a few things, I find I'm reminded of a multitude of blessings that have come my way, most of which I'd never stopped to be thankful for before. I sometimes wonder why it had to take me so many years to learn this lesson.

I've also learned to trust. Oh, that was a hard one for me.

Yes, God, I am on board now.

EPILOGUE

That was two years ago. Our guest ranch is open, and we have the next eight months booked solid. I'm already taking reservations into next year. I've taken calls about the ranch from Canada and Germany, and we've even had guests from the UK—I think Mr. and Mrs. Morgan are probably responsible for getting the word out there.

Kirk's Place is the largest of several structures Thorne had built. The building has a high-pitched roof with exposed rafters. The front is log sided. A large covered porch wraps around the front and one side of the building, where we have placed several old-fashioned rocking chairs. As you enter the building, a massive river rock fireplace greets you with a beautiful handmade fire screen that Thorne had commissioned an artist friend in Montana to make. The heavy metal screen incorporates a doe and her fawn in the intricate metalwork. Thorne tells me that screen weighs over five hundred pounds. Surrounding the fireplace is luxurious time-worn leather nailhead sofas with matching chairs and ottomans. The reclaimed barn wood flooring is accented by a large buckthorn brown-and-blue Navaho-style rug that Thorne had shipped in from Santa Fe.

Beyond the big fireplace is a gaming area with three pool tables, a foosball table, several card tables, and a couple of soda machines. Wi-Fi is available throughout the campus.

On past the game room, Amy has set up her popular juicing and smoothie bar, where she sells delicious and healthy drinks. Her seventeen-ounce glass of juice made with cucumber, celery, parsley, kale, dandelion, Swiss chard, lemon, and ginger will set you back twelve bucks. These youngsters all have plenty of money and don't mind spending it. She's now given up teaching and operates her juicing bar full-time.

Walk past Amy's Juices and Smoothies and you'll come to my Little Cozy Library specializing in fiction from a Christian worldview. Two very comfy wingback chairs occupy one corner, making a perfect place for me to sit and visit with guests about the books I love. This small alcove library just happens to carry my recently published novel, *Will You Love Me Too*, which currently stands at number 9 on Amazon's best-selling list. Who would have ever thought…

Thorne decided the dining hall with kitchen facilities should be a separate building, just to the east of Kirk's Place. The two buildings share an adjoining covered walkway, which is wheelchair friendly, as are all other buildings on the premises.

He recently hired Chef Carlos, from Texas, along with his staff of four. No two meals in a two-week period are ever the same—from luscious barbeque ribs to bruschetta burgers, grilled snapper, and a variety of shrimp dishes. His cranberry blue cheese appetizers are often on the menu. Skipping meals here at the Branding Iron, as we're calling the restaurant, is unheard of. Chef Carlos rings an old-fashioned dinner bell hanging from the front porch when dinner is ready to be served.

By far the most popular meal is Friday night's chuck wagon served out in the north pasture by the natural spring. There are rib eye steaks—Angus, of course—cowboy beans, fried potatoes, cabbage slaw, and warm sourdough bread with honey butter, all around a roaring campfire. Kirk bought the tattered old chuck wagon from our neighboring rancher. Brandon did some repair work on it and installed a new canvas top. Thorne's guitar music tops off the evening out under the stars. We provide blankets for those cooler evenings.

The lodging facilities are first-class. Thorne wanted nothing but the best. I love the bunkhouses, but private rooms are available for those who don't mind spending more. The large bunkhouses are built with logs—one for the guys and one for the gals. Each sleeps twenty-five.

Both bunkhouses have three beautiful restrooms with an equine motif. Mirrors in the restrooms are framed by horseshoes. The washbasin is the top half of a long stainless steel horse trough set on a base made from a large sycamore log. Ten fully separate large tiled showers have the appearance of stables, complete with stable doors. A bucket hangs on the inside of each, holding fancy washcloths, soap, shampoo, conditioner, and even disposable razors. Thorne and Bella designed the shower stalls, and we get lots of comments.

Brandon conducts a weekly hayride. He also does roping demonstrations, conducts horseback rides, and manages the Angus herd. He even solicits the help of some of the guys when it's roundup or branding time. Brandon's cowboy personality is so fitting for this, and his big baritone voice carries out there on the tall grass prairie. Some of the girls always want to know if he is single.

Occasionally, I give tours of our big ranch house to small groups of ladies and talk about Kirk's journey with quadriplegia. I also spend a lot of time in the Little Cozy Library, talking about some of my favorite books and signing my own.

Bella has taken over all responsibilities of website design, as well as all media ads, including TV appearances. Thorne could not have picked a more beautiful lady for TV slots to represent this guest ranch. The English girl all decked out in her Tony Lamas, fancy jeans, and pink cowboy hat would make any guy want to book a stay on the ranch.

Each of us have our own job, but Kirk seems to draw most of the attention. Kirk's Place is his home during the day, as much as his health will allow. I watch in amazement as he wheels among the guests and tells them about his life experiences and his faith. He's become such a comedian. When he's not there, everyone wants to know where he is. Bella has even used him in one of her TV ads for the ranch, which also runs in a six-state area surrounding Oklahoma. The girl is a marketing genius. She managed to get a feature article about the ranch in *Midwest Living* magazine.

Thorne stays busy at the easel and paints. His art is still selling for incredible prices, and his prints are hot items here with the guests. He loves signing them and visiting with the purchasers. The gallery in Santa Fe still displays and sells some of his art, as do Landon and Lena in their Throckmorton Gallery.

Lena Throckmorton makes an occasional visit to the ranch. She brings along that famous painting of the withered hand holding out the Folgers coffee can, displays it on an easel, and talks about Thorne finding his homeless mother. The guests are buying sixty-five-dollar prints of that painting so fast we have trouble keeping them in stock.

Just last week, Lena informed Thorne of his latest sale. *Riding Fences Alone* sold in the gallery for an astounding $195,000. His biggest sale ever.

He and Bella have built a beautiful home up by the big sycamore and the shabby old tree stand. Their architect incorporated a guest cottage out by the pool for Mr. and Mrs. Morgan, who make frequent visits from Cardiff in the UK.

Kirk and Mr. Morgan have become good buds, with the conversation usually focusing on their favorite breed of horse. Kirk always misses him when they have to return home.

Thorne was absolutely right about the amount of income we could expect. Kirk continues to stack up huge medical bills, as do most quads; but now we don't have to worry much about it. It's so easy to trust God when things are going your way. But when they are not, that's the time to slow down and simply count your blessings. It's worked for me.

The financial success we've seen with this ranch pales in comparison to what God has given us lately. Two-year-old Colton Kirk Childers, in my opinion, is Brandon and Amy's greatest accomplishment. And now Childers Guest Ranch has just this past month welcomed little Lana Belle Childers. Thorne tells me he has started working on a painting of his new daughter.

"Don't even ask, Mom," he said. "You aren't allowed to see it until I've finished."

Although this is a work of fiction and no people or incidents in the story are real, the setting for the book was very real. Here are some pictures of the actual ranch:

Milking barn and corrals

John and Lorene Reed, foster parents to 52 [fifty-two (52)] children.

Two of the horses on the ranch (one on the left was Dandy).

The author as a teen on Dandy. This character (the horse) was real.

I enjoy hearing from my readers.

You can reach me at eldon@eldonreed.com

Visit and "like" my author page at https://www.facebook.com/EldonReed

Visit my website at www.eldonreed.com

Member: ACFW (American Christian FictionWriters) CWG (Christian Writers Guild)

Volunteer: CASA (Court Appointed Special Advocate) for foster children

OTHER BOOKS BY ELDON REED

Indebted is about a mother who watched her son for twenty-five years but was never allowed to speak a word to him—he never knew, and she couldn't tell.

The first novel in the Normal series is about a foster parenting couple's quest to heal and replace the scars of abuse and neglect of five-year-old Brandon. But in the end, will money and prestige trump love and nurturing?

Defying Normal continues as the second book in the Normal series. Foster parents Kirk and Katie Childers discover the hidden talents of defiant young Thorne Barrow. But one in his birth family has other plans. Thorne has to decide if he's bound by his heritage or accept God's plan for his life.